WHEN THE
WORLD
WENT
SILENT

BOOKS BY ELLIE MIDWOOD

The Violinist of Auschwitz

The Girl Who Escaped from Auschwitz

The Girl in the Striped Dress

The Girl Who Survived

The Girl on the Platform

The White Rose Network

The Wife Who Risked Everything

The Undercover Secretary

The Child Who Lived

I Have to Save Them

ELLIE MIDWOOD

WHEN THE WORLD WENT SILENT

bookouture

Published by Bookouture in 2024

An imprint of Storyfire Ltd.
Carmelite House
50 Victoria Embankment
London EC4Y 0DZ

www.bookouture.com

ISBN: 978-1-83525-725-8
eBook ISBN: 978-1-83525-724-1

To my editor Claire, with tremendous gratitude.

I know not with what weapons World War III will be fought, but World War IV will be fought with sticks and stones.

ALBERT EINSTEIN

MOTHER

HIROSHIMA, JAPAN 1946

The woman in front of us covers herself in shame, but, naturally, Herr Doktor will have none of that modesty. He needs to measure, prod, poke, photograph, document... anything but what he has sworn to do when he held his hand up and took his oath to do no harm. I took the same oath. Unlike him, I actually believe in it.

The scars on her neck and arms have healed to a molten, thick mass. She covers her pubic area with hands that are twisted and missing fingers which haven't been fused together by unbearable heat. Her hair has begun to grow out, but even that fresh mane doesn't hide the bulge in her neck. It's grown bigger since the last checkup. I can tell without consulting any charts. If these were the old days, the days when the ground was still smoldering and the air tasted of rusty metal—or blood—I would have sent her straight to the surgery with that tumor, for Dr. Sato, a Japanese-American, a volunteer physician like me, to cut it out before it would spin its web of metastases all over her body. But it's not the old days and the American is in charge and all I can do is mockingly address him as Herr Doktor behind his back and click my heels whenever he utters another order.

After all, who will listen to a former German refugee whom the United States begrudgingly took in and gladly shipped off to what was left of Hiroshima as soon as she volunteered? I was here with the first flock of Red Cross physicians coming to aid their Japanese colleagues, mere weeks following the bombings. I still remember the smell of burned flesh imprinted into the very walls of makeshift hospitals. I still remember what children looked like, born to mothers who barely survived the blast themselves. Have you ever held a child so malformed, you couldn't assign its sex, for everything below its severed umbilical cord was fused into a lump of flesh? Have you ever hidden a newborn from its mother, for the sight of its exposed brain would certainly finish her off? Herr Doktor didn't, and yet, he's still in charge here, this well-fed career researcher whose dull eyes only light up when he comes across a particularly interesting case.

"They've suffered enough." I remember telling him as soon as I realized that the new US-founded commission for the atomic bomb casualties was here just for research, certainly not medial aid. "First, the blast itself, then radiation sickness from the fallout, and now this? Being turned into lab rats for the scientific circles' entertainment?"

I also remember the look he gave me. "Research is necessary in medicine."

"So Mengele said when he carved up his twins," I muttered under my breath in German and left him with a puzzled look on his face. There was nothing left to say to him.

We helped as many as we could, without knowing how to help. The burns that wouldn't heal; the wounds that would refuse to close and festered; the sudden anemia and infections refusing to respond even to the new antibiotics that ordinarily cleared everything up in days. Overworked and driven to near hysteria with helplessness, we threw ourselves at this invisible enemy, but the enemy claimed more and more victims with each passing day. It had some greedy appetite. Nothing could satisfy its raging hunger.

Sometime at the end of September, having begged a phone call out of a local US military headquarters, I broke into tears as soon as I heard my husband's voice and couldn't produce a coherent sound for over a minute. And then suddenly it all poured out of me—the desperation, the savage malevolence of it all.

I half-expected him to say that at least the bomb wasn't ours, that the blood wasn't on our hands. But, instead, there was the sound of rustling papers as he rummaged through the desk.

"Here. The radiation sickness study Mina's colleagues smuggled to us back when we were in hiding in Switzerland. Shall I read it to you? It's very short, but perhaps you'll gather something out of it."

He read it and, together with forgotten German words, memories arose like ghosts of the world that no longer was. Our old apartment in Linz we had to abandon in a hurry in the middle of war, like two thieves in the night. Family albums, forever lost together with a library we'd been so proud of. Our cat Libby and the look of betrayal in her green eyes when I handed her to a neighbor, to feed and look after, "just for a couple of weeks while we're away," as if the poor thing knew all about our plans and loathed us for not including her in them. But what hurt the most—what still does—was the blank black-board in our daughter Mina's room. I'd pressed my palm against its surface just before our departure, hoping to hold onto my child, whom the Nazis deemed undesirable and threw her out of school, only to steal her back a mere couple of years later for their own nefarious goals. She was still alive then. She was still alive when someone dropped her radiation sickness report on our Swiss temporary lodgings' doorstep with a short note written in her barely legible handwriting—"All is well with me. Apply for an American refugee visa as soon as possible. When I can, I'll follow."

Last thing I heard, her immediate superior was arrested by the Allied troops a few months ago, right at the end of the war, and is now interned somewhere in England. No woman scientist with him. My only daughter's name is shrouded in the silence in which she lived most of her life. I doubt I'll ever know what truly happened to her. All I have are memories and my work, which I do in her honor. She'd like that, knowing that I'm trying to heal what others tried to destroy.

Johann kept reading in his soft, subdued voice. Nothing interrupted me as I wrote down his words.

It's very quiet now in Hiroshima. Birds don't circle the trees, for there are no more trees to circle. Dogs don't bark, for there are no more dogs. Schoolchildren don't sing their proud songs—they turned to ash together, children and songs alike. One blast and the entire city is a mass grave.

Only silence. This unbearable, dead silence everywhere. My chest aches at the weight of it.

ONE

LINZ, AUSTRIA. OCTOBER 1938

The new headmaster is just like his Nazi Party pin: round, bald, and red in the face. He reddens even further when Mina's father refuses to see the metaphorical writing on the wall that Mina saw a long time ago. She saw it back in March when Hitler's troops waltzed into her native Austria as if it were their own living room, yet her father proceeds to argue with Herr Fahrenholz.

"I understand you have orders." She can only see her father's profile but has grown so familiar with it, she easily reads the words as they fly off his lips in the machine-gun-like sequence. "But I'm telling you, the new decree doesn't apply to Wilhelmina. She wasn't born with her physical defect. She went deaf as a result of measles complications, at the age of five—"

"Precise origins of the girl's defectiveness are of no interest to the Reich."

Herr Fahrenholz is a Berlin transplant. Mina can't hear his accent, but the slight pinch in his lips betrays him. The vowels come out in precise order, like marching troops. Very un-Austrian like. Hard, like the soles of their jackboots.

"All I know is that she takes up a valuable space in a classroom that can be filled by a normal child."

"*Normal?*" Mina feels the shift in the floorboards as her father pulls himself forward, ready to strike. "My daughter is more than normal. My daughter is a brilliant student! For the past two years, her algebra teacher has been giving her university-level assignments because she passed school-level ones years ago. Wilhelmina is—"

"Deaf."

The word shoots through the air like a bullet. Mina almost feels the hiss of it as it flies past her ear. It's burning in its shame —not for herself, but for her poor *Vati*. He had to beg a day off from his work to come here and argue her case, and all for what? She saw the strapping, freckled boy Herr Fahrenholz brought to the class the other day. He breathed through his mouth and couldn't tell a triangle from a square, but he had his *Hitlerjugend* uniform on and was a boxing prodigy, or some such. Apparently, the Reich needed fighters more than thinkers.

And a thinker she is. Nose always in a book, head always elsewhere. Mina has always been this way, for as long as she can remember. A still-warm September day and she, only four years old, running full speed along Mozartstraße toward her house, her kindergarten teacher out of breath on her heels.

"Mina ran away today, again!" The first words out of her teacher's mouth when Mina's *Mutti* came to collect her later that day, smelling faintly of disinfectant and still wearing her white hospital gown atop her green dress.

Back then, Mina could still hear words; staring at her little blue shoes, her mother's hand holding hers, she heard the accusation in them and couldn't make sense of it for the short, little life of her.

"Mina, why did you run away?" her mother asked, squatting on her haunches in front of her.

A shrug. *No reason.*

"Has something happened?" Her *Mutti*, fortunately, always the one on her side, tried to probe her for answers. "Has someone taken your toy? Has someone hurt you or called you names?"

No. She just wanted to be home, alone with her abacus, making numbers go up, up, up with the simple movement of her little fingers—what was closer to magic? She didn't like shouting. Didn't like all of those bodies moving without any rhyme or reason in the playground. She simply craved order and silence; what was so difficult to understand?

But Mina was only four. She couldn't possibly articulate all of that.

Order and silence. When the latter came, on a crisp winter morning some nine months later, after her fever finally broke, Mina took it as a blessing. The world wasn't completely silent yet, just very mute, muffled somehow, each sound reaching her as though from under a pristine blanket of snow. Her body still aching from the battle it had fought and won, Mina lay still and at peace in her bed, gazing out the window and into the snowy expanse outside, overcome with a serenity she hadn't known before. She savored the stillness, even when her parents first rang the alarm, realizing that their daughter couldn't hear them calling to her. She didn't feel she had lost anything of value even when her mother burst into tears at the doctor's verdict: measles complications. Glue ear. Eventual deafness. Incurable.

In Mina's opinion, staying home with her *Opa* Wilhelm, her mother's father after whom she was named, was much better than whatever any kindergarten could offer. The name—Wilhelm—suited her grandfather just fine. Mina still remembered him, tall and imposing, with his emperor-style walrus mustache, his Great War regalia proudly displayed on his chest, regarding his crying daughter and little Mina with calm assurance.

Mina has no memory of what exactly he told *Mutti* that

day. She only knows that on that very first day, he held his beautifully carved walnut cane with one hand and Mina's small
palm with the other and set off into the bookstore, where he
purchased all the books he could find on hearing loss and sign
language. It was there, in his widower's apartment with its thick
carpets hoovered by the maid once a week and rich burgundy
drapes, Mina watched him make a fist—the same fist that must
have intimidated, warned, or propelled men into battle during
the war—and open his mouth while holding a little wooden
alphabet block with a letter painted on it.

"A."

She knew the alphabet already; she wasn't a child, she told
him then and saw his eyes crinkle mischievously and lips curl
under that formidable mustache of his.

He told her something—something kind, no doubt—but she
couldn't make out the words, and for the first time, it frightened
her to a degree she couldn't comprehend. The panic came, the
tears, more words from *Opa* but no sound at all, and there she
sat, scared and trembling and sobbing her little heart out, and
then, all at once, there were *Opa*'s comforting arms around her,
carrying her into the bedroom that was much too big for a single
person.

Mina didn't know her grandmother. She'd died of tubercu-
losis before Mina was born, but her presence was still here, all
around them—in the soft beige wallpaper she had undoubtedly
picked; in the beautifully carved bed and matching armoire;
and the mirror with wings in front of which she must have put
her lustrous locks into an intricate updo—her comb and hair
clips and powder and even perfume bottles were still here, as
though awaiting her return.

It was in front of that mirror that *Opa* set Mina down and
pointed at her tear-stained reflection. A pale girl with chestnut
hair and a smattering of freckles over the bridge of her nose
stared back at her, hazel eyes swimming with tears.

She tried to cry harder and look away; tossed her head obstinately and repeated, "I can't hear, I can't hear; don't you understand? I. Can't. Hear."

His warm hand grasped her jaw. Once again, he pointed at the red-eyed girl in front of her.

"I can't hear."

He nodded, satisfied, and said something once again, now pointing at his own reflection.

"I can't hear!" Mina cried, frustrated, but then something clicked in her mind once she saw her grandfather repeating the phrase as if he, too, was her reflection. "I. Can't. Hear," she articulated, slower this time, watching her mouth closely.

From her grandfather, a smile of extraordinary warmth.

"I. Can't. Hear," he articulated back after her.

This time, Mina "heard" him.

TWO

It is an unusually sunny day for October, with golden, reddish leaves swirling silently in the wind. The schools have been let out and *Hitlerjugend* boys are tossing the ball among themselves as they pass under Mina's window. Their mouths are opening wide, teeth bared in soundless laughter. Mina feels the wall vibrate ever so slightly as the ball bounces off it. Somewhere along Elisabethstraße, the new boy, who sits at her former desk, is walking with his new friends. Mina doesn't quite know how to feel about it.

She was mad at first—mad as she has the right to be—mad at being excluded, and so unfairly at that. Her sense of universal justice, honed by the years she spent under her grandfather's tutelage, was outraged. But, at the same time, she is to be homeschooled for the rest of the school year—the very last one she has left—and that is a relief. She won't have to stifle yawns anymore, bored senseless by the equations on the blackboard that took her classmates forever to solve but which were so very, childishly, obvious; Mina cracked them within seconds in her mind. She won't have to guess the rest of the teacher's phrase when their head is turned to the board instead of the class; won't have to put up with the humiliation of raising her hand to remind Frau Braun to face her so she can take dictation—Mina had long grown used to writing without glancing at the paper, her eyes glued to Frau Braun's mouth the entire time.

Everything that came so easily to her classmates took so much effort from Mina, and yet she excelled in almost every subject, half thanks to the brain she was blessed with and half out of spite, out of a desire to prove herself to be just as worthy. But there were still those snide remarks—remarks that she couldn't hear but she saw the reaction to them, saw the snickering, the lowered heads and half-glances in her direction, elbow jabs and knowing looks. It was easy to tease the deaf girl behind her back. The deaf girl couldn't answer because she couldn't hear.

The teachers were no better. Annoyed with having to face her the entire time, some hinted, in a supposedly helpful manner that reeked of insincerity, that Mina would be better off in a *special* school for *special* children, where she could benefit from *special* education. Some outright reminded her that she was only tolerated in their class because her grandfather had friends in military circles and officers' offspring was officers' offspring—the better blood, even if she's a deaf girl. But then *Opa* died when Mina was only thirteen and the teachers' patience grew thinner by the day.

Only Herr Strobel, her algebra and geometry teacher, made schooldays tolerable. After noticing how quickly Mina finished her classwork when she was only twelve, he began giving her more challenging tasks. After she began solving them in no time, he swapped her beginner algebra textbook for an intermediate one. By the time she reached fifteen, Mina was picking university-level equations apart. But it was at the end of last year, when she offered an easier, much simpler solution to an equation than the textbook did, Herr Strobel, with a half-

bemused, half-awestruck smile on his face, said that there was
nothing else he could do for her. She was university material.

University, my foot. Mina rubs her eyes and rereads the
sentence she must have read ten times before, tries to concen-
trate on Napoleon's army wandering around the city of Moscow
abandoned by its inhabitants, but her thoughts are elsewhere.
Her future, so very certain just months ago, is suddenly evapo-
rating like the morning mist. The Germans came and she
turned into an *undesirable* overnight, a handicapped girl, the
dark stain on the immaculate genetical imprint of the Aryan
race.

Aryan race. "What a pile of horseshit," in her late *Opa*'s
words, God rest his soul, in those rare moments when he lost his
cool and turned from a dignified Austrian officer into a private
with a vocabulary to match.

History is Mina's second favorite subject, and history—
before it was rewritten by Hitler's sycophants—is adamant on
this subject. There is no such thing as Aryan race. There existed
ancient Germanic peoples and Nordic tribes and Anglo-Saxons
and Celts and Teutoni, until the Romans came and then the
Huns from Central Asia with their bloodthirsty hordes and
little was left of any pure Germanic race. Whatever "Aryan"
means, Reichsführer Himmler has to be asked. His education as
a chicken farmer gives him enough authority to speak on the
subject.

A sharp vibration of a doorbell puts an abrupt end to the
current of Mina's snarky thoughts. She feels it travel through
the floorboards and into the soles of her bare feet. Mina scowls
at the cuckoo clock ticking away on the opposite wall. Too early
for either of her parents. Her mother doesn't return until four,
or even later if she has to stop by the grocer's on her way home
from the hospital. *Vati*, too, often stays late in his law office,
unless he decides to bring a stack of files back home, which
Mina prefers, to be frank, because then she gets to share a desk

with him and work in companionable silence until mouthwatering scents summon them to the kitchen before *Mutti*'s call.

Another ring of the bell. It stings Mina's feet and she picks them up, places them on the chair, hugs her knees and contemplates if she should just ignore it. Those unfamiliar with her wouldn't know any better—a deaf girl, alone at home, didn't hear the bell. And it's the unfamiliar that she has grown wary of. Unfamiliar uniforms all around; unfamiliar headmaster replacing the old and kind Herr Wiesenthal; unfamiliar new laws that suddenly singled her out, banning her from receiving education alongside "normal" children. Unfamiliar is all German, marked with that swastika stamp, and generally something Mina wants nothing to do with, whatsoever.

But then a third ring travels along the floor and up the chair legs and echoes through Mina's body. There's no avoiding it any longer. On guard and ready to bolt, not unlike their half-feral cat Libby, Mina pads to the door. She doesn't open it at once, but peeks through the peephole and brightens. On the other side, Herr Strobel stands, his felt hat pressed against his chest.

Mina removes the bolt, opens the lock, throws the door open.

"Herr Strobel!"

"Good afternoon, Wilhelmina." She reads his lips.

"How goes it, Herr Strobel?"

He cringes and moves his hand, palm down, this way and that.

"I see. Me, too." With a knowing grin, Mina steps aside, letting him in.

In a few minutes, a kettle is boiling on the stove. Mina asks Herr Strobel if he still takes his coffee with milk and no sugar.

He used to come here a lot back in the day when he private-tutored her, back when he still had knowledge to offer. Before she became university material, and soon after, nothing at all.

"I tried to intervene, you know," he says as soon as Mina

places a steaming cup in front of him and sits in the opposite chair. His lips turn down in the corners in bitter disappointment as he utters the words. "But there's no reasoning with the new administration. That numbskull—pardon my language—"

Mina hides a grin; nods. She knows precisely what numbskull Herr Strobel refers to. No apologies needed.

"—threatened me not only with dismissal but said he'd report me." A surprised, mirthless chuckle escapes his lips. He rubs his forehead lined with creases and blinks a few times. "I asked him for what and he said for defying Reich policies."

"I'm a policy now?" Mina asks in a flat voice.

Herr Strobel waves his hand, dismissing the detestable word impatiently. He's particularly agitated today, Mina notices. His thinning hair is in disarray and his ordinarily pale cheeks are flushed. But it's his eyes that betray his state the most. They burn with a fire Mina has never thought could possibly ignite somewhere deep in the soul of her algebra teacher. Though why is she surprised, really? He's just like her, all cold logic on the surface but so much hidden passion underneath. Isn't it why they got along so well throughout the years, the teacher and the student?

"To the devil with them all," he says. "You ought to forget them and pay them no mind any longer. They aren't worth the effort." He pulls his chair closer, his coffee forgotten in between his hands that can't stay still. "They will let you sit the exams. And you'll pass them with flying colors; you and I, we both know it."

Mina nods, but still uncertainly.

"But then—listen to me carefully, Wilhelmina—you ought to try the entrance exam to the Faculty of Natural Science at the University of Graz. I know what you're about to say," he interrupts her before she can interrupt him, "but once they see what you're capable of, once they see what I see, they shall drop their pigheaded attitude in an instant."

"Will they, though? Haven't Germans stripped Einstein of his citizenship because he's Jewish?" Mina asks and instantly thinks of her father, who teases her ceaselessly for bringing the scientist up at every chance she gets.

He is right—she simply can't help it. Einstein holds a special place in Mina's heart. She devoured his theories and articles on sunny days when her peers lounged on sandy beaches and played ball by the lakes. And later, at night, when they exchanged first clumsy, wet kisses in dark alleys, Mina climbed onto her building's roof and gazed at the night sky with Einstein's writings pressed against her chest as the universe itself opened up to her through his mathematical equations.

"But you aren't Jewish and this isn't Germany," Herr Strobel counters.

"But it is. We're officially Ostmark now—Germany's appendix. And I am deaf."

Herr Strobel chews on some thought he must have been entertaining for some time—Mina sees it hiding behind his lowered lashes. "What if they don't know that?" he utters at last.

Mina is silent a moment. In front of her, her own coffee cup has long stopped steaming.

"Whatever do you mean?"

Her teacher shifts in his chair, selecting his words carefully. Austrian or not, they still share this infamous German "correctness" with their northern brethren. Deceit of any kind goes against their very nature, but still, Herr Strobel is here, with whatever outrageous proposition he's conceived and he won't let go, because he senses that this is what's right and what's just, and to hell with all that well-bred, Germanic honesty.

"If someone saw us right now, they would never guess that you can't hear what I'm saying but reading my lips instead. All you have to do is forget to mention your handicap in your application, send them your exam results and sit the entrance exam.

It's science. Everything shall be written on the board before
you."

"And once I pass?" Skepticism is audible in her voice. Such
an audacious plan has little chance of coming to fruition—Mina
is too much of a realist to believe otherwise.

From Herr Strobel, a shrug and a conspirator's wink. "Fake
it until you no longer can."

"And when I'm uncovered?"

"When you're uncovered, you are already their best
student. They won't get rid of you so easily. Trust me." With
that, he produces several books out of the valise which had
stood until now undisturbed by his feet and lays them out in
front of Mina. "Second year of Graz University's algebra. Make
me proud."

THREE

Vati comes home from work, in his lapel a new pin, just like the one Mina saw on Headmaster Fahrenholz's jacket. *Mutti* glances at it and averts her eyes, busying herself with setting the table instead. But Mina keeps staring at the offensive item and her father turns away from her, utters a curse under his breath—she's certain of it—and wrestles with the Party pin until it's off, shoved out of sight and into his pocket, together with some loose change, a handkerchief, and a book of matches celebrating the *Anschluss* in remarkably bright colors.

The dinner is set. Mina's mother passes roast potatoes with hands that still smell faintly of rubbing alcohol and chloroform. Mina fills her plate, accepts a slice of roast duck from her father without looking at him, and produces a book from under the table. *Mutti* says something, her dark brows drawn, but Mina ignores the movement of her lips. It's so easy to shut the world out when she wants to. They speak to each other, but Mina is no longer a part of it and that's the blessing of her condition. Sometimes she wonders what the world would be like if she were blind as well. How peaceful it would be, made solely of darkness and silence. She wouldn't have to witness this betrayal that feels so inexplicably personal to her, just weeks after her school dismissal.

But then *Vati* taps her shoulder and there's no avoiding him any longer. Mina turns the book upside down and looks at him. Her mock-questioning pose is deliberate. Her eyes are both ice and blazing fire.

"Don't look at me like I'm the enemy of the state, Mina."

"No, the state would have no quarrel with you now."

"I'm a law clerk, Mina." His lips plead. "They came for us right after they came for everyone in the administration. Only reliable men shall retain their positions. And reliable men means Party men. I have obligations to this family. I have to put food on the table. Surely you don't want us to be reduced to the miserable state we were in back in the twenties? I know you were only a child, but you do remember how it was."

Mina makes no response. There is no arguing with the point, and her father is a jurist for a good reason: he knows how to bring up points that can't be argued. And Mina does remember the endless lines in which she stood together with her mother, a mere child among all of those adults, pushing, shoving, arguing as they crept lethargically toward the counter where they were selling something. *Mutti* didn't know what yet, but whatever it was, they needed it. Could be tripe, could be grain, could be flour or salt, or could be the American preserves they were fortunate to snag. Mina cut her tongue on the tin can licking it clean after they finished rationing the peaches.

They had only survived because Grandfather Wilhelm helped them. As a senior officer in the Austrian army, he was entitled to coupons, and good ones too, most of which went to his only daughter. A coupon for two brandy bottles was traded for Mina's new shoes after the old ones quite literally fell apart. So, yes, Mina does remember how it was.

Her mother gestures for Mina's attention and says, "They

came to the hospital as well. Not for us, nurses, but for the physicians. It's spreading."

A perfect term, Mina thinks. Spreading, like an infectious disease, gangrenous flesh turning black—the color of the SS uniforms flooding their streets.

"I wish I was blind, too," Mina says out loud this time.

"May as well be dead then," her father says, and somehow, it needles Mina when she least expected it.

"Maybe I'd be better off," she retorts acidly. "The state doesn't need undesirables like me anyway."

She slams the book shut, pushes the chair away with both hands, tears already stinging her eyes, throat burning, and storms off into her bedroom. In the hallway, Libby hisses at her as she stomps by. Mina hisses back at the cat and stuns her into silence.

Although it's still too early for bed, Mina is already wrapped in blankets reading a book. Her father tiptoes into the room, the springs of the bed sag as he lowers himself down next to her, and gently takes the book from her hands.

You would not be better off. His hands, as he signs the words to her, are rigid with resolution. *And neither would the world be better off without you. We all come into it with a purpose. We are all needed here.*

Even Hitler? Mina signs back and rests her head on her fist, her arm bent at the elbow.

Her father hesitates a beat, then shakes his head with a smile. "You *are* a jurist's daughter," he says. "And this jurist loves you very much." He tucks her braided hair behind her ear with infinite tenderness.

Mina forgives him the Party pin just then.

"Can we go to the mountains on the weekend?" she asks, suddenly a child again.

It's an awkward age she's at: one day, a young woman; another, still a young girl, and this duality confuses her sometimes. Unlike her equations. Those are always as clear-cut as possible, all easily understood and logical.

There's nothing logical about Mina at this point. She's unmoored, thrown about in a wild ocean like a sliver of wood, directionless, and there's no telling where fate shall take her, if it doesn't drown her altogether.

"Want to ski?" her father asks.

"To ski and to stay in that inn where they let me drink Glühwein last time."

Vati throws his head back and laughs. Mina misses the actual sound of his laughter, but she'll take whatever she can get. Beggars can't be choosers.

FOUR

As the sun casts long shadows on the cobbled streets of Linz, Mina stands, alone and pensive, by the desk she shares with her father whenever he brings work home, a piece of chalk growing warm in her fingers. Their joint study is modest, with heavy velvet drapes that mute the cacophony of the outside world—for her father's sake when he works here. A large armoire dominates one corner, its dark wood a stark contrast to the whitewashed walls. A small bookshelf, filled with tomes of varying sizes and thickness, stands guard on the other side. The only thing out of place in this room is the chalkboard.

A massive structure, it's filled with scribbles and designs, a last present from Grandfather Wilhelm that he made her just before his death. The blackboard is Mina's and Mina's only. Her father gives it a wide berth so as not to smudge the numbers on it by accident and her mother avoids it altogether, only wiping the chalk dust under it on Saturdays, but never touching the surface itself. Sometimes Mina catches them gazing at the thing with puzzled reverence as if it's a complex artifact dropped on their poor heads from some distant future, mysterious and carved with a language of people they do not understand. To Mina, it's amusing, really. There is nothing to puzzle over in her equations. They're the same natural world in which they live and move about daily, simply decoded and confined to a formula. It's sunlight as it travels toward the Earth and sound-waves as they bend around it and the stars that have long died and yet glow so very magically in the warm velvet sky, millions of light years away from their tiny planet.

It's people that are hard to understand. The universe, it's much easier. It's atoms and molecules and that's all there is to it.

Only, today, Mina is stumped herself as she studies the formula in front of her. She copied its origins based on the new findings published by Meitner, Hahn, and Strassmann, the Berlin Kaiser Wilhelm Institute scientists, and walked straight into a metaphorical wall. In their newest research, the German scientists established that different isotopes could be formed by bombarding thorium and uranium by neutrons. But certainly, that can't be right. Because that would mean that thorium and uranium atoms can be split, and any school student with even basic knowledge of physics knows that atoms are the smallest particles and simply can't be divided into anything smaller.

Mina rubs her nose and leaves a white smudge on it. Her stomach issues a loud rumble, protesting against Mina's starving it yet again. She often forgets to eat—or even drink, for that matter—and greets her mother with a guilty look and a palm held out for aspirins, nodding to *Mutti's*, "you wouldn't have a headache if you weren't dehydrated and half-starved; why am I leaving you soup on the stove? All you have to do is warm it up."

But Mina's mind can't be further from any mundane human troubles such as lunch, even if they are necessary to sustain one's very life. In fact, she's been standing so still, two pigeons landed on the ledge just outside her window and began their courting. The sound of their cooing summons Libby into the room. She butts Mina's ankle, asking to be let on the desk, closer to the birds, but Mina scarcely notices her.

"Not now, you little beast," Mina mutters mechanically, eyes still glued to the blackboard.

Libby purrs—a rare occasion for her—and, moving slowly like an automaton, Mina scoops her up and cradles her against her chest as she examines her work.

"Turns out I'm not as smart as I thought I was, eh, Libs?" Mina chuckles, but it's mirthless.

She can't help but feel a pang of sadness. What she wouldn't give to study under one of those brilliant scientists! Like Werner Heisenberg, a celebrated German physicist, who studied under Max Planck himself when he was just a few years older than Mina; like Lise Meitner—a woman!—who published this latest research together with her colleagues. Like Hahn and Strassmann, who walked the same hallways her idol Einstein once walked, and such unparalleled intellect rubs off even on the dullest students. Mina would have easily parted with her right arm just for a chance to pick up crumbs of that shared knowledge, but who will want a deaf girl who wasn't even allowed to finish her school education?

Herr Strobel thought differently, but he was the only voice in the chorus of others that screamed only about her lack of hearing, refusing to notice her other talents. One doesn't need two working ears to understand the problem in front of her; only what's between them.

"Have they made a mistake?" Mina whispers into Libby's gray fur. "Or am I making one, thinking about it all wrong? What if an atom isn't the smallest particle? What if isotopes can indeed be chipped away from it somehow?"

Having had enough of those universal problems, Libby squirms out of Mina's hands and lands gracefully on the desk, frightening the pigeons away. Pulled out of her own world and blinking the real one into focus, Mina follows Libby's gaze—outside, into the big wide world and everything it has to offer.

"You're right, Libs. I'll never solve it from here. Not from this tiny study." Mina chews on her lip, torn between the choice of the familiar and safe and something very risky and vaguely intimidating. "Suppose I listen to Herr Strobel and try to pass the entrance exams for the University of Graz. I'd have to feign hearing. A daunting task, indeed. Suppose it doesn't pan out and they throw me out." Color rises in her cheeks at the very thought of such shame, but Mina jerks the emotion away with one shoulder. "But suppose it does. Suppose, I get accepted." Her very breath catches in her throat at the prospect of it. "Suppose it all works out in the end."

In her mind, Mina's already there, in Graz; she's a student with a pile of books under her arm, walking hastily on campus and inhaling the very scent of knowledge deep into her lungs; savoring the taste of new discoveries as they are born in real time in small conference rooms where students and their professors crack the universe's secret codes. The image is too tempting to resist. She may try to deny it, but she has already decided everything for herself.

"First things first, though. We need money for the entrance fee, don't we?" Mina rubs Libby's ear, buries her nose in the nape of her neck, and inhales the musky smell of cat's fur as she rests her elbows atop the desk. "And I don't want to ask *Vati*. In fact, I don't want him to know altogether. First off, he'll say it's an idiotic idea—and I know that it is—but what if it pans out? If I get accepted, I'll tell him then, and there'll be nothing that he can do then, only be proud, hopefully."

Another bitter smile. The world outside is hostile, filled with prejudice and intolerance. But precise sciences are her sanctuary, a place where the only thing that matters is her mind. The Nazis can label her as handicapped, they can expel her from school, but they can't take away her ability to weave magic with numbers.

"I'm only teasing. *Vati* isn't like that. Of course, he'll be proud. But still, I wouldn't want to worry him needlessly. And

Mutti, she'll be happy too, even if she doesn't understand math at all and looks at me like I have two heads when I begin to talk about it with her. She always taught me to be my own woman, just like she is, earning her own money and having to answer to no man, so she'll be glad I'm settled as well. And you? You won't care one way or the other as long as your dish is full, so I don't have to worry. I suppose, it's settled then."

As Mina's gaze remains fixed on the chalkboard, she finds her answer. With a few strokes of damp cloth, she wipes the board clean, leaving a blank canvas for her to start anew. She will pay for and take that entrance exam. She will feign hearing, she will feign normalcy, for a chance to prove to the world, and to herself, that she is more than a deaf girl.

FIVE

Linz is nothing like Vienna, but it's also not quite small enough for everyone to know "the deaf girl." Certainly, most of the neighbors and store owners around are familiar with Mina, but today, bundled in a raincoat and armed with an umbrella, she ventures further and further out of familiar territory. To pass for someone with two working ears, she needs anonymity.

Despite torrents of rain gushing down from the drainpipes spraying her half-boots with foamy water, Mina stays close to the inside of the pavement. Better risk wet legs rather than being run over by a bicycle rider, like the one that just missed her two intersections ago. A violent swoosh of air, her legs bolting to the side of their own accord and the rider's leg in a mud-splattered boot striking the pavement as he swung toward her. Startled and wide-eyed, Mina only discerned a few words out of his tirade and guessed the rest of the message, likely replete with curses for emphasis. *Daft bat, such and such, head in the clouds, not paying attention to where she's going. Couldn't she hear him ring?*

The real Mina would have narrowed her eyes and spat, in her most poisonous tone, that this was precisely the case and watched in satisfaction the heat rise in the man's face and his lips mumble indiscernible apologies. But this "normal" version of her had little else to do but apologize herself. With a final shake of his head, the bicyclist was gone. And Mina moved as close to the side of the building as her open umbrella allowed and stayed close to it, wet legs be damned.

She had little hope of finding a job on her first try. There is little to do for young girls in any city. They are expected to get married and have children, not work, and those who do work are mostly secretaries, typists, phone operators—jobs for anyone with two functional ears, that is. With the best will in the world, she couldn't feign that much hearing.

A mouthwatering waft of coffee turns her head before she notices the coffeehouse tucked under a striped brown and white awning. The outside sitting area has already been cleaned up for the upcoming winter, chairs stacked neatly by the wall. The tables are already gone—in the cellar for yearly hibernation. One of the French doors remains opened—it isn't too nippy yet and the manager can afford some fresh air in exchange for customers lured inside by the smell of the fresh brew and just-baked pastries. On the glass, a sign that read "servers needed." For a moment, Mina stands and considers. She can try to pull it off, for a couple of hours at least before she gets uncovered, just to see how impossible it really is and discard Herr Strobel's fantastic idea, but she backs away before she changes her mind.

A scene from the past suddenly rises in her mind. Six-year-old Mina, pulling *Opa* Wilhelm's sleeve toward the local theater's entrance, framed with brightly painted advertisements of the upcoming Christmas performances. He had already taken her to the ballet, but Mina didn't like it all that much. She'd known the plot before the performance—who didn't know *The Sleeping Beauty?*—and the costumes were bright and pretty, but watching dancers jump to nonexistent music soon reduced Mina to a state of utter boredom. She wanted a performance—an actual performance, where actors talked and she could "hear" them even if she couldn't hear the music accompanying them. It would be better than ballet, wouldn't it?

But *Opa* Wilhelm, the man whom Mina's mother lovingly chastised behind his back for his inability to say no to his only granddaughter, refused to budge this time.

"Next year, Mina."

Mina had long come to dislike the very first letter of her name, much like she'd grown to dislike Bs and Ps. They jumped around far too much and mixed themselves up in the lips she was still mustering to read. Without context, all she could "hear" sometimes was a jumble. If someone looked directly at her, she knew the word they had said was Mina. But sometimes she'd catch *Mutti* say "Mina" to *Vati* and wonder why they were discussing inviting her over when she was right there in the room, just to realize that they meant Nina, *Mutti*'s fellow nurse. Her new, silent world was confusing. And not so silent, too. Sometimes, the inside of her right ear sounded like a bad radio station that was catching nothing but static and the left one as though it was infested with bees or something clicking, creepy-crawly, scratching, scratching, scratching inside, while the world went about its business as though nothing was the matter. But Mina refused to surrender. She was her grandfather's granddaughter, as *Mutti* liked to rephrase it. She was a tough little soldier. She could handle the performance of the Christmas play.

"If you buy tickets to the first few rows, I'll see the actors just fine."

But *Opa* Wilhelm had a different opinion on the matter. "What habbens whensdey turm towars ishuhther?"

What happens when they turn toward each other? Mina half-read, half-guessed from the context. It had been harder to read *Opa*'s lips than *Mutti*'s or *Vati*'s because of his formidable walrus mustache. As soon as he'd realized this, he'd clipped it short enough to bare his top lip, and to the devil with the look, but sometimes it still got in the way of Mina's lip-reading.

"I can miss a few words."

"Oubee to faraway tozee propelee."

"Not from the front row I won't."

"Eben the from."

He must have seen hot tears welling in Mina's eyes; must have seen her bottom lip beginning to quiver. But, despite being aware of the fact that this was the last resort of his grand-daughter to get the old military man to surrender, he lowered himself to one knee in front of her and spelled so perfectly and slowly, Mina couldn't have misinterpreted a single word even if she wanted to.

"You are not ready yet. Much like the regiment which is not ready for a battle it cannot possibly win. You are setting yourself up for failure, Wilhelmina. And once failed, you may be too scared to try the second time. Understand?"

Grudgingly, Mina understood then.

Much like she understands now, and walks away from the battle that can't be won.

The rain slows to a miserable cold drizzle by the time Mina reaches the busier part of town and steps into a strip lined with specialty stores, inns, cafés, and a moving pictures theater promoting a new Chaplin movie and some ideological German import.

Mina smiles fondly at Chaplin's name. She grew up on his films. They were conveniently silent when she just lost her hearing and provided a blanket of familiarity whenever she walked out on yet another talking picture, exhausted after trying to guess countless subplots flying over her head because the actors either smoked and mumbled, or turned their heads toward the sunset, or covered their mouths with a damned newspaper.

The famed Tramp was a friend she'd never met but knew so very well. He knew her too; the eleven-year-old Mina was certain of it. Else, would he make the main heroine of *City Lights* blind? Deaf, blind—it was all the same to Mina then. All she wanted was confirmation, from someone with authority (and Chaplin was *the* authority, at least in the little girl's eyes) that she could be anything she wanted, even the lead heroine of her own film if—

Mina's dreamy smile first wavers and drops entirely when a theater worker emerges from the entrance and, after swiping a brush with glue over the door's glass, slaps an official notice on it, "No dogs or Jews allowed," before disappearing inside.

I have nothing to complain about, Mina thinks sarcastically. *I haven't been equaled to a dog yet—not that it's an insult.*

She snaps her umbrella closed and walks away. For some reason, she needs to feel the mist on her skin. As though it can wash away the film of something disgusting she has just witnessed and which is coating her skin with its filthy residue. But no matter how far she walks, more and more stores greet her with their anti-Semitic graffiti painted on the windows, behind which hopeless-looking owners stand, gazing into the busy street, bustling with shoppers that avoid their establishments despite ridiculous discounts promised right under the carica-tures of the hooked-nosed *Juden*. There's something ghostly about them, those shop owners, as though they're already fading into nothing; as though they're not long for this world.

Long live Germany, the great Aryan race.

For some time, Mina walks like an automaton as the lights slowly begin to illuminate the merchandise in the windows and wreath streetlamps in golden halos. She no longer wants a job; wants nothing to do with this street or town whatsoever. She hasn't eaten since breakfast and is slightly nauseous. She only wants to find a bus or a trolley—anything to hop on to get away from it all, lock herself in her room, and stay there for as long as it takes. For the rest of her—or her parents' life, after which the state will confiscate her apartment because she won't be able to pay for it and haul her into some institution for "defectives"...

The trolley pulls to a stop not too far away, but Mina doesn't get on. Instead, she crosses the street and walks into a Jewish bakery—the inevitable caricature on the window and all —with a sign on the window: bookkeeper needed.

SIX

Thankfully, the baker who hurries from the back room and into the main one (likely at the ring of the bell over Mina's head she spotted from the outside) is clean-shaven. He stares at Mina in nervous amazement as he wipes his hands over his apron, and Mina stares at the mouthwatering display of his, mostly untouched, goods. This is something that doesn't belong in Linz. This is something that belongs in Vienna or Berlin. She'll be damned, but the masterpieces in front of her could easily be served in the finest Parisian establishments. Everything here is elevated to a level of utter perfection. Every croissant is sliced in half and filled with crèmes and jams of all hues and textures. The assortment of cupcakes that are all colors of the rainbow, topped with berries, sliced almonds, and what looks like colored pearls which are no doubt edible, almost make Mina dizzy. As far as the eye can see are pastries and cookies and breads and the heady smell Mina's floating in. Her senses are stunned to such an extent, she only catches the fact that the baker's lips are moving, but not the phrase itself.

And here's your first test, girl. Fake it until you no longer can, as Herr Strobel said.

Mina smiles, feigning embarrassment. "Forgive me, please. I'm afraid your selection has rendered me not only speechless, but deaf. I didn't quite hear what you said."

The baker breaks into a beaming smile of his own.

"I was only asking if I could help you with something." Mina reads his lips.

"I would like one of each of whatever you have," she replies half in jest and half seriously (the display *does* make her mouth water!), "but I'm afraid I'll have to settle on one croissant for now."

As an excuse, she produces her small velvet purse with artificial pearls sewn on which her *Mutti* gave her on her sixteenth birthday and demonstrates her measly possessions. Ordinarily, *Vati* leaves her some money if he knows that she's going somewhere, but she didn't tell him anything about her plans today.

"Which one would you like?" The baker is looking at a display when he speaks and his head is slightly lowered, but Mina guesses this much from the context.

"Which do you recommend?" she asks.

"My personal favorite is pistachio." He's looking at her again—thankfully—but his eyes are wistful, no longer smiling. "It used to be our staple, but I won't be able to make it for long. The wholesaler who used to sell us pistachios no longer imports to Austria or Germany. And my brother, who handled all the business, gathered his family and is on his way to China now. So, get the last ones that I have. It's bad enough I have to throw them away at the end of the day."

Mina is about to ask why—with such a selection!—but then remembers the red paint warning not to buy from the Jews marring the baker's window and bites her tongue.

"I'm sorry," she says.

The baker shakes his head—not her fault, nothing to apologize for—and slips another two croissants into her paper bag before tying it with a string.

When Mina tries to protest, the baker only shakes his head again. "For your parents. Or a special friend. Or siblings. Sharing sweets is good for both love and friendship."

Mina likes the man despite knowing him only for five minutes. There's something kind and familiar and pleasantly round and harmless about him, much like Chaplin the Tramp. She almost reconsiders deceiving him in such a manner, but then something nudges her, some invisible hand she sometimes feels hovering protectively over her shoulder.

"I'm sorry, I actually came in because I noticed the sign in your window."

The baker cocks his head in confusion.

"No, not that sign," Mina says with a nervous chuckle and a shake of her head. "The sign that says you're looking for a bookkeeper?"

Some tension leaves the baker's face. He's just weary now and also just a tad ghostly, with the faint film of flour coating his arms and left cheek.

"You'd think it's a joke, a Jew looking for a bookkeeper." His smile is crooked and so very sad, Mina feels a lump in her throat in spite of herself. "As I said, it was my brother, Arnold, who was good with numbers. Me, not so much. I love working with my hands and inventing recipes and whatnot, but numbers? Not my forte."

"It is mine."

He regards her dubiously.

"I know what you think. I'm much too young and probably inexperienced and you're right." For a moment, Mina falls silent, but then her eyes land on the abacus lying next to the cash register and a light ignites in them. "Let me show you a nifty trick if you have a minute."

The emptiness of the store in the middle of rush hour and the baker's expression tells her that he has all the time in the world, but Mina waits for his formal permission.

"Go on then," he says, humoring her.

"Hide that abacus under the counter so I can't see it and ask me to add or subtract or multiply or divide whatever big numbers spring to your head."

He arches a brow at her. *Is this a joke of some sort?* she can read in his eyes.

"What else would you ask a bookkeeper at a job interview?"

"Previous workplace recommendations."

"Anyone can type them out at home. And I suspect not many have applied, have they?"

He bristles slightly at that but pulls the abacus under the counter all the same.

"Go on then," he repeats, and Mina can almost distinguish a dare in his slightly narrowed eyes and chin that's jutting marginally out. "Seven hundred thirty-one plus five hundred eighty-four."

"One thousand three hundred and fifteen," Mina replies just as he finishes adding numbers under the counter.

The baker fixes her with a mistrustful stare. Mina sees him lowering the abacus even further, covering it with his apron. "Nine hundred fifty-six minus two thousand six hundred ninety-three."

It takes Mina less than two seconds to produce the answer. "Minus one thousand seven hundred and thirty-seven."

The baker retrieves the abacus and slams all the wooden rolls onto one side before hiding it once again. "Seventy-six thousand nine hundred and twenty-four divided by two."

"Thirty-eight thousand four hundred and sixty-two."

"Divided by four."

"Nine thousand six hundred fifteen point five."

"How are you doing this?" He stares at her with a mixture of disbelief and outright awe.

Mina shrugs with a small, innocent smile. "I told you, I'm good with numbers."

"This is not 'good with numbers.' This is…"

"A pistachio croissant of baked goods?" Mina suggests.

The baker regards her for a few seconds and then, suddenly, bursts into laughter. It looks rusty to Mina, as if he's forgotten how to do it properly. He offers her his flour-coated palm over the counter.

"As you correctly guessed, no one else has applied for the job." He pauses as she encloses her small palm into his. "But even if they did, I'd still take you, Fräulein…?"

"Best," Mina replies, shaking his hand. "Wilhelmina Best. Can I start tomorrow morning?"

SEVEN

She could have started yesterday morning, as far as Herr Freudenberg was concerned. Mina realizes this much as she takes in the sad state of the small room next to the pantry which serves him as a personal office of sorts. The tiny, closet-like affair that barely fits the desk crammed against its furthest wall is dingy and windowless and is only redeemed by its proximity to the kitchen. The aroma of roasted nuts, sweet dough, and freshly baked bread has seeped through its very pores, it seems. Somehow, the smell transforms the room from a dark closet into a secret nook of sorts.

The first thing Mina does is rearrange the heavy desk so that it faces the entrance instead of the wall. By the time Herr Freudenberg arrives with a stack of ledgers and papers, she's wringing with sweat but puts on a bright smile all the same.

"Just wanted to watch you work your magic, if you don't mind."

He seems puzzled, mutters something that Mina deciphers as "could have asked me, would have moved it for you," and deposits the tower of paperwork onto the desk.

"As I said, Arnold dealt with numbers. I'm a tad behind..."

Mina waves it off and opens a wooden case in which she brought several regular and two red pencils and a fountain pen she secretly pinched from her father's desk. According to her arrangements with Herr Freudenberg, she will only work till noon and will be back home before *Vati*. Plenty of time to put it back where it belongs.

"I see you came prepared." He regards her supplies appreciatively. "I do have pencils though. Forgot to bring them down together with all this"—he gestures somewhat desperately toward the ledgers. "Arnold, he lived and worked upstairs..."

Herr Freudenberg is all lost and alone and so very miserable, Mina feels an urge to do something for him, only she doesn't know what. She's much too young and has little experience in the friendship department, and besides, are they really friends or just two people caught on the same side of misery?

Mina can't say, but the urge to help remains, and so she promises to do the thing she knows how to do best. Count.

"You go ahead and work, Herr Freudenberg. I'll take care of everything here."

It appears to be enough. He smiles at her through what looks like mist in his warm brown eyes and nods gratefully before leaving her to her devices.

Left alone, Mina dives into work with the giddiness of a child at Christmas. There's no rhyme or reason to the ledgers or paper receipts, but there's seemingly no rhyme or reason to any problem when it first appears. One only has to move one step at a time and soon the ball of tangled twine begins to unravel if one only knows which end to pull at.

Ledgers into one stack, sorted by the month, with the last one on top. Arnold Freudenberg has been meticulous about records but only up until September. Mina figures it was then that he began gathering paperwork for his family's exit visas and passage to China. She doesn't know much about the process but suspects it's not an easy one.

Wholesale purchase receipts into another stack, also sorted by the date—she'll have to figure out which were the last ones entered into the ledger by Arnold so she can begin entering all the later ones after them.

Expenses—rent, taxes, electricity bills and all such—into yet another stack, the size of which Mina doesn't like one bit, even without looking at the numbers.

By ten, everything's sorted and organized. Armed with a sharpened pencil, Mina dissects the paper receipts all written by different hands and signed by countless people and reduces them to neat numbers in September ledger's columns. The first two weeks are balanced still, but the third one begins to waver, rather to Mina's displeasure but not surprise—she's seen it coming and yet it still bothers her, like anything slowly dipping toward negative. She hesitates for a while, but there's nothing doing and she puts her regular pencil down and picks up a red one. The last week of September is the first one that ended in a loss.

October doesn't look any better. The first week is somewhat similar to the last one of September, but the second one is all but disastrous. It's Mina's guess that it's then that the caricature went up, calling the good citizens of Linz to boycott Jewish-owned businesses. The only sales must have been from fellow Jews and devil-may-care Austrians who paid no heed to politics as long as their buns came in fresh and cost less than Aryan ones. But there were too few of them and the profits dipped even lower, sending Herr Freudenberg further into debt.

Through the numbers on her page, Mina watches her employer's life unravel in front of her eyes. She imagines him swallowing his tears as he dumps his little masterpieces into trash each evening without anyone so much as looking at them. She imagines him watching the SA men standing outside his shop to stop the last foolishly loyal customers from defying new Reich policies. She feels the cold in her fingers as she imagines him trying to wash off the caricature from his display window just to find it bigger and in the same spot the very next morning. Her chest heaves with righteous indignation as she enters a fine from the local police for "an attempt to erase public announcement" (since when graffiti became public announcements is anyone's guess) made out to "Jew Freudenberg" as yet another expense for October. More red pencil; the entire bottom of the ledger is red now, it's dripping from the pages like blood, and Mina slams it closed and sits with her hands pressed against her eyes, in front of which everything is also red, red, red—

A hand touches her shoulder. She yelps, startled, just to startle Herr Freudenberg in turn. The pastries on his plate tilt precariously to one side, but he places the plate down before they slide off it.

"I was calling your name for an entire minute." Mina sees him explain and silently curses herself for such an obvious mistake.

She had turned the table to face the door just so she could see him enter but closed her eyes instead, the daft little thing.

She apologizes for not hearing him; pretends to be overwhelmed with work—"too many numbers, they do that to the brain sometimes"—adds a guilty smile and yet another apology for startling him.

"That bad, eh?" He eyes the ledger she instinctively hides under her crossed arms.

For a few moments, Mina considers her answer. "Depending on how much you have left in the bank."

"Not much. Gave most of it to—" He turns away to gesture to the door, behind which the hostile new word lies, and Mina can't read his lips anymore. Guesses that it went to his brother, who needed it more. He turns back to her. "Rumor has it, they'll seize them all soon at any rate."

"Who'll seize what?" Mina asks, confused.

"New Austrian government. Our bank accounts."

"Oh." And then, when the meaning dawns on her, "Oh! But... can they do that? It's *your* money. Your hard-earned money."

From the baker, a resigned shrug. "Eat, Wilhelmina. Eat and go back home and don't concern yourself with my troubles. I don't pay you for that. Speaking of..." He shuffles in his pocket and fishes out a couple of bills and some change. "Your day's pay. I'll be paying you daily, if you don't mind. Because one day you may come and I won't be here and I don't want anyone hearing that Jew Freudenberg cheated a girl out of *her* hard-earned money."

"You're not Jew Freudenberg," Mina says softly, her cheeks aglow with the same indignation she felt for herself on the day she was thrown out of school. Defective. Undesirable. "You're Confectioner Freudenberg and the best one there is at that."

His lips twitch; he's about to say something but swings on his heel instead and all but runs out of the room. So as not to burst into tears in front of a sixteen-year-old girl. Mina's learned to read body language far too well not to understand that much.

EIGHT

LINZ, AUSTRIA. EARLY NOVEMBER 1938

A tap on her shoulder to call her attention. "Past perfect, Mina. Past."

Mina blinks at her father, then looks at the English translation of a German short story she wrote down in a hurry after her return from work. "What did I say?"

"Present. It's supposed to be past. Where's your head at these days, Mina?"

Somewhere underground, together with the bakery, buried under a growing pile of debt.

They've grown close, Herr Freudenberg and she, in these past few weeks. There hasn't been much business going on and therefore not much baking to do—Mina has persuaded her employer to cut down on the volume of ingredients to balance out the expenses a little—and besides, Mina gets the bookkeeping up to date within the first half hour of her working day. The rest they spend talking, whenever they aren't busy tasting some new culinary masterpieces Herr Freudenberg has produced. The Nazis can keep his business in a chokehold, but there is no suppressing the love one has for their profession. Without a single customer in his store, Herr Freudenberg heats his ovens and mixes the ingredients just so Mina can have something special to finish her lunch with.

"A new recipe today. Taste it and let me know what you think."

He never has to ask Mina twice.

"What is it?" Mina asks with her mouth full, manners forgotten.

A twinkle in the baker's eyes. "Take a guess."

"Blueberries? No, blackberries. Where did you get blackberries? And the cream... it's not sour cream and eggs. It has a texture of ice cream, but it's not cold. What *is* it?" She gushes with enthusiasm.

It's during those moments that Mina sees the shadow of the former Herr Freudenberg emerge. His delighted smile shines upon the entire kitchen like the sun breaking from behind the clouds on a stormy day, basking everything in its warm glow.

"Good, isn't it?"

"*Good?* It's out of this world!"

This is where her head is nowadays. In a world that won't last much longer and a part of which she's become in a few short weeks and which she can't stand to see crumbling before her very eyes.

"*Vati*, do your colleagues bring lunch to work or do they go out to get it?"

"Pardon?" her father replies, mystified.

Mina wets her lips and interlinks her fingers atop the story that matters so very little in this moment. "What if I could bring them fresh bread for their sandwiches every day? And then some pastries they could take home to their families? These are first-rate pastries, *Vati*, I promise. And the baker charges next to nothing for them."

"Those pastries you brought home a few weeks ago?"

He hasn't forgotten. How can he, after all? He and *Mutti* interrogated her for the next two days as to where she got the goods, and for such a cheap price at that. Needless to say, Mina wisely withheld the name and address of the bakery just so her mother wouldn't decide to stop by one evening after work and discover that her daughter has been shopping in the boycotted business. Her *deaf* daughter, who's not particularly on the Reich's good side as it is. And if she found out that Mina worked there on top of that... And so, Mina shrugged it off with some generic explanation amounting to "on the other side of town; was wandering around; don't remember the name."

She wouldn't have ever mentioned it again, but things in the bakery are looking bleaker by the day and Mina isn't in it just for the university admission money and her acting skills. Not any longer, she's not.

"Those very ones, yes."

Her father studies her in the yellow light of the table lamp. "I don't understand. Why would you want to bring food to my office? You're supposed to be studying."

"I am studying."

"Not as hard as before. Your results are slipping."

But what difference does it make if it's past perfect or present when a man's life is hanging by a thread? School doesn't teach how to save someone from metaphorical drowning, does it now? Just some idiotic stuff one wouldn't need in life at any rate. Mina's eyes have been opened in the past few weeks, and she knows this is more important than anything high school curriculum could ever teach her.

"I want to get out more. Want to talk to people more. People who are not you and *Mutti*," Mina clarifies when her father tries to interject. "At school, I could at least be a part of something. Now I'm stuck at home all day like some... invalid." The word is out of her mouth before she can stop herself. It strikes her father, hard; she can see that much in the pained expression his face takes on. "I can't be dependent on you for my entire life.

I need to do something. Find work of some kind. And the baker, he said he'd pay me."

Herr Freudenberg knows nothing of any such arrangement (not that she would charge him anything for such deliveries), but that's Mina's trouble, not her father's.

"He did?" He father looks skeptical and just a bit more protective than Mina wants him to be. "When did you see him again?"

"Oh, a few days ago. Just slipped my mind to tell you."

"You didn't tell me you were out."

"I went out spontaneously. The day was beautiful."

"You should tell me these things beforehand so I can leave you the tram fare to get back home if you end up wandering off again."

"It's all right." She has her own money now, but, of course, she doesn't share this detail with him.

Her father muses something over. "Is he a young man?"

For an instant, Mina is lost. "Who?"

"The baker you travel through half the town to see, Mina."

"Oh." Mina breaks into laughter. If *Vati* only knew of the true nature of their relationship. "No. Not at all. He's your age."

"Well, thank you kindly. I'm an old man now."

"That's not what I meant and you know it."

They're both laughing now, but Mina's eyes are still searching, pleading.

"I suppose, I can arrange something." Her father surrenders at least; tucks her long braid behind her ear. "But you still have to study, Mina. You have to sit your exams."

"Oh, I will, *Vati*."

She's planning to do just that, in the University of Graz, when the time comes.

. . .

Mina leaps off the last step of the tram trolley and all but dances into the bakery. The satchel full with books swings from her shoulder—Herr Freudenberg has long ago suggested she brings her study materials to work, seeing that it only takes her less than an hour to enter all the previous day's expenses and profits into the ledger. He doesn't know she's homeschooled. Revealing the fact would mean a whole chain of questions Mina isn't ready to unravel, for unraveling such a chain will inevitably lead to revealing her handicap and she's doing too well to ruin it all just yet. Besides, Mina simply can't bear the idea of seeing the disappointment in Herr Freudenberg's face once he realizes that she's been lying to him all along. No. Let him think she finished school last year and is getting ready for her entrance exams while saving up money. Half-a-truth doesn't really equal a lie, does it?

She bursts inside the brightly lit front room, inhales a lungful of mouthwatering aroma and proceeds into the kitchen, her face aglow from the frosty air and the news she's about to share.

"I got us our first delivery contract!"

Herr Freudenberg swallows the second half of his "good morning" and stares at her with his mouth slightly agape. "What now?"

"If you let me out half an hour earlier each day, I can deliver sandwiches and pastries to a law office on Hauptstraße. It's across the Danube, but I'll make it there by twelve; I've already checked the tram schedule."

"A law office?" his lips repeat. He's not as excited as Mina expected him to be; more puzzled and concerned. "How did you... Is it a Jewish law office?"

It's Mina's turn to regard him for a few moments in confused silence. "No. Does it matter?"

Herr Freudenberg's lips puff with a mirthless chuckle. "Oh

yes, child." His smile is mild and so very sorrowful. "Thank you kindly for your troubles, but I fear I'm not allowed to cater to Aryans. It's frowned upon for them to shop here, but for me to sell to them is a criminal case."

Mina didn't know that. For a few torturously long moments, her mind is feverishly at work. Her teeth dig into her lip as she calculates the odds and possible outcomes, weighs the risks against the profits.

"What if we do it off the books?" she finally asks.

"Wilhelmina,..." Herr Freudenberg is about to begin, but Mina is ready with an answer.

"It's not an actual written contract. It's you, selling food to me, and me delivering it to whoever I want. And if we don't enter it into the ledger, there's no paper trail, since there are no receipts—"

"Wilhelmina, it's fraud." He regards her, warning clear in his eyes.

"I know that. I'm your bookkeeper, remember?" She's not fazed in the slightest. In an unfair world, it's only fair not to play by the rules. And God knows, this man needs help. "And as your bookkeeper, I bear full responsibility."

He's shaking his head so vigorously, his baker's hat slips onto one side. He catches it, crashes it in his flour-powdered hands. "Not on my watch. You're not risking your future for some Jew you scarcely know. As a matter of fact, you shouldn't be working here in the first place. I haven't told you that much, have I?"

Another bitter chuckle; Mina can't hear it but sees it in the sharp creases around his mouth.

"I tricked you into this affair, didn't I? Took advantage of your innocence. We're not allowed to hire Aryans, but I never asked if you were one, even though I knew that you were, just to claim ignorance later if they asked me. You didn't know, and I desperately needed a bookkeeper. And now you wish to risk your future for a no-good old swindler like me. No, Mina, that just won't do. Go home and study and stay on the government's good side. There's nothing for you here."

Mina says nothing for a very long time. Not to cause offense; if anything, Herr Freudenberg's sudden, desperate honesty fills her heart to the brim and makes it swell with emotion. She supposes she can only repay him with the same.

"It seems both of us are swindlers, Herr Freudenberg. And the government wants nothing more to do with me than it wants with you."

He's confused beyond any measure—Mina sees it in his brows drawn together and his mouth full of questions he's unsure how to ask.

"I'm deaf, Herr Freudenberg. And I'm not taking a year off after school to prepare for the university entrance exams, even though I'm planning to sit them—that much is true. The school's new headmaster has thrown me out without letting me finish my last year because they don't want deaf students among them. Our place is with other 'challenged' ones, they suggested. My father kindly disagreed and so, here I am, studying school material under your very roof, instead of doing so at home, because you allowed me to take this job. And I can never thank you enough for that."

"You're deaf?" he finally repeats after a very long pause. "But you're talking..."

"I lost my hearing at five. Only children born deaf have difficulty with speech, if they speak at all. If one loses their hearing after having learned to speak, the speech remains. So, I was fortunate in a sense."

"But how can you possibly understand me if you can't hear me?"

"I read lips."

The realization slowly dawns on him. "Is that why you

turned the table that very first day? Because you wouldn't hear me enter and call you otherwise?"

Mina nods with a guilty smile. Only, he's not mad in the slightest. Just like she wasn't mad at him for his admission. That's how it is among friends, she guesses. That's how it should be.

"My, but you *are* crafty!" His eyes are full of mirth and—is she reading it right?—admiration, almost. "I thought you had your head in the clouds sometimes when you wouldn't reply to my calling you, but now I see. You couldn't hear me! Ha! I would have never guessed, had you not told me just now."

"You would have. Eventually."

He's suddenly rushing toward her, arms outstretched; tears the flour-dusted apron off his chest not to mar her red overcoat as he embraces her.

"If you're saying something right now, I can't see it," Mina reminds him through her own chuckles as he strokes her braided hair with his gentle, fatherly hands.

He pulls away at once, slams himself on his forehead. "Forgive me, child! I was saying what a poor, sweet little child you are. How could they do this... to *you*?"

Mina shrugs and worms her way out of her overcoat. It has somehow become clear between them that she's not going anywhere. Not anytime soon, she's not.

"Much like they did it to you and your family, Herr Freudenberg. And since there's honor among thieves, it's only fair that two old thieves like us stick together through this. If you don't mind a deaf bookkeeper, I don't mind sneaking your goods to those very hungry lawyers. If the outside world doesn't want to help us, we'll help ourselves, shall we?"

He's quiet for a beat, but, slowly, a smile grows where two harsh lines permanently rest. "Such words from such a young girl, Fräulein Best."

"They made me grow up fast, Herr Freudenberg."

And made him age beyond his years and, just out of spite for them and their damned-to-all-hell laws, they shake on that, two old swindlers in a country full of righteous men.

NINE

For a few days, it works like a finely tuned machine, this little enterprise of theirs. Each morning, Mina arrives with the profits from the previous day—her father's colleagues buy everything she brings, after having had their very first taste of Herr Freudenberg's magnificent bread and pastries—and hands them directly to the baker. After lots of protests, she finally surrenders and takes a few coins for the tram fare, but never anything for the delivery itself. It's no trouble, really, and she loves seeing her father in the afternoons, she claims, and finally, Herr Freudenberg surrenders as well but makes Mina's favorite pistachio cupcakes all the same out of the measly precious crumbs he has left.

Every afternoon, she leaves with bags and boxes that send heads turning in her direction whenever she boards the tram to take her over the bridge. She smiles knowingly when some of her fellow tram riders inquire as to where she got the goods.

"Oh, it's not from the store. My grandmother dabbles in baking. I'm only taking it to *Vati*'s office. His colleagues love her cooking."

"As they should." People nod in disappointment and are about to turn away when another thought occurs to Mina.

"I can deliver it to you too, if you pay for the ingredients and my troubles."

Women's eyes—since it's mostly women who ride the tram this time of the day as men toil at work—light up at the idea and particularly when Mina opens one of the boxes and reveals the edible treasure inside, all creamy swirls and multicolored decorations and glazes that gleam so very appetizingly in the afternoon light. "Why, I certainly would!"

Linz is not a big city and Mina doesn't mind adding another trip to her daily route. As long as Herr Freudenberg's business stays afloat, she doesn't mind it at all.

The sun is slowly drowning in the Danube and Mina is still on the tram, her face turned away from that blood-red sunset. One last delivery and she'll be on her way to Herr Freudenberg to deliver him the day's earnings. He'll be shaking his head, undoubtedly, saying that she should have saved the trip and brought the money the following morning, but Mina is bursting with pride just like her tiny pearl-studded coin purse is bursting with the first paper money it has ever seen. She can't wait till tomorrow. She needs to prove it to him—and to herself as well—that everything will be all right; that even two undesirables like them still have a fighting chance as long as their talents are in demand.

There's a bite in the air when Mina steps off the tram—the winter is at their heels, nipping at them like a pup. Still harmless but with a mouth full of sharp teeth. As she crosses the street, a police truck turns the corner, blinding her momentarily with its bright yellow headlights. Mina bolts out of its way and, safe on the pavement, checks her precious cargo. Thankfully, no cupcakes harmed. The cream is untouched.

Mina pulls her mittens back on and watches the policemen spill out of the truck. Their commanding officer is shouting orders, but all Mina can see is his jaw working. Too far away and all but turned away from her.

Must be a drill of some sort, she thinks to herself and sets off on her way, paying no heed to the detachment any longer.

In the gathering twilight, she finds the right building number, takes two steps at a time all the way to the third floor, rings the bell. No address book needed—her memory stores just about anything in it like photographical snapshots.

When a familiar woman from the tram opens the door, Mina greets her and holds the box with cupcakes to her, proud, as though she's baked them herself. The woman beams as she inspects the contents. Mina can only guess the compliments the happy customer is showering upon the baker as she counts out the money, her head bowed over her purse.

"My grandmother sends her best regards and hopes that you enjoy," Mina chirps and even curtsies a little as she accepts the money.

"Your grandmother has some talent!" That much Mina can make out.

You haven't the faintest idea, she thinks and hides a coy smile.

Her heart sings in her chest as Mina hops on a tram—this one heading to the commercial part of the city, where the big market square is. The streets are all lit up now—the lampposts, the windows behind which Mina can see women setting the tables for dinner and children pressing their noses against the glass as they gaze at the street outside. Too many children. Too many curious eyes peering through the glass, as though expecting something.

That last part suddenly strikes Mina as odd, like a single

false note slipping into a seemingly perfect orchestra performance.

Whatever can they possibly be looking at?

Mina turns her head this way and that as the tram clangs forward but sees nothing out of the ordinary. Yet another police detachment taking formation not too far from the bridge, but that's about all the excitement she can possibly notice. She scans the tram wagon, but it's all the same bored faces around her, some swaying gently in time with the tram motion, some immersed in their books or newspapers. An elderly couple are murmuring to each other at the very back of the car, chained off from the rest and marked with a plaque that reads, *for Jews.*

Mina suddenly recalls her father mentioning something about some German diplomat getting shot in Paris, but that has little to do with Linz, doesn't it? It would explain the police detachments though.

Somewhat pacified with such an explanation, Mina returns to her dreamy state; she can't help but salivate at the thought of the sweet leftovers Herr Freudenberg will inevitably slip into her satchel—"to sweeten everyone's dreams," in his own words. He shows such care for her family, even though he's never met them. He's that kind of a man, Herr Freudenberg. All warmth and light and love. That's why his pastries taste so good.

Mina leaps off the tram's step even before it comes to a full stop and runs into the bakery. She finds Herr Freudenberg in the kitchen, cleaning the counters to a gleaming perfection, ready for the next day's work.

"Herr Freudenberg, look!" she cries, forgoing the greeting, and pours the day's earnings out of her purse.

The look on the baker's face is beyond what words can describe. With trembling fingers, he reaches for the money but doesn't quite touch it, as though he fears it will evaporate somehow if he does. Chuckling softly, Mina pushes it closer to him, spreads the coins and paper bills around so they can both count them. It's not quite profit yet—even he, the one "terrible with numbers," can see that much—but it's something. The beginning of a new day.

And Mina is already far ahead of him, all twinkling eyes and restless hands that won't stop gesticulating.

"I was thinking on the way here: if we switch to order-only production, we can get back to making a profit again as soon as mid-December. And for the holidays—everyone loves a good holiday treat, don't they?—we can double and triple it. Do you know any Jewish bakers you can hire to assist you? Likely, they aren't turning profit either and will be glad to come onboard. And I can find someone to help me deliver the orders. Together, we can get this—"

Herr Freudenberg's sudden jump silences her. He's staring at something over her shoulder, wide-eyed and growing paler by the second.

Mina catches the smell of burning gasoline before she sees it. And even when she swings round and does see it—a smashed bottle forming a small fire in the middle of the front room—she can't quite believe her eyes. It's much too surreal: the shards of the broken storefront littering the floor that has been immaculately swept just moments ago, the Molotov cocktail sending acrid fumes into the air that has known little else but aromas of sweet dough, whipped cream, and roast almonds. The entire scene has a nightmarish quality to it and Mina squeezes her eyes shut to wake herself up.

Only, there's no waking from the brutal reality thrust upon them.

Mina is the first to come out of her stunned state. Her brain is still all fog, but her hands are working of their own accord, sweeping the money off the countertop and shoving it into her employer's hand—"take it, hide it!"—and then off she sprints into her small cubicle to save the precious accounting records. Herr Freudenberg is pulling at the end of her scarf, urging her to drop all that nonsense no doubt, but in Mina's veins, an old Austrian's soldier's blood is pumping.

She's oddly unafraid of the unraveling horror; if anything, everything has come into a sudden sharp focus. She hurls the books into her satchel, sweeps today's receipts on top of them, swings sharply on her heel toward the ashen-faced baker.

"Where do you keep all your recipes?"

Still mortified beyond all words, he taps the side of his head silently. *All in here.*

Mina nods, reassured, and pulls the end of his apron over his mouth. "Try to hold your breath until we're out."

The front room is already chock-full of black smoke. Bent in half, her own scarf over her nose, Mina probes her way along the counter, the glass of which is already hot to the touch. Her other hand, over which the satchel is dangling, is holding onto Herr Freudenberg's palm that is colder than ice. He's pulling back just a tad, like a frightened horse unsure of a dangerous path, but Mina's grip is firm on his hand. She pulls him through the curtain of black smoke and out the door and lets him stumble onto the cobbled pavement and rest on all fours, coughing and gasping for air but very much unscathed. Mina's own eyes are smarting something terrible, but she smiles as she rubs the smoke out of them.

Saved, both of them. All else is material stuff, and material stuff is restored sooner or later.

It's at that precise moment of the first wave of relief that a pair of hands grabs her by the shoulders and sends her hurtling to the ground. Momentarily stunned by her fall—or has she hit her head on the cobbles, she can't quite tell—Mina tries to blink the world back into focus. However, what she sees is yet another grotesque nightmare that just doesn't want to end. Instead of helping hands, black boots reach for Herr Freudenberg. They connect with his nose and temple, all at the same time, from different directions, and send a spray of blood into the air as the baker's body is propelled backwards. Mina gasps as he lands on the street like a broken puppet, but someone yanks her by her braid and she yelps as she comes face to face with an enraged man shouting something at her, spraying her with saliva like a mad dog. She can't see Herr Freudenberg any longer. Her braid is wrapped so tightly around an SA stormtrooper's meaty fist, she fears he'll rip it clear off her scalp.

"...Dirty Jewess..." she catches his lips articulate before a harsh slap comes, sending her ears ringing.

Even in her frantic state, Mina refuses to let emotions take over. If she succumbs to fear, it's all over, she realizes with chilling clarity. And so, with her eyes still stinging from both smoke and unprovoked assault, Mina seeks a policeman out of the gathering crowd. There's quite a few of them around, as a matter of fact, just like there are quite a few SA men, or whoever the hell these jackbooted devils are; only, unlike the SA, the police make no motion to aid either her or her employer. They stand there in indifferent silence, hands clasped behind their backs as they survey the violent mob hurling more Molotov cocktails into the stores Mina remembers being marked "Jewish." They take no interest in the businesses' owners being dragged into the street and showered with vicious kicks and truncheon blows.

Instead of the police, it's Herr Freudenberg who crawls toward his assailant and clasps at his boot with his bloodied hands. His face a disfigured mask, he pleads with the uniformed man, pointing at Mina and bringing his shaking hands together in a prayer and pointing at her again.

Suddenly, she's on her feet, only this time she's held by the shoulder instead of her hair. That patch of her scalp is still burning something frightful.

A different man comes before her. Unlike his predecessor, he seems more in control of himself. Or, perhaps, he's the goons' commanding officer—Mina's too shaken up to tell.

His lips are moving, but, all at once, it appears as though she's lost all ability to read them. He repeats something and finally she makes out a single word—"papers."

"Papers... yes, I have papers," Mina mumbles and gropes about the cobbles for her satchel. It's next to her, its contents spilled onto the wet stones as though from a gutted fish.

The man squats next to her, picks her accounting books up one by one. At long last, Mina remembers that the papers are in the inner pocket of her coat, where *Vati* has instructed her to keep them so that she won't lose them. It's there, to be sure, a small passport book, slightly damp with her sweat, with her photo, name, and address—all in order.

"Please, Herr Offizier, allow me to get Herr Freudenberg to the hospital," Mina says as he peruses her identification closely.

To her immense relief, her employer has been left alone for the time being, the uniformed thugs waiting around him like a pack of dogs, but not attacking just yet. Waiting for the command.

The one in charge narrows his eyes at her. "...were you doing... store?"

Mina half-guesses, half-pieces the question together, her brain is still much too preoccupied with other matters to read lips effectively.

Just what was she doing in the Jewish store? That's a good question.

It's Herr Freudenberg again, shaking his head and pulling the books closer to himself as though to separate Mina from any possible incrimination.

"...good Aryan girl... wanted sweets for the family... when the... exploded... I put... books... satchel..." Mina sees him lie through the blood forming little pink bubbles on his broken lips.

She thinks of interjecting, of explaining precisely what she was doing there, but remembers the law prohibiting Jews from hiring Aryans and closes her mouth slowly. It will only land the kind baker in more trouble. Better she stays an innocent customer who found herself in the wrong place at the wrong time.

The uniformed man shakes her shoulder impatiently and, fearing another blow—he must have thought she was ignoring him, and whatever he was asking while she was staring at her employer, on purpose—Mina blurts out, "I'm deaf, Herr Offizier!"

He's silent a beat. Then, he cocks his head slightly.

"How did you understand me before?"

"I read lips, Herr Offizier."

"And you can talk."

"I lost my hearing as a child. That's the reason I retained my speech."

He nods after all and hands her back her papers.

He taps her shoulder, lightly this time, and articulates, "How did you know the Jew's name?"

Finding her footing again, Mina plasters a dumb smile over her face. "Been buying discounted stuff off him at the end of the day. *Mutti* loves his sweets!"

The man sighs in exasperation. "Do you not know of the law that prohibits Aryans from buying from the Jews?"

Mina only smiles again, even dumber this time. "I'm home-schooled, Herr Offizier. I don't know much about things."

The prevailing stereotype that the deaf are also mentally impaired plays right into her hands then. The SA man shakes his head in apparent disgust and waves her off.

Get lost and don't let me catch you here again—Mina can only guess his parting words as she walks unsteadily away from the bakery, now fully engulfed in flames and Herr Freudenberg still kneeling in front of his assailants.

In the distance, a fire brigade stands, just as indifferent and idle as the police.

TEN

GRAZ, AUSTRIA. SPRING—SUMMER 1939

The night that went down in history as the Night of the Broken Glass (*Kristallnacht*) is long gone from the memory of her fellow townspeople, but not from Mina's. The bruise on her cheek has healed; the one left on her heart still refuses to. The very next morning, she set off back to the bakery, only to find its blackened remains smoldering faintly in the lingering fog. Herr Freudenberg? No one had heard of him, as though the man who'd been a fixture among them for years had never existed at all. Then, the policeman came and advised her to get lost if she knew what was good for her, and so Mina did. It didn't mean that she didn't return every day in the following weeks in the hope of some news, a single word at least. But shortly after the New Year celebrations, some new owner came, gutted the place, and turned it into a leather goods store. On the display where Herr Freudenberg's pistachio cupcakes used to be, gun holsters now gleamed—oiled, fat, and self-important, just like the store owner himself. Jackboots instead of cherry-filled croissants. Leather belts with heavy buckles instead of almond-sprinkled pastries. This was her country now.

Bitter memories of that very last visit rush like a flood over

Mina when she least wants it. A lone girl, in her navy suit and
hair tied into a tight knot at the nape of her neck, she's all but
lost in a sea of rumbustious young men as they push and shove
their way to the auditorium. It's the same one where the
entrance exams were held; the same one where Mina was
forced to take the seat at the very back (there was simply no
pushing through that sea of wide backs and shoulders in front of
her) and squint at the blackboard with all her might to make out
the equations. Her former math teacher was right: it was all
indeed written down and she did pass it with flying colors and
paid her entrance fee with the money earned from Herr
Freudenberg, but now what?

Slowly, the stream of new students of the natural sciences
faculty forces its way through the doors. The auditorium is a
tremendous affair, Gothic and oppressing with its columns and
heavy plasterwork on the ceiling and all heavy, mounted
wooden seats like pews in a cathedral. Much too aware of her
gender, inappropriate somehow for such an establishment
according to all the side-eyed looks she receives, Mina excuses
her way to the first three rows. She managed to squint her way
through the exam, but there is no chance of reading lips from all
the way at the back. And today is the dean's welcome speech.

Fortune is on her side: a strapping young fellow with brilliant blue eyes orders a gangly youth to move his seat so that
Mina can be at the front. The gangly fellow is none too pleased,
but arguing with the towering student would earn him an ear
slap and so he goes, with a contemptuous last look in Mina's
direction, but he does.

"Some people their mothers just don't raise right."

Mina thanks providence that the tall student was looking at
her when he said that and thanks him in return.

Fake it until you no longer can.

She did try to fake it with Herr Freudenberg and look
where it got them both. *No.* Not them both. Just him. Mina—

she's safe for now, despite being tormented with a guilty conscience that keeps her awake most nights and gnaws on her stomach at all waking hours, but she's still here, still living her life. Who can say the same about her former employer?

The dean approaches the podium. Unlike her favorite physicist Einstein and his wild mop of hair and an attire to match, the dean is all polished and groomed, in his silver made-to-measure suit and a signet pinky ring—much more of a politician than a scientist. Mina can't hear his voice but can tell he's quite in love with the sound of it. He smiles much too easily and talks about privilege and the great achievements of their predecessors and the historic pressure that lies on their—this new generation of scientists—shoulders... He stumbles only once, when his gaze falls upon Mina and stays on her like that of a researcher perusing some fascinating but deadly bacteria under the microscope.

"As you have likely noticed, we have quite a few female students this year." He pauses. "Only one in our faculty though." Another smile Mina doesn't care much for at all. "Dear, would you stand up and tell us, please, why you decided to enroll in a university and occupy a student seat which could otherwise have belonged to a man?"

Color rising swiftly in her cheeks, Mina forces herself up. She's both enraged and embarrassed and, for a split second, wishes that she just stayed home and minded her affairs and spared herself all this humiliation that would lead to nothing in the end. But then something else stirs inside her. Her grandfather's officer's pride or the words her mother had said on the platform when seeing Mina off—"You go and make a difference, my girl. God knows you have enough smarts to"—or perhaps her own sense of being, her own assurance that she has just as much right to be here as her fellow male students. All at once, the answer is right there, on the tip of her tongue.

"Come autumn and our first semester, I want to study and

further the development of the theory of relativity. It is my profound conviction that in it lies the future of all precise sciences, starting with aeronautics and ending with peaceful means of fuel production. I'm particularly interested in nuclear science as it's still in its infancy. My biggest dream is to watch it grow into something truly life-changing for all humanity."

The dean smiles indulgently and with a hint of distaste. "Einstein?"

"Yes."

"His theory is Jewish science, as you should be aware."

A few snickers. Mina doesn't hear them but sees them, feels them through her very skin.

"But that's the beauty of formulas, Herr Professor, isn't it? E still equals mc squared whether the man who discovered it is Jewish or Hindu or Catholic or atheist. Same applies to those who use these formulas. Physics is a universal language, the only one that allows no argument."

No one is snickering anymore. If anything, they stare too intently, and such attention Mina needs least of all. And so, she smiles at the auditorium around her, much in the same manner as she did at the SA men on that dreaded *Kristallnacht*, and adds quickly, "I'm a girl, as you have probably noticed. We don't like arguments much."

I'm a girl, just a tad silly and perfectly harmless.

They leave her alone. She's not a threat any longer.

Mina spends summer at home, in Linz and near it whenever her father takes a weekend off and takes his family to the mountains. They rent a small villa, usually near a lake, and soak up the sun on its grassy banks, bodies lathered in lotion, heads tilted up, eyes closed, toes digging into a thin line of cool sand just bordering the lake. If they're fortunate, there's a boat that comes with the villa, and even if it's ordinarily not the fanciest

of affairs, Mina loves taking it out by herself into the middle of
the lake. There, she lets it drift languidly as she lies on its
bottom with a book blocking her face from the sun. She would
surely have dozed off today if it had been a novel, but this latest
acquisition is contraband smuggled by her own father—God
knows from where (he categorically refused to say). It's almost
handmade, with mimeographed pages sewn roughly together,
but it's full of leading American physicists' latest works,
including her favorite, Einstein. He is also an American now, if
not by blood, then by the citizenship he was given after being
forced out of his homeland by Hitler's hateful policies.

Mina devours each article with a hunger that is almost physical, in that private little world of hers where no one can interrupt the flight of her own thoughts. Like a puzzle moved into
places by an invisible hand, grains of discoveries slip into one
another in Mina's mind. What appeared to be an impenetrable
wall just a few months ago when she stared at it, all spelled out
on her blackboard, is suddenly opening wide like a portal to an
entirely new, mystical dimension.

Gulping formulas one by one, Mina sits up, propelled by an
impulse, just like Meitner and Strassmann and Hahn must have
done when their theory was proved correct by the experiments
of their German and American colleagues. There was no
mistake in their calculations, as countless scientists have
claimed, with a self-satisfied look about them, for the past few
months. A Jewish physicist—an Austrian and a woman, just like
Mina!—and a German chemist indeed split the atom. The
smallest particle in the world, they shattered like a glass ball and
marveled at the isotopes and something else it had produced in
the wake of its splitting.

Mina's heart won't settle as she rows as fast as she can
toward the shore to share the discovery with her parents.

"Look at you!" her mother exclaims when Mina finally
enters their temporary home, drunk on sun, fresh air, and the

wildest new ideas bouncing about in her agitated mind. "You've really done it this time. Burned yourself to a crisp. Red like a lobster! Johann, will you look at her?"

Even removed from the hospital, Mina's mother remains a healer. It's no wonder that all of their neighbors prefer to knock on Liv Best's door rather than seek a physician's advice. Mina has lost count of all the skinned knees her mother has cleaned and bandaged in their apartment's bathroom while the children's mothers scolded their offspring for not watching where they ran. There are never lines in Liv's domain and she can diagnose anyone within minutes without all the unnecessary philosophizing and produce a medicine from her personal pharmacy—a cabinet in the corner of the kitchen that is always stocked to its gills. But what must keep them returning to Mina's mother is her bedside manner, which is unrivaled in the whole of Linz, Mina is certain of it. Together with a treatment plan, Liv offers words of reassurance and compassion that are issued from her very heart and a small jar of honey and a few treats—to speed up her patient's recovery—and then checks on them unprompted and unpaid, even after long work hours, because healing is what she was born to do.

Mina admires her mother for her selflessness but pities her at the same time. All Liv does, she does for others. Scatters herself before people until only crumbs are left and they take advantage of her goodness. Mina doesn't have that in her. She's an ambitious little thing who wants to see her name in scientific papers, and as for people? They are a selfish herd and if they want nothing to do with her, why should she worry about them? She's been kicked far too many times to keep searching for love and acceptance where only contempt is found. Let her stick to her scientific studies; they don't judge but reveal instead, if one is bright enough to keep digging. Lise Meitner's example has just proved this much.

"And you are no better!" Liv scolds her husband while

Mina is all but bursting with news. "Could have given her that journal later, when she's getting ready for bed. You know perfectly well how she gets whenever she gets her mitts on those journals. Doesn't eat, doesn't drink, doesn't budge from the same spot. It's a miracle she doesn't forget to breathe when she starts reading."

But Mina's father only smiles at his daughter like a conspirator through the smoke of his pipe (he only smokes it in summer and only in the countryside, for whatever odd reason) and asks if she learned something new.

Mina nods, gulps down the water straight from the pitcher while her mother is rummaging through the multiple potted plants on the windowsill in search of the aloe to apply to Mina's burned stomach and thighs, and thanks him once again.

"The least I can do," he says with the same smile that is half-wistful and half-infinite love. "Now that you got yourself into the university, you ought to have at least some edge over those other students. And where to get that edge, if not from foreign sources?"

He's still upset with her for keeping the entire university business from him—Mina can tell, even though he's trying so very hard not to show it. The conversation they had about it took place a long time ago, but the shadow still hangs over them, even here, in this pastoral, emerald-green valley surrounded by mountain peaks, brown like the best Belgian chocolates dusted with sugar powder on their very tops.

"You could have come to me with this, you know."

"You would have talked me out of it."

"Would I have?"

Mina couldn't answer that back then and still can't now. She carries the guilt around like a suitcase, refusing to let it go, to unpack and forget once and for all, and wonders if she will feel the same betrayal when her own child suddenly flies the familial coup without once consulting her just because it was something that she had to do by herself, something that she could never bear to talk about had she failed, something that was an all-or-nothing sort of deal... If she ever has a child of her own. According to the latest racial laws, anyone "defective" is a strong candidate for "voluntary" sterilization, so as not to "contaminate" the perfect Aryan gene pool. Their family doctor hasn't said anything about this yet. Mina's not quite of age yet, and besides, she lost her hearing later in life and the law is still murky on account of such particular cases. At any rate, it's best not to think of it yet.

"They split the atom, *Vati!* Imagine that? What everyone thought was impossible, they did it—Meitner and Hahn. And if what I'm concluding from their recent studies is right, they're talking about the possibility of sustained atomic explosion that can be generated from splitting the nucleus of uranium. Berlin scientists called the splitting process itself 'fission' in the February issue of *Nature* magazine and it perfectly fits with Einstein's formula—"

"You lost me right after the words 'recent studies'." Her father smiles.

He always looks a bit sheepish when Mina enters ones of her "states," as she herself calls it—the unrestrained stream of scientific terms flying off her feverish lips, wild gesticulations accompanying them. She's in her own universe in moments like these—the universe her father is in awe of, as though it's positively mystifying to him just how exactly he and his wife could produce someone so unlike them. Extraordinary, that's what he called it.

Mina takes a breath to slow herself down a bit, remembers her audience and smiles a tad guiltily. "Imagine that a uranium atom is a drop of this water." She picks the empty pitcher up and tilts it until a sole drop forms on its narrow nose. "It's very wobbly and unstable and ready to divide itself on the slightest of provocations, such as the impact of a single neutron." She flicks at the drop with her fingers, disrupting it and making it land on the table in a spray of four separate drops. "Not the perfect example with the water, but just imagine that there's two of them because that's exactly how the uranium atom is split." She wipes the extra drops off the surface to illustrate her explanation. "Now, the two nuclei formed by the division of a uranium nucleus together would be lighter than the original uranium nucleus by about one-fifth the mass of the proton. Why would that be?"

"The by-product is lighter in mass than the original product?" her father asks tentatively.

"Yes."

He gives it some thought but ends up spreading his arms in a helpless gesture.

"Because the energy is released," Mina finishes in a whisper that, for some reason, sends goosebumps down his arms, as though in his daughter's eyes he suddenly sees some grave and formidable discovery that could potentially change the entire world. "After the atomic split, the two nuclei are forced apart by their mutual electric repulsion and acquire high speed and hence very large energy. And now imagine if you bombard a million uranium atoms with neutrons at the same time, forcing them apart, creating all this energy and directing it to whatever one's mind can conceive."

Mina didn't realize her mother was listening to her the entire time until she steps in front of her, a sliced leaf of aloe all but forgotten in her hand. "You could light up the entire world."

Mina nods at her, delighted to be understood. "Yes, *Mutti*. The entire wide world."

ELEVEN

GRAZ, AUSTRIA. AUTUMN 1939

The auditorium is only half-filled on the first day of theoretical physics studies. On the first day of September the war broke out, the war that was in the back of everyone's mind for the past three years but as some vague, unrealistic threat that would somehow divert itself from its course and never come to fruition. Only, it was here at long last, marching past the university windows in its steel-lined boots, robbing its halls of yesterday's students.

Mina looks around while Professor Erbacher is sorting his papers for the lecture and sees only thick lenses, hunched backs or eyes averted in shame—the army rejects who might as well stay put where they are as far as the High Command of the Wehrmacht is concerned.

Mina is surprised to find her introduction day's champion among them. Whatever is he, the perfect physical specimen who belongs on the draft campaign posters plastered all over the city, doing among their pitiful lot?

He notices Mina staring and winks at her from a few rows back.

"How goes it, Einstein?" he mouths.

Mina gestures toward the street where the echo of the boots is sending the other students into a black depression, then toward him and adds a shrug as an extra measure.

He grins coyly and begins to scribble something on his notepad. In a moment, a paper ball is flying into her hands. No one ever threw notes to her at school. She was always the odd one out, the girl no one wanted to communicate with, neither in words nor in writing. Perhaps that's why the note feels so special as she unwraps it, smooths it out on her lap.

Too smart for the army, it reads and Mina can't help but quickly bite down a smile.

That's not a diagnosis, she writes back and throws it clumsily back at him.

Apparently, it is, the following note reads. *By the way, I'm Siggy.*

Mina, she writes, throws the note and turns just in time for Professor Erbacher to lift his head to scan his scantily attended class.

"At least taking of attendance won't take long," Mina watches his lips mutter as he flips open the attendance book. "Good. More time for physics."

The lectures are all right and easy to keep up with as long as the professors address the students directly, and even when they turn their backs to their class to scribble lengthy equations on the blackboard, Mina still follows those and puts two and two together well enough. It does give her headaches, this constant hyper-vigilance, eyes straining with effort as they try to take it all in at once: professors' lips, students' answers she can scarcely make out as they're always standing up and are sideways to her, keeping her head high enough so that she doesn't miss the professor calling her name while trying to copy the latest formula off the blackboard. It's not an easy job, to "listen" with her eyes all the time, but being thrown out of the university for her "defectiveness" before she can prove her worth would be even worse. And so, Mina stocks up on the pain pills ("thank you, *Vati*, for your generous allowance and *Mutti* for your home pharmacy I can raid!") and gulps coffee in the student canteen in between lectures to keep herself as alert as humanly possible.

"You can't survive on coffee alone, Einstein."

Siegfried—or Siggy as he introduced himself in his missive —is next to her today in the student canteen line.

"Do you have enough money for food?" he asks with an almost endearing directness when Mina grabs her coffee off the counter with a timid smile.

"Oh yes," she rushes to assure him. "I'm just not hungry during lectures."

"Because if you don't, just tell me."

In place of a reply, Mina produces her little purse and pops it open. Bills and coins are stuffed into it without any rhyme or reason, but there are plenty of them.

He nods, visibly satisfied, and barks something at the canteen worker, who most likely made a mistake of telling him to move it.

"Before we were so rudely interrupted," he continues, touching her elbow in a confidential way and lowering to her ear—to ask something in secret, as normal people do.

But Mina twists herself free and gestures toward the window instead, "Let's talk there if it's all the same to you," and hurries out of the line.

By the window, Siggy nods almost imperceptibly toward one of their fellow students who's busy working on his eggs at one of the tables. "What do you make of that one, Einstein? Don't stare at him so closely, he'll notice. They have eyes in the backs of their heads, his type of people."

Those last words send unpleasant tingles down Mina's spine. "Those types" was how Jews were called just before the

Nazis went and attacked them openly, clubbing them to near death and burning to the ground whatever they still had left right in front of Mina's eyes.

She's hoped so naively that Siggy is different, that he doesn't have that kind of hate in him, but just how well does she really know him?

"What do you mean?" she asks slowly, on guard.

He widens his brilliant blue eyes theatrically, an amused smile slowly creeping onto his clean-shaven face. "Don't tell me you haven't noticed anything strange about him. Not with your smarts, Einstein."

Feigning five working senses takes up a lot of time from her schedule, Mina wants to say, but, naturally, doesn't.

Siggy sighs in mock exasperation. "He always sits at the back. He barely scribbles anything down. Professors never ask him anything. He's on the attendance list, but I've never seen him submit any papers when we do."

"So?"

"So? He's a government spy or some such!"

"Pfft." Mina rolls her eyes but is relieved that he meant something quite different from what she originally thought. Not a Jew hater then. Just a young man who reads too many spy thrillers, which is fine as far as she's concerned.

"Be skeptical all you like, Einstein, but I'm telling you. Watch him."

Mina does, as subtly as possible for the next few weeks. However, in between Poland falling to the German war machine and the preparations for the upcoming midterm paper submissions, she eventually loses all interest in Siggy's suspect and soon forgets him altogether. Her new obsession preoccupies her mind, pushing everything else out of its orbit. Her mind, in its hyper-focused state, is constantly spinning entire spiderwebs of theories, with a single protagonist at its center—the mysterious uranium—but they're not quite there, not quite good enough, and it's driving her to distraction because she feels that she's onto something incredibly radical and vaguely frightening and yet so very elusive.

Mina attends other lectures, but her mind is barely there nowadays. All she craves is physics—the science of nuclear power, to be even more exact—but even in their lecture halls, the professors don't give her enough. All they offer during the first year is the history of nuclear physics, something that was discovered decades ago and is such old news, Mina feels like tearing her own hair out in desperation. Starved of knowledge, she spends most of her time in the dusty libraries, seeking out every new scientific magazine on the topic with the most recent research results. Crumb by crumb, she collects precious information, slowly but surely adding it all into her notebook, which she carries close to her chest at all times, like a lover would carry their sweetheart's love letters.

"Why uranium anyway?" Siggy asks her during one of their luncheons in the student canteen. They've been running into each other quite often and invariably ended up sharing a table and a conversation. In front of Mina, a buttered bread roll with a single bite taken out of it, while Siggy is tucking into a hearty goulash. He bought the goulash for her—"You're wasting away, Einstein, I swear!"—and only agreed to finish it off when Mina took a single spoonful before pushing the plate away and explaining that she just can't eat when she's... "like this."

"Like what?"

"Can't think about anything else."

Mina considers the uranium question. Why indeed?

"I didn't choose it. It chose me. It's difficult to explain but..." She picks up the roll but puts it back on the plate, annoyed with herself for her inability to find the right words. "You like your codes, right?"

He gives a noncommittal shrug. "They're fun to solve, but I'm not obsessing over them every second of the day."

That much is true. Siegfried Mann is a darling of their cryptanalysis professor, who drives most of the other students mad with his ciphers and codes. His course is a fringe one, added almost as though it was an afterthought to the natural sciences because there was nowhere else to fit it, and most students—and, to be frank, even professors—treat it as such. The joke around the faculty is they'd all like to be paid to solve crossword puzzles all day. That's how they see it, but not Siggy. And, apparently, not the Wehrmacht either, judging by the fact that Siggy is still here, studying it diligently, instead of digging trenches together with the less gifted lot.

"But that's the whole trouble," Mina says, pulling forward. "You do solve them and it gives you satisfaction. But no one has solved the uranium puzzle yet. And it's like an itch I can't scratch. That's why it's so maddening."

Siggy laughs, and, for a second, Mina regrets that she can't hear his laughter. She bets it's easy and contagious; that's why everyone's so drawn to him. And yet, here he is, sharing a table with Mina instead of bantering with the fraternity fellows two years their senior in the very back of the canteen where they always sit in their smart uniforms. He has an open invitation from them, but, for some reason, Siggy likes it better here.

"But that's my initial question precisely." He still laughs. "Why uranium, of all things? What's so special about it? Yes, it releases energy when split. All right. Big round of applause. Now what? How can you possibly apply that energy? Your own favorite Einstein said it's inapplicable."

It's Mina's turn to grin. "But that's precisely it, you affable nitwit! Inapplicable *yet*. There must be a way to contain it and direct its use as we see fit. Can you even conceive what a miraculous, marvelous discovery it would be? Like a perpetual engine that never stops, it would provide energy for everything as long as you have fuel. It can power entire electric grids, and seemingly at no cost. Or, at least, much less cost than the fossil fuels we're using—" Mina stumbles upon another thought and swallows it mid-sentence.

Yet, Siggy notices all the same. He pulls forward and searches her eyes that were feverishly bright but are suddenly extinguished and full of shadows of the past.

"It's selfish, I suppose, but that's the only way I can see myself being useful. The only way I can leave my mark," she admits.

Siggy scowls, visibly confused. "That's an odd thing to say."

"For you." Mina smiles wistfully. "You're the golden child."

"What nonsense," he says, but recedes when he sees the look on Mina's face. "Is it because you're a girl? Marie Curie was a woman and she discovered radioactivity. Lise Meitner is a woman and she split the atom together with those Berlin chemists."

It's because I'm a deaf girl who is likely prohibited from getting married and procreating in this new German Reich and that discovery can be my only child, the only thing I leave after myself before disappearing back into nothing, Mina wants to say, but, in the end, doesn't.

Sometimes it's easier to agree than argue and so, she nods and does just that.

"Yes. Because I'm a girl."

Linz. December 1939

Dismissed for winter holidays and homeward-bound once again, Mina doesn't quite know what to do with herself. In her hand, a suitcase, not so much packed as stuffed with miscellaneous items she's hastily thrown in without much thought. All around, crowds of commuters bustling chaotically in the evening rush hour, but she stands on the platform as if paralyzed, while something is clicking inside her mind, some sequences and theories still embryonic and unformed, inspired by that very chaotic movement. She's in everyone's way; they stumble into her and mutter inaudible curses under their breath, while Mina decides between the trolley and a taxicab—she has the money now, thanks to the university's generous stipend—but...

So many bodies around her; they bounce off one another and heat the entire vast hall with their frantic energy. And Mina stands there and remembers her mother seeing her off on this very *Bahnhof* and just how chilled the morning air was despite the Indian summer still lingering in the streets.

"Because we are contained," Mina's lips mutter as the realization dawns on her. "Atoms must be contained in a chamber of sorts to produce all that energy. A controlled fission, a chain reaction that won't slow down because—"

A policeman in his winter green overcoat positions himself in front of her and touches two fingers to his helmet. "Visiting? Need help?" Mina watches his lips say.

In wartime, anyone standing out from the faceless crowd is suspicious, and here she stands, mumbling to herself like someone who escaped from the mental asylum.

Grasping the new discovery by the tail and pinning it down in the corner of her mind for further investigation, Mina feigns normality as much as she can and bares her teeth in a bright grin. "No. Heading home to my parents. Thought I left the light on in my lodgings at Graz and was thinking to call my landlady, but I just now remembered that I didn't. All is well. Thank you."

He steps away and off Mina flies, into the crisp darkness of the street, where snowflakes swirl—more particles and waves, that's all she sees nowadays—and climbs into a taxi. The cabbie tries to talk—Mina sees his lips moving in the rearview mirror, but, for the first time in months, she taps her ears and openly admits that she's deaf. He shrinks back into himself like many do whenever they encounter someone or something different from themselves, but Mina couldn't be less bothered by his visible discomfort, mixed with pity for an even measure. Left to her own devices, she sketches designs in her little black notebook, designs of the machines that are yet to exist.

The short walk home, up the flight of stairs, is all a fog. But then, as soon as the front door opens and her mother throws her arms around Mina's body, she is enveloped in a light and love that knows no bounds.

"How much I missed you," she whispers to her mother, who she is certain whispers it back.

Mina drinks it all in—the festive dinner in her honor as though she is some foreign princess, the freshly turned bed and a quilt her mother knitted for the occasion—and doesn't realize for the next two days that the tea with honey is always hot on her desk where she works, the vacation be damned, and her mother is always hovering just over her shoulder, ready to serve her lunch or a sandwich or a fresh stack of papers from *Vati*'s cabinet. It strikes Mina as extremely odd now that she pauses to think of it. Holiday season has always been the busiest for Liv Best at her hospital, with alcohol poisonings, fireworks burns and broken and dislocated limbs after a bout of festive, and not always sober, ice skating. Mina begrudged her mother her absences as a child, but now she's both happy and perplexed with the fact that *Mutti* is here decorating the tree *Vati* brought from the market a day ago instead of getting ready for her daily shift. And the quilt? Just when did she have the time to knit?

"Are you on vacation as well?" Mina asks, handing her mother a string of tinsel.

Something shifts in her mother's countenance and disappears behind a bright smile. The smile of the same fake quality Mina offered the policeman just days ago.

"You could say that."

Mutti doesn't elaborate, but Mina lingers close until her mother realizes that there isn't any avoiding her.

"I quit," she finally offers and stands there, her jaw jutted forward as though in a challenge.

Mina looks at her mother's face but sees herself, just a couple of decades older. Just as principled and quietly obstinate, her mother's daughter.

"Congratulations?" Mina probes with a question in her voice.

Not the right remark for the occasion; her mother's glare attests to that.

"May I ask why?"

"You may." *Mutti* chews on her lip as she considers an explanation. "A new law recently went into effect." Her eyes are two smoldering pits, and she holds herself with both hands as if against a gust of arctic wind.

"Something to do with the Jews?" Mina tries once again, as gently as she can. The subject is much too tender; she sees that much now that she finally looks—actually looks at her mother with fresh eyes.

"No, not with the Jews. They came for our own this time." Another pause, longer and colder than the previous. "I was assisting a routine C-section. Both child and mother survived, fortunately. Left for monitoring, as is always the case with such surgeries."

Mina nods, wishing they weren't standing next to this festive tree with its bright balls and shimmering tinsel and glossy-faced angels and electric candles highlighting something truly hideous about to be revealed.

"During the routine assessment, Dr. Braun discovered the newborn was blind. I was there, in the room, together with a pediatric nurse..." She swallows hard, twice. "Dr. Braun ordered her to fetch phenol. Phenol is a strong antiseptic, lethal in high doses—"

"Yes, I know what it is," Mina interrupts, just because the wait is worse than the end of the story, which she can already see. Mina feels the floor shifting under her feet. And yet, this sickening sensation of free fall is still nothing compared to what her mother must have felt that day.

"I asked him whatever he intended to do with the child, to which he produced a paper from the health ministry. Apparently, they have just issued a euthanasia decree for all of the medical institutions in the Reich and the occupied territories. I read it while the baby wailed on the scales—Dr. Braun just left her there without her nappy and it's so frigid now... the window was opened, too..." *Mutti* passes her hand over her forehead, but grabs hold of herself with some inhuman willpower. "It stated that all the defective newborns are to be destroyed immediately. Mothers are to be told that the infant didn't survive. Otherwise, a perfectly healthy girl; so what if she can't see? She'd make do with the cane just fine. People have lived without sight for thousands of years, what harm can they do to anyone?"

Poisoning the well of perfect Germanic genes, the answer hangs between them like a drop of a venom. Mina has heard the explanation many times, with sideways looks in her direction, whenever they don't know her full story.

Before, the Nazis only detested her handicapped kind. Now, they are outright killing them.

"You're safe," Mina's mother's hands are upon her in an instant, as if sensing the direction of her thoughts. "You weren't born deaf, they won't touch you."

Mina can't quite tell whom her mother is so desperate to persuade, Mina or herself. But she nods all the same and congratulates her mother on quitting the whole rotten business.

"They didn't give you any trouble, did they?"

Mutti gives half a shrug, selfless once again. "Reported me for insubordination, but that's the last I heard of it. Don't fret about me, worry about your atoms instead. Tell me again how they're our future. I so missed hearing you talk."

Atoms are the furthest thing from Mina's mind now that she's learned of a state-authorized murder happening in hospitals, the very places that are meant to save lives instead of taking them. Still, she puts on a smile for her mother's sake and talks of a future in which atomic-engine cars can fly, in which borders no longer exist, where wars are no longer waged for limited resources and where people live in harmony with nature and each other.

TWELVE

GRAZ, AUSTRIA. SPRING—SUMMER 1940

In the south-west, France is being bombed into submission, and in Graz, the lilies are in full bloom and crimson flags are streaming from the buildings in victorious cascades. In the university, all windows are thrown open and the warm breeze is ruffling the hair on the students' heads, bowed over their exam papers.

Mina enters the auditorium as soon as a fellow student exits it (face beaming, "barely passed!") and approaches Professor Böhm's table.

"Here's the subject for your oral presentation," he says, handing her one of the papers from his table, "and the equations that you are to solve are on the blackboard. What's that?"

In her exam-induced anxiety, Mina has completely forgotten to leave her little black notebook behind. It has almost become part of her, she literally sleeps with it under her pillow in case one idea or another springs into her mind in her sleep (quite a few do). Naturally, she left all of her textbooks and lecture notes on the bench in the hall, but the notebook somehow slipped her mind.

"It's nothing," she mumbles quickly, "just my notes on uranium."

The exam is on trigonometry, nothing to do with nuclear physics, but Professor Böhm still pats the corner of his desk. "Leave it here, Fräulein Best. You can collect it after you finish with your examination."

There's nothing doing, and so, Mina reluctantly parts with the notebook and takes her seat by the open window to figure out the distance between a submarine and the enemy warship based on both locations' latitudes, longitudes, and the Earth's curvature. The sun is warm on her face and Mina wonders why it always has to be warships and submarines and troop movements calculations, but then reminds herself that they're at war and her country now is all about uniforms and overt masculinity, and, naturally, a state such as this new German Reich needs to utilize everyone. Which means that if one's body isn't fit enough for the front, they'll just make use of their brains. Girls have never even been taken into consideration, so there's little she can complain about. *Ought to be grateful for being here at all, occupying a seat that could have been some young man's,* according to their dean.

Lost in thought, Mina's done before she knows it. The rest of the students—there's only ten of them taking Böhm's exam at the same time as some professors choose to keep a hawk's eye on them to ensure they don't cheat—regard her in stunned silence as she raises her arm well before her time is up.

"Ready, Fräulein Best?" His initial surprise is instantly replaced by suspiciously narrowed eyes.

"Yes, Herr Professor."

"You may approach."

As she does, Mina notices with a sudden sense of ice around her heart that her trigonometry professor is leafing through her notebook, his expression unreadable. Eventually, he puts it down and turns his attention to Mina. With ease, she rattles off uses of trigonometry in radiology and isn't even halfway through when Professor Böhm raises his hand to stop her.

"Your papers with solutions, please."

She hands them over and watches the professor as he carefully scans them.

"Very elegant solutions, Fräulein Best. Not quite by the book, though."

"I skipped a few steps," Mina admits. "I noticed some time ago that they aren't really relevant to the final result."

"Those steps are necessary for eliminating possible mistakes." He's peering at her over the rim of his glasses.

Mina doesn't look away only because she needs to see his lips. After a few moments of silence, they're moving again as though he's chewing on something unpleasant.

"There's a reason for everything we teach you here."

"I understand, Herr Professor. I can rewrite my solutions—"

"That won't be necessary."

He passes her despite lowering her mark for her "improvisations," and waves Mina toward the exit. "Invite the next student in once you're out, please."

Mina hesitates a moment, shifts from one foot to another.

"You may go, Fräulein Best."

But she can't. "May I have my notebook, please?"

A smile barely touches Professor Böhm's lips, blander than a soup *Mutti* used to make back in the twenties when a single dollar traded for a billion crones. He places his hand atop the small black notebook and swipes it across the desk and into the drawer, which he promptly shuts. "This shall stay here for now, Fräulein Best."

"But—"

"You may go."

This is not a mere dismissal now but an order—Mina sees that much in his steely eyes.

Suddenly lightheaded and feeling as though both violated and robbed, Mina stumbles out of the auditorium and into the hallway and barely nods when Siggy asks her if she passed.

Linz, Austria. Two weeks later

"Is that Paris?" Mina asks her father, whose face is hidden behind the newspaper. On its front page, German troops are marching against the backdrop of the Arc de Triomphe.

He lowers the paper, nods somberly, and mutters something that Mina can decipher only as "thought it would take longer."

It still strikes Mina as something out of a bad dream, just how much her father has changed over the past year. From an energetic, elegant lawyer with eyes full of good humor, he has become a former shadow of himself, his hairline quickly receding on his temples and turning prematurely gray and a light blue vein prominent along his forehead, like a scar that refused to heal. It doesn't escape Mina just how ill-fitting his summer suit is on his gaunt frame, and *Mutti* just bought it a year ago for his birthday. Back then, it fitted him just fine.

Mina doesn't ask him about work because all his firm deals with now is Aryanization. There's a new gray BMW convertible that stands under the Bests' windows, but when Johann Best took Mina for a ride out of town, his face remained as clouded over as the sky overhead.

"Money is very good now," Mina's mother's letters filled her in on what couldn't have been said in person. "But he has terrible acid reflux now and can barely eat anything, and he smokes far too much and can only sleep with those new pills Dr. Weber prescribed him. Lawyers, they get a percentage from each Aryanization deal."

Not quite blood money, but close enough. Mina remembers quite well what preceded that very Aryanization; remembers Herr Freudenberg's face as she walked away and he was still smiling in relief that at least she was unharmed and free to go, even when he, himself, was kneeling in a pool of his own blood, his face smashed, just like his beautiful displays. She still blames herself; still has nightmares over it, and it was just one night and she was just a young girl whose only fault was walking away when she should have stayed and stood by her former employer, and to hell with the consequences. But everyone is a hero in their own mind. In reality, once someone in jackboots with murder in his eyes backhands you and holds you by the hair like a helpless pup, all heroism flies out the window. How could she blame her father for writing the contracts that robbed Austrian Jews of their businesses and properties when she was no better, running away with her tail between her legs? They were a family of cowards, it seemed.

No. Not *Mutti* though. She handed over her resignation as soon as her supervising physician ordered her to prepare a phenol injection for a blind newborn. Apparently, while Mina was away in Graz, busy with her idiotic uranium, certain government people in civilian clothes came over to the Bests' house to politely inquire as to what precisely Frau Best had against the euthanasia program approved by the Führer himself. Frau Best was a smart woman. Instead of telling them just what she thought of their barbaric practices, she cited her Catholic upbringing and must have annoyed them so much with Bible quotes and crossing herself that they left her well alone. No further investigation followed.

Mina is still digesting it all as her father closes the paper and folds it neatly. He puts it on the table and doesn't shoo Libby off when she jumps on top and starts cleaning herself.

"Want to go for a ride, Mina?" He taps her shoulder before asking.

Mina doesn't, but humors him all the same.

The ride in the new car is smooth but joyless and silent. Mina attempts to break the quiet between them a few times, pointing out a freshly groomed poodle here and a new store opened there, but her father doesn't seem to hear her or notice anything around them. At last, she gives up and turns her searching gaze away from him. If he wants to, he'll tap her shoulder to talk.

For the entirety of the ride, he doesn't.

When they come back, an unfamiliar fellow in civilian clothing is sitting in Mina's father's chair. Mina's mother is on the sofa, pale as a ghost, her back ramrod straight, hands clasped around her knees with a force that turns her knuckles white.

For an instant, Mina thinks that he's one of the original pair that came to see her mother, but then *Mutti* jumps to her feet and almost drags her husband toward the man. She launches into a shaky and tangled explanation that whatever it is that their daughter did, her husband is a lawyer and a Party member and certainly something can be sorted without them having to take Mina away—

The fellow in the dark suit is on his feet too now, a hand in front of the couple as though to ward off the flood of Mina's mother's pleas. "Frau and Herr Best, I'm not here to arrest anyone, and your daughter hasn't done anything wrong. I'm only a messenger, sent here by the University of Graz administration as they wish to talk to Fräulein Best on some urgent matter. Even I don't know what it is, but I assure you, it's not a police matter."

Silently, her stomach in knots, Mina packs a small bag— mostly her documents, a toothbrush, a change of clothes, and a sandwich her mother slips her. The "messenger" is lingering in the hallway, making some sort of small talk with her father, judging by the looks of it.

Tense as a spring, Mina lets her *Mutti* envelop her in a tight embrace and stiffly promises her to call as soon as everything is sorted. *Vati* offers to drive them to the train station, but Herr Messenger—it just then occurs to Mina that he never introduced himself—politely declines. He has his own car.

Of course, he does. There it stands, just outside the building's entrance, with a government license plate on it. They parked right next to it upon return, but paid it no heed and now Mina curses herself for her inattentiveness, as if it would have changed a thing. She gets in and casts a glance to her second-story windows. Like two despondent specters, her parents gaze back at her through the glass. Mina raises her hand in a final salute. A terrifying feeling overcomes her as the car begins to pull out that she shall never see them again.

The sun still hangs high in the sky when they arrive in Graz. Mina is somewhat comforted by the fact that it is indeed Graz where Herr Messenger has brought her and not one government prison or the other, even though for the life of her she can't possibly conceive what it is that she's done to anger the Reich. Certainly, failing to mention one's handicap on admission papers doesn't constitute a prison sentence. Besides, she hasn't been found out, has she?

Mina spends the entire trip from the station to the university on the edge of her seat in yet another government car, staring in her escort/driver's rearview mirror so as not to miss him saying something. But he's as mute as a Buddhist monk with a vow of silence and his face is as blank as freshly fallen snow, untouched by any footprints or marks. She picks the skin around her nails until it bleeds, but at least the raw physical pain distracts from the fear of the unknown that's creeping all over her body like tiny insects, leaving her skin wet with sweat by the time they reach their destination.

To Mina's amazement, it's Graz University indeed. She's not arrested then? But why such secrecy, such hurry?

With a lump of dread in her throat, Mina follows her escort

along the empty hallways and into the dean's office. She's never seen the inside of it—and thank heavens for that!—but now that she steps through the heavy wooden doors, the dean himself is not even there. Instead, three sets of unfamiliar eyes are suddenly on her; all well-dressed men she's never seen before gathered around the dean's desk in a semicircle. The only familiar face in the room is Mina's trigonometry professor's, Herr Böhm's. He welcomes her with a tight smile and offers her a seat in one of the plush visitors' chairs.

It's only when Mina is about to take her seat that she notices yet another person she never expected to see in this bizarre setting. In fact, she's forgotten about his existence altogether, ever since her conversation with Siggy months ago—their fellow student who always sits at the back. Only he isn't a student any longer. In place of the shirt and a pullover he always sported, a sharp green-gray uniform now sits on his frame. With a growing sense of horror, Mina takes in the two lightning bolts on his lapel—the SS—and the black diamond SD marking on the sleeve. She hasn't the faintest idea what that means, but whatever it is, it can't be anything good.

He rises slightly and nods at her with a smile that's meant to be reassuring—"Sit, sit"—but Mina feels anything but reassured.

Siggy was right after all. Should've listened to him instead of discounting his intuition to be a product of his love for spy thrillers. This is where your arrogance gets you.

Mina doesn't know if such knowledge would help her in any way but can't help berating herself for her own stupidity. And, in the meantime, one of the strangers produces something in front of her and Mina recognizes her small black notebook, the one with all of her uranium notes and equations. In her state of excitement, eyes glued to the notebook as though to a long-lost lover, Mina misses her cue and doesn't catch whatever the stranger is asking.

He's kindly enough, with his round face and ruddy cheeks, to repeat his question—"where did you get this research?"—and this time Mina recovers herself enough to mumble that it's hers, but not research really, just notes, something she thought of, theories that are severely lacking, something to occupy her time—

She's interrupted by the older gentleman's colleague (or whatever the devil he is) and this one, seated to the gentleman's right, is as gaunt as death and just as sinister-looking. With his scrawny paw, he picks up the notebook and shakes it in the air, demanding answers. Mina suspects that he's wearing dentures or is missing a few teeth, because his diction is so badly impaired, she can barely read his lips. She thinks that he is accusing her of lying. Mere first-year students don't produce such theories.

"But they aren't even good theories," Mina tries to protest. "Just scribbles, really. They don't prove anything—"

The third fellow introduces himself and Mina only has time to catch the end of his title—something of nuclear research at Berlin University. The name is already lost to her. He's the youngest of the three and attired with an effortless elegance that only German Empire old-money families possess. On his left pinkie, a black signet ring with a familial crest. He asks her something from the notebook, but he's reading from it and Mina can't possibly see his lips and is silent when he looks back at her, and then all three begin to talk at the same time and the world begins to spin faster and faster around Mina until she's dizzy and feels physically sick. Her forehead is damp with sweat, she's shifting her frightened eyes from one man to another and back until the SS man is leaning over her and saying something in her ear that she naturally can't hear.

From his place by the window that he has occupied this entire time, Professor Böhm begins to shout something, his face creased with fury, until finally Mina bursts into tears and cowers in her chair as though expecting a physical blow and screams back at them all—"I can't hear you, I'm deaf!" and weeps into the silence that descends upon the room for well over a minute.

First, they stare at her in great mistrust. Next, they confer among themselves.

Mina jumps when her former "fellow student" touches her shoulder to get her attention.

"How can you hear us then?"

"I can't," through sobs and tears. "I read lips."

"How can you possibly talk then?"

"I wasn't born deaf. I lost my hearing as a complication from measles, when I was five." Mina feels as if she has lost count of all the times she has offered this explanation in the past two years, when, in fact, it was only Herr Freudenberg who knew her secret. The memory of his sweet, fatherly face sends her over the edge once again.

Once again, a hand on her shoulder. Mina looks up.

"How were you able to attend the lectures here?"

From Mina, a miserable shrug. "Read the lips, filled out whatever I missed from books or other students' lecture notes."

"Seems to be a lot of work."

"I really wanted to study."

The SS man regards her for some time. "You didn't mention your handicap in your application."

"It only asked if I had any hereditary conditions," Mina barely whispers. "My condition isn't hereditary."

The young elegant Berliner waves his hand in the air to call attention to himself. "That's a lot of trouble to go to just to study physics."

"I love physics."

"Nuclear physics."

"Yes. I love it the best."

"Can you explain what you tried to do here?" He flips the

notebook open in the middle and points to one of the designs she sketched on her way home, inspired by the Linz *Bahnhof*.

Mina recognizes it in an instant. "I was trying to figure out the design of the fission machine. To release any meaningful amount of energy, uranium atoms must be contained in an apparatus of sorts. But since uranium is highly radioactive, the materials that need to be used need to counter the force of the radiation released. Like lead aprons protecting the vulnerable physicians' flesh whenever they take X-rays? And also to control the chain reaction itself..." She looks up at him and continues, somewhat assured by his nod. "I tried to calculate the formula of the controlled fission, but my numbers just aren't good yet. I don't know enough to get even a little closer to a somewhat feasible design. All I know is that uncontrolled fission has a possibility of turning into an unrestrained chain reaction with the possibility of destroying the planet itself—that much I calculated, but how to rein in that process to convert it into energy? There needs to be an engine of some sort that drives the particles and contains them at the same time. Something that surrounds, I don't know... the core, I suppose? The heart of the machine. And around it, lead cylinders or discs or something." She makes a desperate gesture with her hands. "You see how lacking my ideas are."

For a few moments, the three wise men (for some reason, Mina baptized them as such in her mind) are exchanging remarks and glances, purposely covering their mouths with their hands.

At last, after their discussion, The Death Mask folds his arms on top of the desk and arches his brow at the SS man. "You think the girl's lying?"

Mina stares at the uniformed man as though her very life depends on it. Perhaps it does—who can tell?

But the SS man only shrugs and grins like a cat.

"You're the scientists here. You tell me."

Mina notices the kindly gentleman producing her report card and a list of her works submitted to different professors. Unbeknownst to her, they have an entire file on her, and have clearly studied her like some dangerous strand of plague this entire time.

"Well, she is an excellent student," he says at length.

They converse some more; grill her some more on different theories written in her sloping, barely legible cursive.

The sun begins to cast golden shadows into the room when Professor Böhm turns the lights on and the Berliner announces his verdict.

"Well, Fräulein Best, since you like nuclear physics so much, I suppose you'll be glad to continue working on your research in Berlin."

This isn't a question, Mina sees that much from all of the faces around her. Still, she gazes around herself like a frightened hare. "Wouldn't it be better if I stayed here and studied some more?"

This time, it's the Death Mask who replies to her. "Your little book has proved that you already know whatever they could possibly teach you here on nuclear physics, child. You'll be working under Dr. von Weizsäcker's guidance." A nod toward the Berliner. Nobility, just as Mina has suspected. "Naturally, the government shall provide you with housing."

It's the SS man's turn to nod. "Naturally. Only the best for the brightest minds."

Yet, when Mina is whisked away on yet another train—to Berlin this time—she doesn't feel like a brightest mind or a fortunate one whatsoever.

More like a prisoner, with a life sentence to serve.

THIRTEEN

BERLIN, GERMANY. SUMMER 1940

Throughout Mina's journey, her escorts change, but their uniforms don't. They never introduce themselves; simply pass her from one to another, from the train to the car, from building to building, office to office, where she's questioned, finger-printed, photographed, weighed and measured by the physicians and interrogated again. Family history, education (both hers and parental), health. She hardly slept on the train—too many unknowns bouncing off each other inside her poor skull pounding with a headache—and is drained of all energy. But perhaps that's precisely how they want her: disoriented and sleep-deprived in the breaking Berlin dawn.

"You weren't in the Girls' League while at school." Another white-clad doctor.

"I'm deaf. They don't take deaf girls." Mina is exhausted, hungry, and desperately wants a hot bath.

"But you wanted to join?"

She regards him. "Naturally." The lie slips easily off her tongue.

He inspects her ears, shines the light into her eyes and her throat—"Pull your tongue out. More"—probes her neck under her jawline and along her windpipe until it's sore, then dismisses her.

Another uniformed escort. Another office, with racial charts all over the walls. This time, her skull is measured, the distance from the tip of her nose to her lips, lips themselves and the jaw. This physician doesn't ask her anything, communicating with her SS escort only.

"No known Jewish influences in the bloodline?"

"None that we know of, so far. Birth and church records have been requested, all from the mother's side. The father is a member of the Party; his ancestry was submitted to the Race Office a long time ago. Maternal father was a colonel in the Imperial Army and comes from a long-standing Catholic family. The only concern is maternal grandmother, though we're quite convinced there won't be any faulty blood there."

Mina watches the physician write, "Nordic race; Alpine subtype," next to her measurements in his chart. He puts a faint question mark next to it, in pencil—likely to be erased once he receives her complete ancestry records.

Next, an office, not a doctor's exam room, and it's already a relief. A uniformed man flips a file open. Mina's photo and fingerprints are already in it.

"Political affiliation?"

She has none, but it doesn't seem like a correct answer here.

"NSDAP sympathizer. My father is a member of the Party."

"Youth organizations?"

"They wouldn't take me because of my handicap but I did want to join."

He nods, satisfied. Grills her some more on the National Socialist German Workers Party history, the Putsch of 1923 after which the Führer was arrested. Asks her if she studied the manifesto the Führer wrote while incarcerated.

"We studied it in detail at school." Mina stifles a yawn just at the memory of it. "And I read it at home, naturally," she adds, just in case.

Another office, much more welcoming this time. There's a soft couch by the window and heavy velvet drapes blocking the sunlight. The man who welcomes her is in civilian clothing, with a kindly face and manner.

"Ordinarily, I sit behind the head of the couch," he says as he takes her narrow palm in his. "Ordinarily, I would have invited you to lie down and relax so you would be perfectly at ease, close your eyes maybe, but that would render all of our communication useless."

Mina can't help but smile in response. After being treated like an object for the most part of the morning, a tiny sliver of human warmth is melting her in spite of herself.

"So, let's both sit on the couch and have a little chat. Is that all right with you?"

She knows she doesn't have a choice but appreciates the illusion of being offered one.

"Tell me a little about your childhood."

"It was good. Regular. Happy."

"You contracted measles when you were five, correct?"

"Yes."

"How did you feel when you lost your hearing?"

A *psychiatrist*, it occurs to Mina then. Evaluating if a deaf girl can be trusted with handling radioactive materials and isn't depressed to the point where she blows the entire facility up.

"It didn't affect me as it would an ordinary child."

"What do you mean by that?"

"I'm very introverted. I've always preferred books to friends, so, to me, silence was a blessing of sorts. Of course, it became an inconvenience later on, when I had to go to school, but otherwise I've always felt perfectly normal. Not as if I lost something of great value."

The psychiatrist cocks his head. Not the answer he

expected. He finds her to be an interesting case, Mina can tell. "You like silence then?"

"It's very comforting."

"What else do you like?"

"Physics. But, I suppose, you know that much already."

He's very easy to talk to. Mina wonders just how many scientists or government workers have been cleared or vetoed by him before her.

"Why do you like physics so much?"

"It's science. It's impartial. One can never get into an argument about it because there can't be two different opinions about the fact that two by two equals four."

"You don't like conflict, do you?"

"I try to avoid it at all cost. Is that a bad thing?" Mina wonders what it is in him that makes one so predisposed to such uncontrollable honesty.

"Why, if anything, it's rather typical for your gender."

"But science is not."

He smiles wider and with an extraordinary charm. "There are always exceptions."

They chat some more until Mina feels her eyelids drooping. She feels the warmth of the sun on her back even through the heavy drapes and doesn't mind at all when kindly Herr Doktor offers her a chance to rest her eyes while he writes her report. Through her half-closed lids, she sees him write "well-balanced personality" and something about self-introspection but doesn't get any further than that.

By the time a hand gently taps her shoulder, Mina is in such a deep sleep, it takes her a few moments to remember where she is and why. The psychiatrist bids her goodbye and wishes her all the best and bristles slightly when the SS man reaches for Mina's forearm.

"Take the girl to the hotel if her accommodation is not ready, for Christ's sake. Sleep deprivation is torture, you know."

Mina's sure that the SS man knows, but somehow, he nods and even has the decency to look mildly chastised. Yet Mina takes no pleasure in this. She is much too tired.

The sun blinds her briskly as they step outside—at long last! —but once Mina's whisked into the back of yet another staff car, she can't stay awake even with the best will in the world. She's still fast asleep when the car pulls to a stop and perceives the hand shaking her shoulder as part of her dream.

When it can't be ignored any longer, she snaps her eyes open and silently drags herself after her escort as he walks through a dark archway and into a courtyard of yet another building. No guards at the doors this time, only staircases and doors with name tags next to them. *Residential?*

Before Mina can ask anything, the SS man opens the door on the third, top floor with his key and gestures for her to go inside.

"You'll be staying here for now. Your handler shall arrive shortly, but you can rest in the meantime."

With that, he clicks his heels and pulls the door after himself. Sometime after he leaves, Mina tries the door. It's locked.

FOURTEEN

The apartment is clean and perfectly devoid of any personality. It only takes Mina a few minutes to inspect it: a small but neat kitchen with a fridge in the corner, a living room doubling as a dining room, a bathroom and a bedroom with a single bed near the window. Mina tries to open it, but it's painted shut.

"Unsurprising," she mutters to herself.

What is surprising is that there are no bars on it—Mina half-expected them. There are also no knives in the kitchen, only dull ones for smearing butter on bread. Mina snorts softly but has little energy left to exchange sarcastic remarks with herself. The mattress on the bed is new and firm. She tucks herself under the covers without undressing and sleeps.

When Mina finally blinks her eyes open, the room is wreathed in light. Her head full of cobwebs, she gropes at the bedside table for an alarm clock and squints at it. Twenty past seven. Morning or evening? It was dusk when she was brought here and surely, she couldn't have slept through an entire day, so it must be morning.

She lingers in bed a little longer, soaking up the luxury of being able to stretch her limbs after the previous two days' ordeal. But then the thought of her parents jolts her upright. Did the government people have enough decency to inform them of her whereabouts? Did they tell them that she's safe and sound and hasn't been thrown behind bars, or shot for that matter?

At once on her feet, Mina rushes out of the bedroom, without any coherent plan but driven by the urge to do something. Startled, she stops in her tracks with a gasp stuck in her throat. In the chair by the dining table, a man sits with a cup of tea in front of him. At the sight of Mina, he rises to his feet, rather slowly, as though not to frighten a wild animal looking ready to bolt and bows his head with a smile that is both polite and apologetic.

"You can read lips, right?" The first words out of his mouth. "If not—" He quickly produces a notebook and a pencil from the inside pocket of his summer linen jacket.

"That won't be necessary," Mina finds herself saying despite her heart still beating wildly in her chest. "I can understand you just fine."

"Forgive me for barging in on you in such a manner," he begins with a hand against his chest. "I'd be startled out of my wits myself if I discovered a stranger in my living room."

Her emotions somewhat under control, Mina studies him. He's tall and dark-haired and handsome in a very classic way, with every feature perfectly in proportion. But it's his eyes that draw Mina's interest the most. There's a shadow of something terribly painful in their dark depths, something that spread around like an incurable disease and drew two sharp vertical lines above his nose, painted creases around his mouth, pulling it down, and turned the hair on his temples gray. He's dressed in civilian clothing, but his ramrod-straight posture betrays his military bearing. Mina's grandfather went to his grave with his shoulders still perfectly square; she can recognize a career officer in a single glance.

"My name is Nikolaus Taube." He offers her his hand but without moving an inch from where he stands. He reminds her of the psychiatrist just then, equally as good at handling people —unlike his counterparts from the SS.

"You're my handler then." Mina approaches him and shakes his hand. It's soft like her father's; the hand of a man who has never carried a burden of physical labor.

"I don't quite like that term." Taube cringes slightly as if smelling something foul. "Sounds like it should come with a leash."

"Only logical, if you think of my accommodation as a large, comfortable kennel. One that locks from the outside." Mina smiles, but her smile is bitter.

"I apologize for that. That was only for the first night. The SS can be... rather insufferable with their security protocols." With that, to Mina's great surprise, Taube produces a key and puts it on the table.

"So, technically speaking, I'm free to come and go as I please?" Mina looks at him.

Taube considers this for a few moments. At last, he takes a deep breath and says, "You must be starving. I brought some bread rolls and eggs and the kettle should still be hot. Why don't you eat first and then I'll explain it all to you in detail?"

Mina tucks into everything that's been spread out in front of her with the appetite and manners of a starved stray. The rolls are fresh and still smell of the bakery and it stirs memories in Mina she doesn't care for just now because she's weak as it is and if she bursts into tears, there will be no saving the first impression she wants to give, and Mina needs Taube to think that she's strong, very strong.

"You don't work for the SS, do you?" she asks with her mouth still full.

He wrinkles his nose once again—a fleeting expression that tells Mina all she needs to know about his attitude to the SS.

"The *Abwehr*. Intelligence Office."

"What does the *Abwehr* want with me?"

"We don't want anything particular with you. We're only tasked with providing..." He's searching for the right word. "Guidance for individuals—scientists mostly—working for the Reich."

"And I'm working for the Reich now?"

"You are."

Mina ponders this as she chews on her buttered roll. "Why do I need guidance from the *Abwehr*?"

"Because the science department is on the government payroll and we are tasked with ensuring that scientists know—"

"Who they're working for if they know what's good for them," Mina finishes for him.

Taube hides a grin but not very successfully. "You do catch up quickly. I'm glad you understand your position."

Mina doesn't like his frankness. If he tells her this much within an hour of meeting her, it can only mean one thing: she's not going anywhere. Not now, not anytime soon. Despite the seemingly open door.

"Can I write to my parents to tell them that I'm alive?"

"Most certainly."

"I assume I can't tell them where I'll be working now."

"Afraid not."

Mina nods, sips her tea. "So I can never leave here?"

"Your apartment, or the Institute?"

"Berlin."

"Why, you may leave, for your yearly vacation or a weekend out of town. All you have to do is submit a request to your department's head. If he approves it, I'll be happy to approve it as well."

The length of the metaphorical chain around Mina's ankle is impressive, but its invisible weight is still there. "And if I want to quit at some point in the future?"

"I'm afraid that request will be denied. I'm sorry."

He looks like he is, but it doesn't change the fact that she's in essence a prisoner now and he is the very thing he loathes to be called—her handler.

"What does the SS have to do with all this?"

"They have their own program where they put their men into different universities and workplaces and collect people who can be of use to the state."

"The *Abwehr* doesn't do that?"

"We have plenty of other work."

Something clicks in Mina's mind then and falls into place. Taube wants to be here just as much as she does, but as long as there are orders from above, he doesn't have much choice but to babysit a girl who can count better than others instead of doing the work he'd liked to occupy himself with. But at least he's being a good sport about it and doesn't take his frustration out on her. Just for that, Mina is grateful.

"Can I borrow some paper to write that letter?"

"Of course."

After a moment's hesitation, Mina looks up at those sorrowful, haunted eyes of his. "Can I please write another one too?"

"To whom?"

"A friend."

He's about to say no—Mina sees it before he utters the word—and so she pulls forward and all but begs.

"Just a few lines, I promise. Just to let him know that I'm alive and well."

A wistful smile passes over his face, leaving him looking even more pained than before. "Ach. That kind of friend."

"No, it's not like..." She's blushing and tangling in her own words and curses herself for it but goes for it all the same. "He *is* just a friend, just... a very good one."

The only one.

Taube's silent for so long, Mina is about to accept her defeat, when suddenly he releases a tremendous breath and shakes his head—at her or himself, Mina can't quite tell. "Just a few lines. Tell him you transferred to Berlin. We'll have to go over both letters before I can approve them; you understand that."

It isn't a question and, yes, Mina very much understands. In the span of a few days, her biggest talent has suddenly turned into a curse of unimaginable proportions and there will never be privacy in her life—a life itself that now belongs to the state—but at least she still has her uranium. If she cracks its code, she'll die with a smile on her face. Let them do whatever they please with her afterwards.

Dear Siggy, the words spill from under her pen. *Forgive me please for disappearing without so much as a goodbye, but the Fatherland calls and now I'm in Berlin to answer it. Don't worry about me, I'm studying and trying not to skip meals. Knowing you, you'll likely get yourself in an uproar and try to call every university in the book until you find me, but I fear I won't be able to answer, no matter how much I would love to. I don't know if you suspected and never said anything out of the goodness of your heart, or if my lip-reading is indeed that good, but I'm deaf and have been concealing it from everyone in Graz to stay at the university. I hope you will forgive me this little deception for the sake of knowledge. I miss you dearly and hope to see you one day.*

The note reads far too much like a goodbye and Mina isn't even sure if it will ever reach the recipient, but she slashes her name under the text and resists the urge to kiss it before handing it over to Taube.

FIFTEEN

The following day, Taube takes Mina to the Kaiser Wilhelm Institute for Physics. The trip doesn't take long, only fifteen minutes, but he wants to make sure she doesn't get lost. *Or runs off*, Mina thinks to herself as they drive through a visibly affluent neighborhood.

In a thick envelope in her lap, Mina's new papers are tucked: her Institute pass and a special pass into the research facilities, and another identification with her new Berlin address on it. It's the one she'll be showing to the police—the regular Kripo or the Gestapo—if they stop her in the street.

"Do people get stopped a lot in the streets in Berlin?" Mina asks.

Taube gives half a shrug. In the rearview mirror, his lips are sealed. The silence speaks volumes.

Mina memorizes each bend in the road as she'll be taking it every day—not in the car, of course, but on the bicycle Taube promised to deliver later that day. There's also a U-Bahn line that goes from her apartment to the Institute, but Mina would rather stay above ground for now.

"Welcome to the German Oxford, Fräulein Best," Taube

finally says as a constellation of red roofs appears in the square of the windshield. "It's not an official title, of course, but rather a testament to the concentration of the great minds working together in its facilities. Which now includes you," he adds with a smile through the rearview mirror. "See all those buildings to our left? Most of them are part of the Kaiser Wilhelm Society. You'll be working in the Institute for Physics—we can't see it just yet as it's hiding behind the one for Chemistry. The row of buildings to our right is research establishments for biology, anthropology, and medicine. The rest are libraries, workshops, lecture halls—you name it. Naturally, the laboratories are equipped with the latest instruments and the libraries are stocked with the newest research materials from around the world. Also, there are weekly lectures from foreign scientists invited for the occasion, from what I'm told. Our scientists find those most stimulating. I'm certain you will too."

"Foreign scientists, meaning those from occupied territories." Mina regards Taube through the mirror.

"No." He shakes his head, to Mina's disbelief. "From neutral countries as well. You won't be hearing much about war here. Here, it doesn't really exist."

Through the nerves and fear fueled by the events of recent days, excitement begins to emerge. Clasping Taube's seat with her hands, Mina pulls herself forward to see the miraculous hub of knowledge and research, reminiscent of the esteemed English university, with her own two eyes. There's some ephemeral, magical quality to the miniature town. Small figures of scientists appear doll-like and unreal as they stroll through the landscaped gardens with books under their arms or pour out of elegant buildings deep in discussion, oblivious to everything around them, including Mina and her escort in their slow-moving car. No swastika banners fly here. No steps of hobnailed boots echoing along its alleyways. Taube didn't lie. The war indeed is nonexistent here, in this little town of enlightenment which stands as a flickering candle in the gathering darkness. Still burning brightly—for now.

Mina has seen photos of the Kaiser Wilhelm Institute for Physics many times in her favorite scientific journals and yet, she doesn't recognize it at once when it slowly rises in front of her eyes out of the lush greenery surrounding it. It's smaller than she expected and yet more fascinating somehow, in its turn-of-the-century elegant simplicity. As they pull up to the entrance framed with four white columns, Mina feels her skin tingle with nervous excitement. Will she truly be walking the same halls that Einstein walked? Will she be working in the same laboratories in which he made the discoveries that earned him the Nobel Prize and the title of the Institute's first director?

Mina has all but forgotten about Taube when he pulls the handbrake and turns to her in his seat. "Fräulein Best."

"Yes?"

"Do not mention Albert Einstein to anyone. The Reich likes to think he never existed."

Mina swallows uncomfortably, slightly unnerved by the fact that he can so easily read her and even more so by the fact that as far as the Reich is concerned, the greatest physicist of the century has been erased from its memory solely because he happens to be Jewish.

She thinks of saying that without Einstein and his theory of relativity, neither the Institute nor nuclear fission itself would exist, but she keeps her mouth shut in the end. It looks like she'll have to learn to be mute in addition to being deaf if she knows what's good for her.

Silently, she follows Taube inside. Despite the hot June morning, the halls of the Institute are pleasantly cool. It's nothing like the University of Graz and yet, the air here smells the same—of some secret knowledge, wood wax, chalk, and old dusty libraries. Mina soaks it all in like a sponge and for a few short instants doesn't even mind her involuntary transfer and the invisible chain around her ankle, forever binding her to this gilded cage.

Before long, they enter a room in which several men are standing bent over a round table littered with papers that take up all of their attention. Taube must have cleared his throat or rapped on the doorframe—Mina didn't see which one it was, absorbed in taking in her surroundings—for them to finally lift their heads and stare at the newcomers. Mina recognizes one of them: Dr. von Weizsäcker, the young fellow from the three-man assembly that interrogated her in Graz. Just like his colleagues, he wears a white lab gown over his civilian clothes. Unlike them, he greets Mina with a brisk nod and a well-bred smile.

"What is it?" one of the scientists, who looks vaguely familiar, demands of Taube. Mina can all but hear the irritation in his voice.

Taube must be introducing her, but Mina keeps staring at the scientists, not to miss anything they're saying.

The same physicist who looks so very annoyed huffs before Taube can finish.

"This child?" Mina watches his lips crease in distaste as he utters the words. "So, let me get this straight: first, they send away half of my staff to the front and now they send me little girls as replacements? What mockery is this?"

Von Weizsäcker comes to her aid then. "Dr. Heisenberg."

Mina blinks in disbelief, but the name and the face come together at once in her mind. Dr. Heisenberg, yet another Nobel Prize winner, probably the brightest mind behind the present-day fission theory development, stands before her with his hands shoved into the pockets of his white coat. It's devastating somehow, this displeasure of his at the sight of her, the young girl who has admired him greatly from afar.

"Fräulein Best has demonstrated great ability in theoretical physics despite her young age," von Weizsäcker continues in the meantime. "I looked through the notes that she worked out by herself and she shows great promise otherwise, I'd never have agreed to her joining our team here in Berlin—"

Mina's still reading von Weizsäcker's lips and misses whatever Dr. Heisenberg asks entirely. Only when Taube taps her shoulder and calls her attention to the physicist, explaining at the same time that Dr. Heisenberg's new charge is deaf, does Mina see him open his mouth and close it without another word. With great emotion, he shakes his head and turns his back on both Taube and Mina, concentrating all of his attention on his papers once again.

Hot tears flood Mina's eyes. Heisenberg is disgusted with her, that much is clear.

It's Taube who gently turns her toward himself and presses her shoulders ever so slightly. "Give him time," she sees his lips say. "He'll come round." To Heisenberg, he reminds him that he's under the Reich grant and orders and has no say in the matter, but the physicist's back remains turned to the *Abwehr* official. It's Taube's turn to shake his head as he nudges Mina forward. "Dr. von Weizsäcker will fill you in. For now, you'll be working under his direct charge at any rate, fortunately for you."

Dr. Heisenberg ignores the bait.

The more the day progresses, the more Mina feels like a shadow slowly disappearing under the midday sun. Von Weizsäcker promises to be with her right that instant; he just has to finish something here—she's more than welcome to listen—he catches himself and corrects the word to "watch," but there's not enough space around the table and Mina is too self-conscious to work her way in between the scientists' elbows and into their circle. Soon, they forget about her altogether as they slash at some designs with their pencils and argue with one another heatedly. And so, Mina melts into the air, just as invisible, and gradually backs into the wall lined with shelves containing hefty tomes, by which she remains until it's lunchtime.

The physicists file out of the room still deep in conversation and even von Weizsäcker doesn't remember to bring Mina along. That's fine with her. She went without food before and for much longer stretches of time when, immersed in her studies, she would simply forget to eat. If anything, their forgetfulness is a blessing. Now, Mina can approach the round table and study the papers on it unhindered.

They're blueprints; she sees it at once and gathers what they're blueprints of the very next instant. They're trying to devise the uranium machine, the engine inside of which the nuclear fission could be sustained for as long as the scientists needed. Except the calculations surrounding the machine are all off, just like they were in her little black notebook. But here, inside those very formulas, Mina sees something that makes her halt her breath in utter awe: moderators, at which she couldn't arrive with the best will in the world. Moderators that will slow down the neutrons generated from fission and lead to a controlled chain reaction.

She jumps as a hand lands on her shoulder and she swings round on her heel, hand still pressed to her chest, inside which her heart is beating wildly. Mina expected von Weizsäcker, but it's Dr. Heisenberg who's regarding her with his clear, gray eyes.

"Found something interesting?" he asks and Mina realizes why she didn't recognize him right away. In most photos, he's blond, handsome, and smiling, genuinely and easily, but today his face is a stern mask, aging him beyond his thirty-nine years of age.

"The moderators," Mina whispers and is grateful that she can't hear herself, for her voice is certainly shaking—with nerves or the discovery, she can't quite tell.

Werner Heisenberg arches a wide brow. Mina notices that when he's not posing for staged photos in celebrated scientific publications, his hair is in just as much of a natural disarray as Einstein's in his youth. It's reassuring somehow, even if Einstein is a verboten subject in his own former Institute and Heisenberg, who followed in his footsteps, doesn't like her all that much.

After a sigh, she proceeds with an explanation. "I could never arrive at what could be used as moderators. And here you have carbon and D_2O, the 'heavy water' and I'm thinking what an idiot I was and..." She passes her hand over her forehead and blows out her cheeks. "You're right, Dr. Heisenberg. I don't belong here. I'm only a student with a passion for physics, but I could never even conceive anything close to what you're working on here. I can see it now. You can tell Hauptmann Taube that I'm useless to you and don't waste your time with me."

Dr. Heisenberg regards her with interest for the first time. After an infinitely long minute, he moves a clean sheet of paper toward her.

"My colleague, Dr. von Weizsäcker, says you're a prodigy."

Mina tosses her head at once. "I'm not."

"He says you were sketching something very similar in your notes." He indicates the reactor in the blueprints.

"No, nothing even close. It was all wrong—"

But Dr. Heisenberg is not listening. Or he's ignoring her, on purpose. "Now that you have your missing moderators, tell me which one would work best." He all but encloses a pencil in her hand and gestures toward the table, as if to say, "Use our notes, don't be shy." Whether he's being helpful or mocking, Mina can't possibly tell. Most likely, the latter.

She starts with carbon. The physicists are back from their lunch break and are back at work but not for long. Soon, they disappear one by one after shaking each other's hand until only Dr. Heisenberg is left. Mina feels his presence, sees him on the periphery of her vision, but she is so absorbed in her calculations that she doesn't bother with him or the impression she's making, almost a child sitting cross-legged on the floor, surrounded by books on chemistry in addition to physics and scrawling, scrawling in her papers as her braid repeatedly falls over her shoulder.

The room grows dark and the lights come on, but Mina's still deep in her studies. Only when Dr. Heisenberg squats next to her does she force herself to unbend her back and feels the creaking in her spine as she does so. Her entire midsection is numb, just like her neck. Her toes have long gone to sleep and are beginning to tingle now and she works some blood into them inside her sandals.

"Any progress, Fräulein Best?"

"Some. I'll need more time."

"Naturally, you'll need more time. I didn't expect you to solve this in one day."

Mina solves it in one night. The following morning, without having slept a wink, she knocks on Dr. Heisenberg's office door and presents her findings without preamble.

"Only an actual experiment can confirm it, but according to my calculations, carbon in the form of graphite isn't a stable enough moderator. At first, I couldn't understand why because it *is* supposed to work, but the calculations invariably proved otherwise."

Dr. Heisenberg puts away the paper that he was reading and folds his hands atop his table. He's listening.

With renewed inspiration, Mina continues, "I went through lots of organic chemistry books and I think I found the answer. When they manufacture graphite, they use electrodes of boron carbide. Now, one atom of boron absorbs about as many slow neutrons as a hundred thousand atoms of carbon. Thus, these tiny boron impurities would 'poison' the graphite for use as a

moderator. It's these impurities that always skewed the calculations. It's my profound conviction that, if tested, the theory will
prove itself."

A faint smile appears on Dr. Heisenberg's face. It grows
slowly, turning the physicist into a veritable Cheshire Cat.
"You'd be delighted to hear that one of our colleagues, Dr.
Bothe, did test this theory. The experiment has proven precisely
what you've just stated. We got the results two months ago."

For a few moments, Mina takes it all in in stunned silence.

"Why haven't you told me?" she finally asks.

"How would I have known that you're worth anything as a
future scientist otherwise?"

Mina rolls the papers in her hands into a tight scroll, not
quite knowing how to feel. She's annoyed and delighted at the
same time and it's all somehow making it harder to breathe.

"Have you tried it with heavy water yet?" he asks.

"I did. It has its own troubles, but it works much better as a
moderator."

"And what troubles are those?"

Mina sighs. He already knows; what he showed her were
old findings just to test her, but, fine, she can play his game if it
means she'll finally be admitted into the team and this time it
will be due to her own merits instead of Taube's threats.

"Ordinary water only contains heavy water at a rate of
about one part in ten thousand. To separate the two by means of
repeated electrolysis, one will need large amounts of electric
power in close proximity to a watercourse. An entire hydroelec-
tric plant, in other words. But Germany doesn't have any, as far
as I know."

"No, it doesn't," Dr. Heisenberg concedes surprisingly
easily. "But Norway does. And Germany has just occupied it a
couple of months ago."

SIXTEEN

The next morning, the atmosphere in the scientists' quarters is altogether different. Instead of aloof turned backs, warm smiles greet Mina upon her arrival. Von Weizsäcker interrupts his conversation with one of his colleagues to hop off the desk on top of which he was perched and asks Mina how she likes her coffee.

"Or you can come with me to the canteen if you like so you know where it is."

But Dr. Heisenberg inserts himself between the two before Mina can form a reply. "Let the girl catch her breath; she just got here, for heaven's sake. Fräulein Best—"

"Please, it's just Mina."

"Mina." Dr. Heisenberg is more like his photos today, easygoing and so very approachable. He motions the other scientists to gather round. "Let me introduce you properly to our little Club."

"The Club?"

"Why, yes. The Uranium Club. Don't laugh, it's an official name." He feigns to be offended. "As you have probably gathered from the absence of machines and the abundance of chalk dust, we are theoreticians. Which means we come up with theories and formulas that work on paper but can only be proven by experimenters. Now, their group—except for a couple of gentlemen from the chemistry department here—works in the other wing, where they have all of the labs."

"Does Dr. Meitner work there too?" Mina's breath flutters in her chest in spite of herself. The woman behind the splitting of the atom itself, one of Mina's idols who inspired her to this very path, working just across the hall from them? That's just too good to be true.

It appears to be precisely the case, judging by the eyes lowered all around her as if in mourning.

"Dr. Meitner doesn't work here anymore," one of the scientists explains. His stance is like that of a physician breaking the news of an incurable illness to a patient that has an entire life before them. He even looks like one, with the heavy forehead of an intellectual who spends his life in thought and a narrow mustache covering his top lip. He's the only one out of the entire group who appears to have been born in the past century. The rest are all young men, not a single gray hair among them. "She had to leave Germany a few months ago."

"Jewish," von Weizsäcker mouths in response to Mina's confused look.

"But... she's brilliant," is all that Mina can say.

Lise Meitner's the reason why they, this little Uranium Club she's a member of by some miracle, can sketch all of these uranium machines in the first place. Without her, there wouldn't be fission, there wouldn't be any chain reactions that could light up the entire world with their purest, cleanest energy.

Yes, Lise Meitner might have been brilliant, but so was Einstein and look how far it got him, it suddenly occurs to Mina.

"You don't have to tell us that," the same scientist says with a grim smile. "I worked with her ever since she came here to study. Much like you, just a young little mite she was." His smile is fond and wistful now—a father recalling a daughter who is long lost but not forgotten. "But what a brain on that woman!"

"You're Dr. Hahn," Mina guesses then and covers her mouth in a gesture of reverence far beyond her control. "It was the three of you who split the atom," she finishes in an awestruck whisper.

"Only me and Dr. Strassmann left," the chemist acknowledges with a hand atop his colleague's shoulder.

In the downturned corners of Dr. Strassmann's eyes, Dr. Hahn's sorrow reflects. His swarthy complexion would contrast so wonderfully with his white lab gown and his just as bright, open smile if it didn't drop in an instant at the mention of his colleague. He must sense Mina's disappointment at such injustice and steps forward with his hand outstretched. "Come. Lise may not be here, but the lab still stands. I'll show you where it all happened. It'll give von Weizsäcker time to fetch you that coffee he promised."

Mina appreciates the attempt at humor, but Lise Meitner's absence is still felt too much among the group. A newcomer, Mina can still sense her ghost walking beside them along the Institute's hallways. She isn't dead, just gone, to one friendly country or another and yet... and yet.

Taube was wrong when he claimed the war didn't exist here. It does; it's just invisible and sometimes, that's even worse.

Dr. Hahn pauses in front of a locked door and rummages in his pocket for a key while Mina and Dr. Strassmann wait beside him. The chemist pushes the door open as though to a tomb and enters a room that is hauntingly quiet without its mistress' steps and fast hands cracking nature's codes open with admirable ease.

"We'll be working here sometimes," Dr. Hahn says, hands

jammed in pockets. "If you like, you can assist. How is your chemistry?"

"Worse than my physics and math, but much better than my calligraphy."

That gets her a double smile and the temperature in the room rises just a few degrees.

"Pardon my curiosity—or ignorance, but why are there rolls of toilet paper hanging next to..." Mina feels her cheeks grow warm. "Pretty much everything?"

"Before we moved into the Institute, Lise and I used to work in an old wood shop where we had our experimental facilities. Compared to this new lab, it was a proper pigsty! So many radioactive liquids spilled and gasses that decay turned into dust that settled onto every surface imaginable—there was no working there any longer, for its presence made sensitive measurements all but impossible," Dr. Hahn explains. "We knew little of radioactivity back in the day. Now, we don't even store highly radioactive materials here. They're in a separate storage facility."

"We call it *radium house*," Dr. Strassmann adds with a friendly wink.

"And whenever we conduct experiments here, there's an entire new safety protocol to follow. No shaking hands, no touching anything—including phones or door handles—until you decontaminate yourself."

"Hence, toilet paper," Dr. Strassmann concludes. "We use it to turn door handles or answer the phone while inside."

Dr. Hahn regards Mina and her expression, which hasn't grown any less quizzical for some time. "What did they teach you about radioactivity?"

"Just the basics, I'm afraid," Mina acknowledges with a taste of shame on her tongue. "Radioactivity is the release of energy during certain atoms' nuclei's decay. I never knew it had such a long half-life. For the particles to remain on surfaces long enough to contaminate them, that is."

The scientists in front of her exchange looks.

"It appears you're in luck then," Dr. Hahn declares. "Dr. Geiger is giving a lecture on radioactivity today. Is it in Harnack House?"

"Harnack House, yes," Dr. Strassmann confirms. "It started at ten, I believe."

"You'd better hurry then, Fräulein Mina. Learning about radioactivity is just as essential for a future physicist as visiting an autopsy for a future physician."

"I'm sorry?" Mina tilts her head, confused once again.

"So you can decide for yourself if you want to get into the whole rotten business before it's too late."

Dr. Hahn's strange words still ring in Mina's ears as she trots along lush, meticulously manicured lawns toward Harnack House, consulting Dr. Strassmann's hand-drawn map from time to time. The lecture hall is already full by the time she enters it, but Dr. Geiger, a bespectacled, middle-aged man with a neatly trimmed mustache and a shaved—or prematurely bald head? Mina can't quite tell from the distance—directs her to a free chair without interrupting his lecture. After excusing her way to it, Mina sits as quietly as she can and flips a notebook open, all eyes on Dr. Geiger and the small apparatus on the presentation table in front of him. *A Geiger counter?* she wonders.

"Reduced voltage in this newest model—only 450 to 650 volts opposed to 1200 volts in older units—allows for a smaller size and a longer battery life. The clicks identifying the number of ion pairs created every sixty seconds—our 'counts per minute'—can still be counted through accompanying headphones, but there's also a neon lamp flasher that serves as an additional indicator."

A Geiger counter, indeed. Fresh off of an assembly line and much more sophisticated than the models she's seen in physics magazines.

Mina tries to dive into all of the new information headfirst, tries to absorb it into the already existing pattern of her previous knowledge, but the waters are much too murky and she's drowning in terminology she can barely decipher, let alone understand. She stays patiently put, writes down something about the natural background count of ten impulses per minute and twenty impulses for a single milligram of radium at thirty feet with no shielding but is soon lost completely, overwhelmed and feeling inadequate for the umpteenth time in just a few short days—an impostor among truly bright minds. She's grateful to Dr. Geiger when he writes down in bullet points the possible uses for the new model of his original invention, even then finds herself confused when certain words appear on the blackboard.

Harmful gamma rays from X-ray equipment? The study of radium poisoning for toxicology studies for physiology students? Mina has never heard of either. In the scientific world presented to her, there was nothing harmful about radioactive particles. They were the alchemist's dream, something that turned metaphorical coal to gold. They are the answer to every-thing, the future of mankind, the ultimate tier of the periodical table.

While she remains in her chair absorbed in contradictory thoughts, some students around her file out of the lecture hall and some crowd around Dr. Geiger to ask him further ques-tions. But soon their numbers melt as well, and Mina still sits, eyes staring in contemplation, and she doesn't realize that it's only her and Dr. Geiger who are left. Only when he passes his hand in front of her face half in jest does Mina jolt herself back to reality and offers the physicist a guilty smile.

"I see I bored you to sleep."

"No, not at all," Mina rushes to assure him, rising to her feet that are all pins and needles. "I'm afraid I'm simply horribly unqualified to understand your lecture just yet. And deaf on top of things." She gestures to her ears with a mirthless chuckle. "It doesn't help things, as you can imagine."

She expects him to nod in a well-bred manner and walk away, but instead Dr. Geiger pulls up a chair for himself and gestures Mina to the opposite one she's just vacated.

"You can read lips, I assume?"

"You assume correctly, Herr Doktor."

"And what is your name and title?"

"No title yet, Herr Doktor. Wilhelmina Best. I'm a junior assistant in the theoretical physics department at the Kaiser Wilhelm Institute for Physics."

"Working under Dr. Heisenberg?"

"Yes, Herr Doktor. Just started. Dr. Hahn directed me to your lecture today, but I fear I'll have nothing to show for it." Another bashful smile she simply can't help.

"Fräulein Best," Dr. Geiger begins with the gravest air of sincerity about him, "there is absolutely no shame in not knowing something, only in not being willing to learn. Now, what is it precisely that confounded you so?"

"The harmfulness of radioactivity."

"What about it?"

"I don't understand what is harmful about it."

Dr. Geiger pulls back with a light grin, as though glad that she asked. "You have heard of Dr. Röntgen who invented the X-ray machine, haven't you?"

"Certainly." Mina nods, all willingness to learn.

"He was so fascinated with the picture of his bones, he decided to take it a few more times, from different angles. And then making different gestures. And then just for the fun of it. Until one day he awoke with blisters on his hand, as if after a bad burn. Only, he was nowhere near fire. Any ideas what might have caused it?"

Mina slowly shakes her head, even though the first tiny worm of suspicion already begins to twitch somewhere in the pit of her stomach.

"He thought it was free radicals produced in the air by X-rays from the ozone."

"Something tells me that wasn't the case," Mina says.

"No, it wasn't. A certain Dr. Walsh, who was also very much mystified by the phenomena, established that it was free radicals produced within the body that are the cause. To sum it all up for you, certain particles are extremely harmful to the human body. What's even worse, their half-life is so long, they remain attached to surfaces for days, weeks, and sometimes years. I can attest to that; I went to Paris to test my counter on Marie Curie's journals they keep there for visiting scientists. I expected to hear a few clicks, but what happened to my head-phones was a veritable machinegun fire. I needn't explain that I wouldn't touch the damned things after that. And that's years after her death... which was also caused by longtime exposure to radiation."

"I thought that was only rumors."

"No, not rumors. Radiation penetrates our tissues and damages the very inner structure of our cells. Leukemia is the most common occurrence among our scientific lot though there are other, more horrible ways to die of it. Have you heard of a certain American gentleman called Byers?"

Mina admits that she hasn't. And, frankly, doesn't want to, now that Dr. Geiger's tales have released a horde of ants under her skin. They creep everywhere and turn her cool, logical mind into a frightened hive that is sentient enough to understand that the danger is there, but the nature of it remains a mystery, making it all the worse still.

"The poor chap was suffering from a painful wrist from

playing tennis too much. A wrist or an elbow, don't quote me on which one, but the joke is, his physician, who was very *progressive*, prescribed Mr. Byers to drink radium tonic every night to help with his pain. Take an educated guess at what happened?"

"He got leukemia? Like Marie Curie?" Mina almost hopes it's the right answer.

But Dr. Geiger is already shaking his head, chewing on a story too ghastly to tell.

"First, his jaw began to ache. Then, he started losing his teeth, spitting them out by the handful each morning until nothing was left. Next, the bones in his jaw began to rot, seeping poison in his stomach with every swallow. His throat swelled up three sizes too big. Soon, he couldn't get down any solid foods out of fear of suffocation. Breathing itself was now a chore." Dr. Geiger pauses, but it's not for effect. He contemplates something, which Mina is still too petrified to decipher. "Fortunately for him, the fellow didn't suffer too long. Within days, his jaw disintegrated entirely and his white blood cell count dropped so low, the doctors could do nothing to revive him. That's radium for you, Fräulein Best."

Mina takes a few minutes to collect herself. The hellish images still stand before her eyes, but the scientist in her finally begins to triumph. She files the new information into the corner of her mind and nods slowly, with great resolution. This is what Dr. Hahn meant with the autopsy metaphor – he wanted to see if she had the guts to stomach it all.

"All right, that's the radium poisoning you mentioned. What of the harmful gamma rays produced by X-ray equipment?"

But Dr. Geiger cups her hand in a gesture reminiscent of her grandfather. "Read Walsh first. He titled his study *Radiation Sickness*. It dates back to 1897 and is in our library. It is rather fascinating and particularly for its time. Forty years ago and the man knew better than hotheaded idiots hoping to slap together a bomb out of uranium fuel."

Mina is stunned into silence for a few moments. Now, this is something new entirely.

"A bomb?" she repeats in an undertone. "No one is thinking about making any bombs. We are working on a uranium machine to produce electricity, for peaceful purposes. No one has ever said a word about any bombs."

She recedes eventually as she sees the look on Dr. Geiger's face. He pities her, genuinely pities; Mina can see it written clear as day in his intelligent eyes behind their black, round spectacles.

"I do see that you're indeed new here," he says eventually. "I'll compile you a list of things to read on radioactivity and leave it with my assistant by the end of the week. My advice to you, stay out of experimenters' facilities. And away from them in general. And particularly from Director Diebner."

Mina is about to ask who Director Diebner is and why she should avoid him, but Dr. Geiger is already on his feet, checking his wristwatch.

"I'm late for a meeting, I'm afraid; else, I would have stayed and chatted here with you longer. Come back anytime, Fräulein Best. Oh, and while you're checking that study out of the library, ask them for Wells' *The World Set Free*."

"What is it about?"

Dr. Geiger pauses just long enough to answer and bow slightly before placing his hat on his gleaming scalp. "Atomic war and what comes after."

SEVENTEEN

Outside, the world is bursting with color and sunshine, but in the Institute, pale-faced and harried physicists from the Uranium Club are deep at work. Due to her handicap, Mina has always been an outsider, a loner excluded from every imaginable group, and it takes her weeks to catch up on the inner life of the Institute. It would have taken Siggy a few days at best. Mina finds it both strange and melancholy how often he pops in her mind, uninvited.

She misses most of the snide remarks, but from what she does catch—mostly muttered under one's breath, inaudible to the others, but ones she can easily decipher through lip-reading —Mina learns that experimenters, with Dr. Kurt Diebner as their director and their oscilloscope, despise theoreticians such as Dr. Heisenberg and their "insufferable blubbering about quantum mechanics only three people in the world understand" and blackboards full of mathematical formulas that "make their eyes bleed." In turn, theoreticians call experimenters "Wehrmacht bootlickers" behind their backs and roll their eyes at their requests for "a formula that would finally put the atom to good military use." Dr. Geiger wasn't exaggerating

after all. There *is* an idea of an atomic bomb; though, as soon as
Mina expresses her concerns, Dr. Heisenberg dismisses them
with a smile and a shake of his head.

"The dream of an atomic bomb exists in Director Diebner's
imagination only. It's an impossibility. We have already counted
and recounted multiple times. It simply can't be done."

"Physicists were claiming the same about splitting the atom
not that long ago. They were also saying that it can't be done."

Dr. Heisenberg's grin widens. It reaches his eyes and wrinkles their corners.

"You question everything, don't you? No, don't get embarrassed; it's a compliment for a scientist. I'd say, it's imperative
for our kind to constantly question things. And you are correct.
There is nothing definite about the future of nuclear physics
just yet. It's in its infancy and still very much a mystery to all of
us. I should have phrased my statement differently. It simply
can't be done with our current knowledge of the atom and its
behavior. Maybe in the future, years from now... But not in this
decade and not in this war. So, don't lose sleep over it."

Mina tries not to, but she reads Wells' novel in bed every
night and thrashes around in tangled sheets when vivid nightmares of explosions wiping everything living off the face of the
earth grip her in their vise. In her dreams, she tastes air
poisoned by radiation and climbs through ruins which entire
civilizations have been reduced to and feels her skin burn and
blister when she touches radioactive dust, and corpses, charred
corpses everywhere...

But then the morning comes and the world outside is still
standing, going about its business as usual, and Mina shakes the
cobwebs of the nightmares off her eyelashes and bikes to the
Institute, pretending that nothing is the matter.

Instead, she follows Dr. Heisenberg like a shadow and
absorbs every word he directs at her personally and cleans his
office blackboard herself at the end of each day. He doesn't trust

janitors. Anyone can be a military spy and particularly with Director Diebner breathing down their necks with his grand ideas. Dr. Heisenberg isn't concerned about the distant possibility of any bombs. What he's concerned about is someone reporting his group for sabotaging war efforts, even if there is literally nothing that can be done for the military at this point.

"He has every right to be paranoid," von Weizsäcker quips cryptically one day as he takes Mina for a midday walk on the Institute grounds.

"Why's that?"

Von Weizsäcker widens his eyes at her. *Which rock have you been living under, girl?*

"Shaky political grounds," he replies before puffing the smoke out of his thin, elegant cigar into the clear summer air.

"Dr. Heisenberg?" *Impossible.* Mina has seen him greet his colleagues with a Heil Hitler salute each morning and break into a smile whenever inspectors from the War Office descend on them.

"The very same," von Weizsäcker nods sagely. "His quarrel with Stark has brought the entire SS on his poor back. If it wasn't for Heisenberg's mother, who just happens to know Reichsführer Himmler's mother, it's anyone's guess what ditch our dear Herr Professor would have ended up in with a garrote around his neck."

If this conversation had happened during her first few days at the Institute, Mina would have seriously doubted the validity of such claims. But now that she's been made aware of von Weizsäcker's father working for Foreign Affairs Minister von Ribbentrop's office, she simply can't write them off as regular gossip. Still, she gives him a doubtful look.

"You're joking, certainly."

"My dear, I'm as serious as a heart attack."

"Your father told you?"

"We did have quite a few chats about it, but even without

him, it wouldn't have been a secret. Have you not read newspapers in the past few years? Their feud played out in front of the
entire population of Germany, right in the pages of *Beobachter*."

No, she hasn't. She was a mere schoolgirl a few years ago,
with other worries on her mind than scientific feuds, Mina
reminds him.

"With your big brain, I keep forgetting you're still a child,"
he teases and yet regards her fondly, with almost brotherly
affection. After Dr. Heisenberg has granted his silent approval,
they have all taken to her, these theoreticians from the Uranium
Club. "Let me fill you in then. There was this experimenter,
Johannes Stark his name is, who took offense at all theoreticians
and particularly those who followed Einstein's quantum
mechanics theories."

Mina stops abruptly at the mention of her idol's name, but
von Weizsäcker doesn't skip a beat. They're in the open, with
no unfriendly ears around them. And with her, untainted by
political affiliations and guided by her love for science only, he
can talk freely.

"And Herr Professor, he went and signed a petition
protesting the dismissal of Jewish scientists from their posts
back in '33. That, combined with Heisenberg's being a theoretician who swore by Einstein's 'Jewish physics'," von Weizsäcker's eyes narrow mockingly as he uses the term, "sent Stark over
the top. He made it a point of honor to insult Heisenberg's character in every possible way in every issue of the newspaper.
Now, Dr. Heisenberg, being the laidback fellow that he is, took
it all in his stride and simply refuted whatever 'scientific'
nonsense Stark was spouting just to discredit Heisenberg to the
general public that didn't know any better. But it all went
downhill when Stark began calling him a 'white Jew,' the title of
which Herr Professor wore with certain pride about him, mind
you. However, once Himmler's secret police got involved,
things got ugly and fast. The SS were publicly calling for paying

Herr Professor a visit and doing away with him like they did away with the Jews he liked so much—their words, I'm merely quoting."

Despite the warm day, chills creep down Mina's spine at the mention of the SS and the Jews. Herr Freudenberg's bloodied figure once again comes to mind, kneeling in front of the smoldering façade of his bakery, surrounded by black jack-boots. She hugs herself with both arms; wants to avert her eyes but needs to see what von Weizsäcker has to say.

"The Gestapo began investigating him on the grounds of being an enemy of the Reich. It was then that Frau Heisenberg intervened and called on Frau Himmler for help. Must have worked, because all charges were dismissed and his status restored. But it still haunts him, you see. The feeling how fast it can all go to the devil if he's not careful enough."

Mina looks at Dr. Heisenberg with new eyes from then on. And he keeps sketching his designs for the uranium reactor prototype. From the west, through the cool Norwegian forests, cisterns with heavy water begin to arrive. In the experimental department, under Director Diebner's watchful eye, they work on something hidden and vaguely nightmarish. Mina stalks around their premises on her way to lunch and back, but the doors are always locked. The air here smells of metal and mistrust.

EIGHTEEN

With a stack of literature collected from Dr. Geiger's assistant under her arm, Mina takes two steps at a time to her floor and nearly stumbles into a uniformed man waiting just outside her apartment's front door. She recognizes him instantly: he's the SD "student" who picked her out of the university class and had her shipped off here under a military escort. He's smiling like he did that day, but Mina is all cold sweat under a summer dress, frozen like a doe in the headlights of a swiftly approaching car.

"Good evening, Fräulein Best." He's all civility and formality, clicking his heels and saluting her from the top step. "Forgive me for such an unexpected visit, but when duty calls, we have to answer."

"What duty is this?" Mina forces her lips to part. In front of her chest, a stack of journals like a shield.

"Why, to check on your well-being, of course." His eyes are wide and sincere.

Mina doesn't believe him for one second, but there is nothing doing but to open the door and let him in. That's any dictatorship's law of the land: the uniforms hold all the power. Civilians are to shut their mouths and obey.

Once inside, Mina deposits the studies on the kitchen table and asks the SD man if he would like some coffee.

"Don't bother with it." He's already in one of the chairs, leafing through Dr. Geiger's recommended reading list. "Sit, sit; it's your own apartment. By all means, make yourself comfortable. X-ray and gamma rays? Now, that's interesting. I was just at the meeting where Dr. Brand—you do know Dr. Brand, no? The Führer's physician? Such a brilliant fellow. But I digress. He was giving a lecture on the newest methods of sterilization and mercy death methods to use in euthanasia centers. You do know of the euthanasia program, I believe? Your mother quit her nursing position over it, if I'm not mistaken?"

Mina is thoroughly cold now, borderline shivering, despite the sultry evening seeping through the open window with the last rays of the blood-red sun.

"Yes. She's very religious, my mother."

"A pity." He tilts his head to one side, a picture of compassion. "She was an excellent nurse, from what I heard."

What else have you heard of us? slips through Mina's mind on high alert.

"At any rate," he continues, "whatever the stance religious institutions hold on that matter, euthanasia is done for the sake of our people, not because we like sending invalids to God early." He stops abruptly and laughs with ease. Only, unlike when Dr. Heisenberg does it, the SD man's eyes remain sharp and cold, like shards of ice. "You must have seen the documentaries that are running all over Reich territories now. Those mental patients, they are of no use to society. They only consume resources without giving anything back. Can't put them to work, can't send them to the front. And, in the meantime, our best genetic stock, the youngest and healthiest men are dying for the Fatherland on the frontline."

Shouldn't have started the war in the first place then no one would have to die, Mina thinks but nods emphatically instead.

"Before the war, it was a different case, but now we simply can't divert valuable resources to waste in such a cavalier manner. You're a scientist; if you had to choose between a healthy German citizen and an invalid, what would you have done in the government's place?"

This time, Mina simply can't swallow the truth. "I'm considered an invalid," she reminds the SD man quietly, wondering if he purposely nudged her toward the acknowledgment of the fact. For what purpose, it is anyone's guess.

The SD man's smile is all benevolence and goodwill. "Not that kind of invalid. You're not mentally retarded; quite the opposite, in fact. And we don't euthanize anyone with minor handicaps like yours. There's a sterilization program for that, just so they wouldn't pass undesirable genes to their offspring. That's exactly what I was saying about Dr. Brandt—he suggested using X-rays as an effective and accessible sterilization tool that can be used in any hospital, even in the most remote locations. They still have to work out the details, but it's all very scientific—you do recognize the importance of eugenics for the health of the nation, don't you? I do hope your mother hasn't infected you with her religious zeal."

"No. I'm an agnostic."

"Splendid! We are on the same page then."

Mina stares at him for what feels like eternity. "Am I to be sterilized?" she asks at last. Better to be out in the open with it, whatever the outcome. The wait is much too insufferable.

The SD man pulls back in mock horror. "Whatever gave you that idea?"

"What you just said."

"Bah, I said eugenics. Undesirable genes. You don't carry those. You weren't born with a defect. Why sterilize you?"

What do you want from me then?

And he does want something; else, he wouldn't be sitting here, chatting with her about pseudo-science and her mother's crimes. The air between them is charged with invisible threat as though before a rainstorm.

"How do you like your new position?"

The change in subject is so abrupt, it takes Mina a few moments to form a coherent answer. "It's good. Wonderful, actually. I feel truly fortunate to be working under the guidance of such brilliant scientists. Thank you for placing me with them."

"No need to thank an ordinary civil servant for merely doing his job." He's all smiles once again. "And it's my pleasure to hear how well you're adjusting. They don't give you any trouble, those new superiors of yours, do they?"

"No, not at all." Mina's vehemence is sincere this time.

"Good. What are you working on, if you don't mind me asking? Likely, I won't understand a thing, but I'm so very curious."

"Uranium machine prototype. It's an engine of sorts that would work on nuclear energy. No need for any fossil fuels to power electric stations or sea vessels—they can work by using the energy released from splitting uranium atoms."

"Sounds incredible."

"It really is." Mina feels a tentative smile tugging at the tense muscles of her face.

"Such vast amounts of energy... one wonders what else they can be applied to."

Mina stills herself, sensing precisely what he's probing at. Military use. The bomb. But if that's what he came for, he won't get it from her.

"Yes, one does. Hopefully, with time, we'll find even more methods of uranium application. Dr. Heisenberg's team is working tirelessly on it, I assure you. We're just as curious as to what else can be done with such power."

"Whoever discovers it shall be held in the Führer and Fatherland's greatest esteem. And handsomely rewarded, of course. All kinds of grants, facilities—you name it." He leans forward in a faux-conspiratorial manner. "You didn't hear it from me, but that's the talk in higher circles."

"I'll make sure to be discreet." She plays along.

"And please, don't hesitate to contact me if..." He pretends to ponder something while playing with the card he produced from his inner pocket. "Say, some rogue element decides to put a wrench in the research's gears. Don't get me wrong, we have thoroughly vetted all the scientists working on nuclear research, but there is always someone who can slip through the net. A covert communist sympathizer or a pacifist who will sabotage the entire team's work for his own selfish reasons. Don't be intimidated by them, whatever they tell you. Call me, night or day. I'm always here for you and your colleagues and shall always provide all the help and support you need for the most seamless research."

"Thank you kindly—" Mina realizes that he never offered her his name. She reads it off the card embossed with two lightning bolts in its corner. "Untersturmführer Gürtner. I certainly will."

He slaps his knee and is on his feet, ready to depart, satisfied, when he suddenly pauses with his cap under his arm. "Oh, before I forget. Was there anyone else at the University of Graz that you would recommend joining the Institute and your research team? Someone as brilliant as you."

The sugar on top of the compliment turns Mina's teeth, but she smiles compliantly all the same. "I'm afraid I was the only one interested in nuclear physics. The rest, they preferred something more orthodox."

"Yes, that's what I thought. Oh well. Thank you for this most pleasant conversation, Fräulein Best. Goodnight."

"Goodnight, Herr Untersturmführer."

She locks the door after him and goes to collect her research literature, only her hands tremble something frightful. There is no reading anything tonight.

At past three in the morning, it seems like there's no sleeping either.

NINETEEN

BERLIN, GERMANY. AUGUST 1940

"Have you read *The World Set Free* by H. G. Wells?" Mina asks
Taube.

They're at the Ethnological Museum, which Mina expected
to be teeming with people on Sunday, but it's all but deserted.
Only uniformed museum workers stand guard over the precious
art collections like forlorn guardians of the dead as Mina and
her escort make their way through the labyrinth of museum
rooms.

"Not that I recall."

They pause in front of the statue of Buddha. The serenity
in his downcast gaze almost persuades Mina for a short instant
that the war isn't gaining speed all over Europe.

It was Taube's idea, to show her Berlin while it was still in
its summer splendor, before October rains swaddle the city in
drab grayness and reduce it to a shell of its former self altogether
when winter comes. To Mina, such explanation carried an echo
of something far more profound and sinister; something that
made her think of Wells' novel just now.

"Dr. Geiger recommended it to me. Wells wrote it before I
was born," she tells Taube. "In 1914, if I'm not mistaken, right

after the very first works on the atom were published. The premise is that humanity develops atomic engines that drive progress forward. But being the doomed, self-destructive species that we are, people develop a new type of atomic weapon—a bomb—which eventually leads to a world war. The last one of its kind."

Mina looks at Taube, but he's silent. Silent and so very still, watching her intently.

"In the end, the planet is reduced to a toxic wasteland."

Not a particle of air moves around them. Time itself seems to have come to a stop.

"Why are you telling me this now?" Taube asks after what feels like an eternity.

Mina moves her shoulder. "You know who Dr. Diebner is?"

"Naturally. He's the director of the Nuclear Research Office."

"You know who appointed him to the post?"

"The Army Ordinance Office."

"Who answers directly to...?"

"The Führer." Taube flicks his wrist—*what's with the interrogation?*

Mina nods and wets her lips—*bear with me, Herr Hauptmann.*

"Do you know the purpose of the Nuclear Research Office?"

"Nuclear research, I would assume?" His irony is accented by the arch of his brow.

"And namely?"

He gestures in desperation. *How would I know? I'm not a scientist.*

"That's the whole trouble," Mina says quietly and tugs at his sleeve. Museum workers are silent as statues and can lull anyone into a false sense of security, but the further away from their ears, the better. "Dr. von Weizsäcker told me that Dr.

Heisenberg wasn't initially invited into the Club. At first, it consisted only of scientists who shared Dr. Diebner's idea of nuclear research."

"Which is?"

"That with fission, one can produce bombs. But you ought to know that already."

Judging by the look of unguarded horror on Taube's face, Mina's calculations must have been off, at least by some degree.

"Don't tell me you didn't know that, Herr Hauptmann," she presses. "You're the intelligence branch of the army. Surely, you ought to be more informed than regular brass?"

"When I came on board, Heisenberg was already in the Club," he says and holds his hands in front of himself without realizing, as though to shield himself from such accusations.

Growing up without hearing, Mina had to rely on such body language to compensate for her inability to distinguish the emotion and pitch of a voice. People don't recognize how much they reveal through such gestures, but Mina sees it all, always has.

"And from the reports I received, Heisenberg and his team are working solely on the development of the uranium machine," Taube continues. "I'm no scientist by any means, but from what they have explained to me, it will be used to replace engines driven by coal and oil, something more efficient from an energy point of view but by no means destructive. Do you truly think I would have brought *you* on board to develop an atom bomb?"

"And what makes me so different?" Mina is about to laugh. Untersturmführer Gürtner had no qualms on this account, why should Taube?

And yet, there's something different about the *Abwehr* officer. Something that makes this very conversation possible.

"You're a young woman, for God's sake! Women bring life

into this world, not obliterate it—" he ceases abruptly, his face a mask of agony for reasons Mina can't quite comprehend.

She sees his throat constrict and eyes mist over, but that isn't on account of her. Just like his entire countenance, ever since she met him, a picture of permanent grief has become embedded deep into the very lines on his face.

Taube passes his hand over his face, forcing the emotions under control. It's not easy, but he does it—stuffs the suffering back into his heart, where he carries it day by day, heavy as a stone.

"Forgive me for the outburst, please." He's stoic and straight-backed once again, only his eyes are still veiled with pain. "My wife passed away in childbirth. Just a year ago. So, it's all still a bit... tender."

Now it all comes together at last.

Mina's gaze softens. She isn't suspicious of him any longer; not of what she feared from him, at any rate. She thinks of pressing his hand in a silent gesture of comfort, but they aren't that well-acquainted and so she doesn't, but regrets it somehow.

"I'm very sorry for your loss."

He nods briskly; swallows. Mina sees his jowls clench. It *is* still tender; she sees it well enough. Without another word, they pass through the hall and enter another room, all draped in red and full of stone-carved demons.

"Yes, Dr. Heisenberg and his team are working solely on the development of the uranium reactor," Mina begins as quietly as possible. "But Director Diebner and his team of experimenters, they want something far more different. They have the facilities at their disposal—Director Diebner is in charge of that too. Fortunately for us, they need theoreticians to work the formulas for them. Without us, they're simply extremely gifted engineers, but it won't do them much good. The point is, Herr Hauptmann, I'm not all that certain that they won't eventually come by some other student who can guide them through the process, or come by the correct formula themselves after experimenting on it to death. Your SD colleague, who paid me a visit, hinted at such a possibility."

"Gürtner came to see you?" Judging by Taube's look, the visit wasn't authorized.

"Yes. We had a most stimulating conversation about sterilization and euthanasia."

Taube's countenance is all storm clouds ready to burst. "You should have told me at once."

"And let him know I reported our conversation?" It's Mina's turn to arch a brow. "To all but announce that I'm against such inquiries and am therefore the very wrench in the gears he was talking about? I'm young but not stupid, Herr Hauptmann. I mentioned it for your sake, not for you to pick fights with the SS, or SD, or whatever secret service he's working for." Mina shakes her head.

They both study the artifacts in front of them without properly seeing them until Mina decides to speak again. She's brave with Taube. Much braver than with Gürtner, even though the latter smiles so easily, and the former is hard as granite on the outside and just as mournful, as he carries his late wife's and child's names engraved on his very soul.

"They want their bomb, Herr Taube. The men who use X-rays—one of the greatest inventions of modern medicine—to sterilize their own citizens whom they perceive as racially defective. The men who murder newborn children with phenol for the slightest handicap. The men who took everything from the Jewish citizens and took their lives when there was nothing else to take. No, Herr Hauptmann. Say what you will, but Germany—this Hitler's Germany—cannot be the country that builds this bomb first." The look that she gives him is full of meaning.

"Can such a bomb be built?" Taube asks after a pause, gazing past her shoulder at one of the demons sitting on top of the world, ready to devour it with its forked tongue. "Theoretically?"

"Maybe. In a few years. That's what Dr. Heisenberg says. But, then again, he isn't actively working on its design and I thank God every day for this greatest mercy."

If anyone in the entire Reich can build such a bomb, it would be Werner Heisenberg. Mina doesn't say it out loud, but there is no need to. Director Diebner wouldn't have invited a politically unreliable "white Jew" to the Uranium Club if he had any other choice. Dr. Heisenberg is the brightest mind of German nuclear physics. He's also its conscience, at least for now.

Taube knows it as well; Mina can see it in his eyes, see multiple thoughts running over their surface as he takes it all in.

"And just how destructive would such a theoretical bomb be?" he finally asks.

For a long time, Mina gazes at the demon as well.

"Just like in Wells' book," she finally replies.

In the periphery of her vision, Taube's face turns gray as ash.

TWENTY

With the fall, comes the promised rain. It starts one day in mid-September and doesn't stop for what seems like weeks, drenching the streets in misery. No more sunny bicycle rides for Mina by Grünewald, with freedom itself kissing her freckled cheeks as she gains speed. She takes the U-Bahn exclusively now, swaying to and fro in a crowd of Berliners looking like drenched crows in their black raincoats. The entire capital is one big funeral.

Along the train's walls, old advertisements for shaving creams, amusement parks, and department stores are plastered over by new ones—Luftwaffe and SS recruitment offices mostly and Red Cross drives. In the newspapers her fellow commuters read, the same patriotic nonsense. Most of them skim-read through it and turn to something more interesting in the back of the paper: UFA film stars and football scores. The more Mina gets to know Berliners, the more she likes them. They speak what's on their mind and joke about what's not supposed to be joked about. Sardonic and adaptable to all, Berliners infect Mina with their irony-infused resilience, and even on such rainy days, the future doesn't seem too bleak when she's among them.

It's almost her stop; she's inching closer to the doors when someone catches her attention. Tall and blond and towering over the crowd with his hair combed just the way he always wore it, but it can't be Siggy. Surely, it can't? The arm with which he's holding onto the leather strap is obscuring his face and there isn't enough space around Mina to maneuver herself just a bit to see him better, but something keeps nudging at her to try, even though Siggy's in Graz – he must be.

The train pulls to a stop. The doors open and people push Mina without ceremony, like only Berliners can—"Are you coming out or what? Don't block the exit, girl!"—but she fights the current and stays put and begins to work her way toward the blond fellow when he suddenly turns.

Their eyes meet briskly before he looks away but turns right back and stares at Mina in stunned amazement.

"Einstein?" She sees his lips form the nickname she hasn't realized how much she's missed.

As though awakened from slumber by a magical incantation, Mina elbows her way toward him and he toward her until they meet in the middle of a car carrying its human cargo through a dark tunnel and grasp each other with a strength that could fuel the engines of the entire world. Even the Berliners don't curse them out any longer but smile knowingly and avert their eyes to give the two some privacy.

"Siggy."

"The very same." His smile is just as brilliant and goofy. Only the clothes under her hands have changed. Gray-green and very smart—thankfully not the SS ones but with some patch on the sleeve Mina doesn't recognize.

Radio division.

Mina doesn't realize it at first that he doesn't say it but signs it instead.

When did you learn to sign?

As soon as I got your letter.

Why?

Missed you.

Such an easy explanation, but Mina's heart swells with emotion as if an entire universe with all its beauty was enclosed in two simple words.

What are you doing here?

Serving.

That explains the uniform.

They came for you like they did for me? Mina signs.

Siggy nods. His lips form one bloodless line. *Told you that bastard was the SS.*

I know. I should have listened.

Where did they take you?

Kaiser Wilhelm Institute for Physics. Here, in Berlin-Dahlem.

What do you do there?

Nuclear research. You?

Codebreaking for the Abwehr.

Why am I not surprised?

They miss another stop and don't even notice. Around them, the sea of humanity is shifting and flowing, in and out, and they still stand, oblivious to everything around them, talking with their hands and eyes, and, it is Mina's profound conviction, hearts as well.

Only after the train pulls out of the tunnel and into the overhead tracks do they remember themselves and quickly exchange addresses they don't write down but commit to memory and promise to visit at the first chance.

"If I don't get off now and change trains back, they'll announce me a deserter," Siggy says, just because he needs both hands to hold Mina.

She, too, grasps at his arms and refuses to let go even when the train begins to slow down. "You won't get in trouble, will you?"

He brushes it off. "It's not the regular army. They won't make me peel potatoes in punishment all night, if that's what you're asking."

"Be careful, all right?"

"You too, Einstein. We'll catch up later this week."

"Yes."

"It was so good to see you."

"You too."

The doors open. Siggy releases her at last, takes a step back, but then changes his mind and grasps her once again by the shoulders and holds her so close, Mina's head begins to swim. And then, before she can utter a single word, he jumps through the closing doors and gazes at her through the glass with infinite longing and, for some reason, worry as the train pulls away.

Mina rides it to its last station and only then stumbles out of the car, her hand still pressed to the sleeve of her coat where Siggy's hand rested as if to hold onto something inexplicably precious.

Siggy comes by at the end of the week, Mina's apartment his first stop after his Friday shift. He's still in his uniform and it fits him like a glove and yet it still pains Mina to see the detestable eagle on his shoulder, much like it pained her to see the Party pin on her father's lapel. Like a cancerous growth, it ate into her father's very flesh and is slowly consuming him from the inside —she saw it with her own eyes during her last visit—and his work is nothing like Siggy's. It's terrifying to think what that patch shall do to her friend.

He's still very much the same right now, only somehow even bigger and stronger. Or perhaps it only seems that way to Mina and it's she who's slowly shrinking, like Alice who drank the magic potion, turning into one of the invisible atoms herself until they split her, use her for energy, and discard her like they do with everyone else. People are disposable in this new Germany. It's ideas that ought to live forever, and where one person falls, another should pick up his banner and carry it further until he, too, drops and so on and so forth until the end of time.

"Are you terribly hungry?" Mina asks. She, too, has just returned from the Institute and is still in her work clothes. "I haven't had time to whip up anything for dinner," she explains apologetically and hopes that Siggy won't notice the telling absence of pots and pans. She's not her mother and there's no one to cook for here, and on most days, she survives on sandwiches smeared with whatever she can find in the fridge, or a pretzel bought on the way from the U-Bahn. Sometimes she forgets to eat altogether.

He is terribly hungry, Siggy says. But not for food. For conversation.

"Nuclear research then, eh?" he asks.

Mina nods. Despite his protests, she did put a kettle onto the stove and is stealing glances at it over Siggy's shoulder. Between them, a pack of half-eaten crackers and an ocean of state secrets.

"Peaceful?" Siggy asks and tosses his head with a chuckle that looks bitter. "Of course not. Whatever hasn't been converted to the war effort is scrapped. Who's in charge of the facilities?"

"The OKW."

"Wehrmacht High Command." Another knowing look. Just as he has suspected.

The heat is creeping up Mina's cheeks. She knows he blames the system—after all, it's the system that has essentially kidnapped her and put her to work—and yet she can't shake the feeling of being interrogated. Accused.

"We're not making weapons or anything of the sort," she says.

"Oh no, I didn't mean to imply anything," Siggy says hastily. "Who am I to say anything at all? Look at where I work." Another grim grin. He gestures toward the radio corps insignia sewn onto his uniform.

But he's right all the same. The army does want the bombs, together with Director Diebner—the former, for the victory; the latter, for personal prestige. It's humanity's fortune that Dr. Heisenberg keeps all his scientists' attentions on the reactor research only. Only, how long shall that last? And what shall Mina do when posed with the task of developing anything other than a so-called "peaceful atom"?

"I'm sorry for being defensive," Mina says eventually and goes to the stove on which the kettle is now boiling. For some reason, it's easier to talk without having to look him in the eyes. The guilt is still there—the guilt for something that hasn't even happened yet—but the die is cast, and with each new discovery, they're approaching something that shall forever change the very life on earth... or cause its annihilation, if such a discovery falls into the wrong hands. "I haven't lied to you. We are working on a nuclear reactor design as of now, something that would supply energy to entire cities without oil or coal, simply by splitting atoms."

A faint smile appears on her face as she pours the hot water into the two respective cups. For some time, Mina watches the tiny shrunken tea leaves unravel and turn the water to liquid amber.

"It's beautiful when you think of it. Something that you can't see with the naked eye lighting up entire cities, continents in time. One doesn't get closer to magic than that." Mina places the two cups on the table and lowers herself heavily into her chair, her smile slowly fading away. "And yet, the same energy can level those cities—and continents—if one turns its good to evil."

"And it's possible?" Siggy probes gently as he cups the tea in his hands. "To turn its good to evil, that is?"

The same question Taube asked.

Mina gazes at the languid dance of tea leaves in her cup. "Everything is possible. Given enough time."

"And how long do you think it will take until someone cracks the code?"

Mina feels her lips quiver ever so slightly as she smiles at him. "That's the question that keeps me awake every single night."

The sun's slanted rays paint the room in golden stripes as they sip their tea and reminisce about the good golden days of Graz, when life was simple and the only problems they had to solve were the ones written on blackboards in chalk.

"I miss the cafeteria food," Siggy confesses with a chuckle. "I loved the Hungarian chef's days the best. The goulash he used to make!"

"To die for," Mina agrees readily. "And the plump cook who used to dye her hair with henna? She made the best cupcakes, didn't she?"

"Oh, don't remind me!" Siggy pats his stomach with a look of mock suffering on his face. "How I suffer from the absence of Austrian sweets here! Germans are as tight as a hussar's trousers when it comes to sugar, and particularly now that they ration everything."

Mina nods emphatically. "I would kill for an authentic Viennese pastry just now! Whenever *Vati* would take us to Vienna, pastry shops were always our first stop, as soon as we'd hop off the train. The only sweets that ever came close were—" She stops abruptly, her eyes, just now brimming with light, are suddenly extinguished.

Siggy sees the change in her at once; pulls forwards and catches her hand in his. *What is it?* His eyes search hers.

It pours out of her then, the story of Linz and Herr

Freudenberg's bakery and the fall of 1938 and the SA boots on the ground and the smoke obscuring the baker's kneeling figure while she ran, ran like a coward—

Siggy's instantly on his feet, holding Mina by her shoulders, saying something urgently to her, but she refuses to see what.

"A coward is what I am," she insists and swipes at the hot tears already spilling down her cheeks. "I was then, and I am now. Anyone with a conscience would have done something—"

He turns her toward himself and cups her face in his hands. Mina freezes for an instant, forced to look into those infinitely bright blue eyes. Only now, instead of the tiny specks of mirth always present in them, they're as grave as they can be.

"You would have done something and ended up on the same truck as your employer," Siggy says. "When thugs like the SA get bloodthirsty, no one is safe. And sometimes running is the only logical thing to do."

"Trucks," Mina repeats. "What trucks?"

"The trucks they put most of those poor devils in that night," Siggy says. "Whoever they didn't kill, they sent to concentration camps like Dachau."

Intent is slowly creeping back into Mina's devastated eyes. It's always been a curse of hers, falling apart whenever she didn't have a purpose, a visible goal in sight. A visible problem, no matter how complicated, can always be solved.

"Do you think he's still alive?" she asks, hope trembling at the tips of her fingers that clutch the gray-green cloth of Siggy's sleeves. "Herr Freudenberg?"

Siggy shrugs, pensive in the gathering twilight. "He might be. He's a baker; if he lucked out, they might have put him on kitchen duty, and that's always the best. No hard physical labor."

"Do you think it's possible to find out?"

"For me?" He looks almost amused. "I'm confined to the radio quarters at all times. All I get are coded messages to decipher. I don't know any higher-ups in the *Abwehr*, and even if I did, fat lot of good it would do. It's the SS that man the camps. So, unless you know someone in the black uniform—"

"No."

He nods, looking oddly satisfied. "And good for you, Einstein. Stay as far away from them as possible."

"The trouble is, they don't want to stay away from us. That's how we ended up in this entire mess, you and I."

TWENTY-ONE

BERLIN, GERMANY. AUTUMN 1940

No one has been told about the meeting. It comes as much of a surprise to Werner Heisenberg as it does to his team. It's early in the morning. The coffee mugs are still steaming on tabletops and the blackboard is still black, untouched by the chalk. But Director Diebner's adjutant—Mina can only think of him as such as there's positively nothing secretarial about the fellow, with his military bearing—is standing in the doorway and telling them to gather their papers and follow him to the conference room. There's nothing to be done but to exchange glances and grudgingly gather their research under his hawkish stare.

Mina's more in the dark than anyone else. She hasn't heard Diebner's underling barging in and relaying Diebner's orders. She can only sense the instant change in the air, the tension that suddenly charges it like electricity. She peers into each face, but they're as closed off as ancient tombs. Only in the hallway she seizes her chance and catches von Weizsäcker by his sleeve, pulling him to the very end of the dismal procession.

"What is this about?" she whispers.

"Damned if I know," he mouths back. "Diebner wants us all in the conference room."

Mina wants to ask whatever for but swallows the useless question. Von Weizsäcker doesn't know, and she'll find out soon enough. Hopefully, Diebner simply wants an update on the uranium reactor progress. However, the stone that's suddenly sitting in Mina's stomach warns her of something more sinister brewing in the circular tower of the Institute.

They take the stairs one flight up and enter the experimenters' domain. It's a different world here and the air is heavier somehow and smells faintly of metal and, for some reason, singed hair. They pass laboratories and their fearsome machines and, as one, long for their blackboards, papers, and numbers; that's what they know and love—the theoretical work that solves the universe's riddles. Here, they feel out of their depth and vulnerable somehow. For a split second, Mina wonders if that's what the chemists who produced mustard gas felt when they realized it could melt the very flesh off a human's bones. Writing a formula on a board is one thing, seeing physical results from it is something quite different.

Thankfully, the conference room is just that: one big rectangular table surrounded by chairs and two big blackboards on opposite sides. Above one, a portrait of the Führer. Above the other is that of Max Planck, the father of nuclear physics and the first director of the Institute. It's much smaller than the image of Hitler.

It's the first time that Mina has seen Director Diebner in person. He rarely graces the theoreticians' quarters with his presence, and on the rare occasion that he does, it's Dr. Heisenberg office that he heads to, always briskly and thoroughly ignoring anyone he passes by.

An ever-receding crown of dark hair barely covering his skull, his eyes concealed behind thick black-framed lenses, Director Diebner looks to be in his late fifties. Seated opposite him, Dr. Heisenberg, who's four years his senior, resembles a student fresh out of college. To Mina, the contrast is almost surreal.

They take their seats like two warring camps at the negotiating table: theoreticians all clinging to Heisenberg, and Diebner's experimenters opposite them.

Mina's palms are wet with sweat. She could do well enough in a university setting when it was just one person speaking, but with the best will in the world, she won't be able to keep up with this round-table conversation. She tries to pacify herself with the thought that no one could possibly be interested in what she has to say—she's just a student, all of eighteen years old, and a girl at that—and later von Weizsäcker shall explain it all to her like he always does whenever—

Dr. Heisenberg suddenly raises his hand to call everyone's attention.

"I apologize for interrupting, Herr Professor"—he's looking at Director Diebner—"but one of our esteemed colleagues, Fräulein Best, is, unfortunately, deaf. She can easily read lips, so I shall kindly ask anyone who wishes to speak to raise their hand first so that she can pay attention to that speaker. Just thought I'd get it out of the way before we begin."

Mina's skin turns hot from all the attention suddenly on her, and yet, her chest swells with gratitude for such a simple gesture which she feels she doesn't deserve. Far too many times she's been told, mostly by her school teachers and fellow students, and even strangers in the street, just how much of a nuisance her handicap is. Despite being told otherwise by people who actually cared, the feeling of inadequacy is much too deeply etched into her very self-conscience that even such small acts of kindness touch her profoundly.

The theoreticians are all used to communicating with her in this exact manner, calling her attention with gentle shoulder taps or raised hands, but the experimenters' chests heave with a collective sigh of annoyance. *They have work to do and, instead, there's a handicapped girl they have to accommodate, wherever the devil dragged her in from.* They don't say any of it, but Mina can read it clear as day on their faces.

Director Diebner's arm rises next, with a consideration that can't help but appear mocking. When he's certain of Mina's eyes on him, he begins to speak.

"Esteemed colleagues, first of all, I apologize for the brisk manner in which you've all been summoned here, but I assure you, the news didn't allow for delay." He pauses dramatically and smiles like a magician who's about to perform his most stunning trick. "When we first founded our so-called Uranium Club, our work was still in its infancy. I still look fondly on those very first days, during which we were stumbling in the dark like blind kittens, having only ideas and theories to juggle instead of anything concrete to work on. And what progress we have achieved since! Each report I write for the OKW is a testament to all of your hard work and dedication to the war effort."

Another pause, even longer than the previous. Mina notices that Diebner's hands are clasped atop the thick folder.

Diebner nods and his adjutant disappears, only to return moments later with a stack of similar folders, which he proceeds to place in front of each scientist. No one opens them yet, just regards them as though they've been given hand grenades instead of innocent binders.

Once more, he raises his hand.

"Everyone here recalls the very first two questions we posed. The first one was whether we can use the newly discovered uranium fission as an energy producer. It has only been two years and, thanks to Dr. Heisenberg's efforts, not only do we know for certain that we can, but we're already developing a prototype of such a uranium engine—or a reactor, as we now call it."

After each word of his, Mina's head grows lighter and lighter. She can't shake the feeling of being trapped on a train that has lost control of its brakes and is heading for a derailment at full speed, and in front is death—death as far as the eye can see.

"But it's the second question that we posed which is the reason for the Uranium Club itself. It's the reason why our generous OKW now transports heavy water from the Norsk-Hydro plant in Norway, the production of which has been increased to 1,500 liters a year. It's the reason why all of the uranium obtained from mines in both Czechoslovakia and Belgium is now being put at our disposal. The question was whether a uranium bomb can be built. Well, my dear friends, it appears that we finally have our answer."

He opens the binder and Mina feels the bang of its cover travel through the wood of the table and into her very fingertips.

"It was none other than Dr. Heisenberg's protégé, Dr. Carl Friedrich von Weizsäcker, who answered this question."

All heads turn to the young scientist and Mina sees the blood drain from his face in front of her very eyes. In a matter of seconds, he's turned as white as a sheet, staring at Diebner without a hint of comprehension.

"There must be some mistake," Mina sees him mutter. His lips tremble something terrible, but it's still possible to understand him. "I never said anything about a bomb. I wasn't even researching it. My current work is still very much fission, and namely, the decay product of neutron capture in U-238—"

Diebner raises his hand and, having captured Mina's attention, finishes after the theoretician with a smile that is positively wolfish. "A new element which you've named Eka Re—a very befitting name, if I may say so, for an element one step above rhenium in the periodic table."

He's silent a moment and Mina wonders if she is the only one who's holding her breath or the entire room.

"Thanks to your latest report, my team—we are called experimenters for a good reason—we decided to test your calculations. And what do you know? Eka Re not only fissions, but it's also chemically separable, which would make it perfect for usage in bombs. Now, if you please open the binders you've been given, I shall take you through the process and results of our experiment step by step. And after we've all caught up, we'll discuss further steps. Finally, the news the OKW will love to hear. Thanks to us, dear colleagues, German victory shall be swift and decisive."

Cold sweat breaks on Mina's temples. Her hands shake uncontrollably as she flips the folder open. There are formulas and diagrams, but it's all alien to her right then. Her brain, seized with horror, refuses to process the information which ordinarily reads like a book. And in the midst of all that chaos only one thought is beating itself against the cage of her skull: *Impossible. Impossible! It can't be; it's much too soon.*

She throws a frantic glance at Dr. Heisenberg, but he, too, is staring at the pages with a look of quiet horror about him. Mina sees his eyes jump from line to line, from page to page. He's obsessively trying to find a mistake—there must be one—but his silence speaks volumes. He chose Dr. von Weizsäcker as his protégé for a good reason. The young man is much too brilliant. Unfortunately, he doesn't make mistakes.

But still, Mina rivets her gaze back to the formulas, praying for the impossible. They can't be the first ones to produce such a weapon. The fate of the entire world depends on the pitiful few of them, gathered around the table, heads in their hands. How to stop this in its tracks? How to prevent the catastrophe from unraveling the thread of life on the planet itself?

Suddenly, they're all talking at once, forgetting about Mina's existence in the heat of the moment. Caught with their pants down, lured here without announcing the reason for it, and now face to face with the results of their own research they thought to be perfectly harmless. From time to time, von Weizsäcker taps her on the shoulder, but Mina throws his hand off, swatting at it as though a pesky fly. She's thankful for her handicap in this moment of crisis. She turns the room off and focuses her gaze on the pages of research, cutting through it like a scalpel.

Rarely has she moments like these, but when they come, the adrenaline rush is something she imagines comparable only to the bliss opium addicts chase in their drug-induced dreams. Her skin is suddenly alive, with every hair standing on end. She feels every pump of blood her heart is sending through her limbs. She was born for this and now dives into the numbers like a fish into water. For the next few minutes, the world around her ceases to exist; all that remain are formulas and numbers. And, to Mina's immense relief, here it is, the break she's been so desperately looking for.

"You can't report it just yet."

All eyes are suddenly on her. They fall silent as she snaps the binder closed, mirroring Director Diebner's gesture.

"Unless you wish to find yourself in a whole lot of trouble when you can't deliver the results, and you won't. Not in the next few years at least," Mina finishes and folds her hands demurely on top of the study.

"What's this?" Director Diebner's lips twitch.

"You did make it work in a laboratory setting—I'm saying nothing against it. But—" Mina is suddenly on her feet. She approaches the blackboard under Max Planck's portrait and begins to scribble calculations with a speed that used to leave her school teacher in wordless awe. "You have only performed it with a small amount of uranium just to test Dr. von Weizsäcker's theory. This is the reported number of natural uranium you used. Now, let's multiply this by the number of neutrons one would need to use to bombard enough of said natural uranium to lead to any significant uranium isotopes that would decay further into Eka Re."

A small circle is forming around Mina as she works, but she

doesn't really see them, her eyes glued to her hand that seems to have gained a life of its own. Numbers spill from under her chalk in rapid succession, machinegunning through Director Diebner's hopes for the recognition as the world's most feared physicist.

"Keep in mind that you need a sustained chain reaction to keep the fission going, which leads to the numbers growing exponentially—"

She turns, annoyed, when a hand grabs her shoulder and finds Director Diebner himself looking over her shoulder at the curve she's begun to sketch alongside the formulas. His fingers claw at her in impotent rage as he, this time, desperately searches her calculations for a careless mistake.

But, to his misfortune, Mina has been born to count. She also doesn't make mistakes—she sees it from the faint outline of a smile that is slowly lighting Dr. Heisenberg's face with hope.

"It won't matter! A bomb is a runaway reactor," Diebner shouts in her face. "Once we launch it, it'll detonate—"

"—While it's still in the air, rending your entire enterprise useless." Mina wipes specks of saliva from her cheek with a nonchalance that would have surprised even her. Only, she's on familiar ground now, among numbers that don't lie and don't care for anyone's ambition. "Say we mount the so-called runaway reactor inside the rocket case just so. I'm saying rocket to increase its speed; I'm trying to minimize the amount of material to use, see? If we put it into a sphere, it'll be even more unyielding and cumbersome and you'll need even more of the... But never mind that. Let's stay with the rocket for now. Dr. Heisenberg, you have the numbers for a reactor prototype we're working on. How much are we talking here?"

Breathing easier now, the chief theoretician is writing it all down for her in a separate paper and Mina is already sketching the rocket and its dimensions and takes the curvature—thank you, Professor of Topography from Graz!—into account and the force of the blast to be at least somewhat comparable to, say, a landmine, let's be modest here...

And ends up producing such a monstrosity, the very idea of building it would be a laughing stock for the entire scientific community. Not just the scientific community, the Wehrmacht top brass would laugh Director Diebner out of their reception if he dared to demonstrate to them its warship-like dimensions.

"Yes, the bomb is a possibility," Mina concludes, stepping away from her calculations and sketches the experimenters are perusing with glum frowns, "but this is what it shall look like. That's why I asked you not to report it just yet, Dr. Diebner," she softens her tone on purpose, hopes that she sounds apologetic. "We can't show this to the Führer and his war ministers in good conscience just yet. We ought to research it further, build a reactor first, see how that works and proceed from there. We're in the Stone Age of nuclear physics now. And we need something out of this century."

Saved, for now. The air in the theoreticians' quarters is lighter somehow, the charge gone out of it. The men smoke one cigarette after another—they've been at it since Diebner dismissed them—but even the smoke that stings Mina's eyes is familiar and welcomed and, in a way, celebratory. It smells of New Year fireworks here, not of bombs, thankfully—not just yet. They all pat her on her back, kiss the top of her head, and press her hand as they speak and speak, but their words don't register with Mina anymore. Like a runner after a marathon, she drops into a chair and stares into space with a smile that is both exhausted and infinitely relieved.

Instead of Institute walls, the universe itself unravels in front of her like a majestic flower. The purpose of her birth is revealed to her; it's written right here, among the pages of humanity's history, with which her own fate is tightly interwoven. She, Mina Best, was not born to crack the uranium code—it was others' destiny. No; she was born to buy some time for mankind, until the scales tips so good outweighs evil, and after that, she can go peacefully back into galactical nothingness and become one of its dying stars, the light of which shall shine upon the earth for centuries to come.

The fight is not over, however. She realizes that much with a sense of bittersweet melancholy, but the battle is still raging and she is on the right side and her comrades are brave and self-less, and so, tomorrow doesn't look all that bleak.

TWENTY-TWO

Mina is staring out the window while Taube, seated opposite her, is reading through her letters. She's learned how to write them by now; they're all about Berlin and new museum exhibits and her health and daily mundane routine and nothing at all about science or war. Taube has nothing to strike out with the black ink used by censors all over the country. Mina's letters to her parents are as clean and as innocent as they can be. And full of lies.

Outside, a street sweep is smoking as his broom rests against the wall. Birds are fighting for a place under the roof. Children are rolling marbles next to the building stairs. A neighbor, her hair in rollers, is watering geraniums mounted just outside her window. And just a few train stops away, builders are hammering at the new experimental facility that will soon house one of the very first atom reactors.

Despite the setback, Director Diebner hasn't lost hope of his bomb becoming a reality. On the contrary, he demanded, and promptly received from the War department, the new facility in which Eka Re can be bred from uranium. Thankfully for the whole world, he hasn't the first idea of how to create a chain-reacting pile to produce enough of it, let alone put it into a bomb, but he shall work his experimenters to death all the same. Until someone builds him a working chain-pile. Mina shivers and rubs her shoulders with both hands.

"When shall they finish the reactor construction, do you know?"

"They're working round the clock to finish by the winter holidays," Taube replies. "If they outpace the production quota, they'll get a nice bonus, so they're working as fast as they can."

Mina nods, looking like a patient who has just been given a death sentence.

"Why did they put a sign up saying 'virology lab' outside the reactor construction?"

Taube looks up from the letters, folds them neatly, and puts them into envelopes which he seals in front of Mina. Her parents' address is already on them, so too a blue stamp with Hitler's profile. "So that other scientists who aren't a part of the Uranium Club wouldn't be tempted to poke their noses where they don't belong," he responds half in jest. "The project is top secret. If people think highly contagious viruses are being studied there, they'll take good care to stay away."

"Little do they know what a nuclear reactor that goes rogue can do then."

Puzzlement comes over Taube's face. "It's essentially a highly sophisticated engine, is it not?"

"Yes, only your regular engines don't produce deadly radiation when mishandled."

"What do you mean, mishandled?"

"Do you know how Marie Curie died?" Mina asks.

Taube tucks the envelopes into the pocket of his uniform jacket as he considers his answer. "I remember something about radiation poisoning, but, to be frank with you, it means little to me."

"Meant little to me, too, until I attended Dr. Geiger's

lecture on radioactivity and later collected study materials from his assistant. Not something I would call 'light bedtime reading,' that's for certain." Mina's smile is small and wistful. "But coming back to Marie Curie. When she discovered radium, she hadn't the faintest idea what it could do to her. In fact, she used to carry tubes with radium in the pocket of her dress and kept them by her bed at night because she found the green light they were giving off comforting. Dr. Geiger, who's always been rather fascinated with her, traveled to France to look at her notebooks, only to discover that they were still so highly radioactive, he advised them to be kept in a metal case. He wouldn't touch them himself after he saw a reading on his counter."

"Dr. Geiger's counter counts radiation?"

"In a broad sense, yes. It detects alpha, beta, and gamma radiation. In small doses, radiation isn't dangerous. That's your X-ray machine, for instance."

Taube brightens at this. "I had my wrist X-rayed after a skiing accident. Back when—" *He was still married*—Mina reads it from his suddenly anguished eyes. He quickly takes hold of himself though and resumes. "It was only badly sprained, but I must say, it was fascinating, seeing my own bones when my physician showed me the print."

"It is fascinating. And such a brilliant discovery that revolutionized modern medicine. And yet, deadly all the same."

Taube regards her in confusion and, on instinct, glances at his right hand as though to ensure that it is still intact.

"Don't fret, Herr Hauptmann, you're perfectly fine." Mina smiles once again. There's something incredibly vulnerable and tragic about her, this girl who knows too much for her own good. Who sees into the future and recoils each time at the macabre pictures it paints. "As I said, an occasional X-ray is perfectly harmless to a human body. However, Dr. Röntgen, an X-ray inventor, who was also very fascinated with the prints of his bones, kept taking them one after another. Soon, he noticed that his hand began to swell, then blister, and then turn black, as though he'd sustained a bad burn."

Mina suddenly wishes she smoked. She needs something to occupy her restless hands with, something to taste and smell just to steady herself. With a casual, "You don't mind, do you?" she reaches for Taube's cigarette case and helps herself to one.

Without a single word of protest, he lights it for her.

Mina inhales, not too deep just yet, and smiles at the bitter smoke flowing out her nostrils. It feels suitable somehow. A comforting poison.

"He did, in a sense," she continues at length. "That's what you'd call a radiation burn. Only, unlike the burn inflicted by fire, radiation goes much deeper than that. Gamma rays penetrate everything in their path. They get into your bones and destroy their very marrow—the marrow that's responsible for producing your blood cells, including white ones, those responsible for fighting infections starting with the common cold and ending with sepsis. No white blood cells, no immune system. Your body is left defenseless. First symptoms of aplastic anemia —that's the most common result of ionizing radiation—is excessive bleeding from the smallest cut, hematomas appearing all over your body seemingly without any cause, extreme fatigue, rashes, dizziness, bleeding gums, and, later, frequent and prolonged infections that eventually kill you." She's silent as she takes a full drag, her eyes narrow and so very old for a girl her age. "That's how Marie Curie died."

Hauptmann Taube thinks it all over for a good minute, silent as a grave. Then he, too, reaches for a cigarette. It's unnerved him, Mina can tell; it unnerves anybody who first hears about it—this invisible death people know so little about and yet, they keep prying open the Pandora box containing it instead of hurling it somewhere far and deep and forgetting it all like a bad dream.

Mina can't blame them. She, too, used to be enamored with

uranium not that long ago. Now, she fears it with every cell of her body despite being chained to it fast and good.

Taube waves his cigarette in the air to call Mina's attention. "I still don't understand what it has to do with the reactor."

"Uranium decay products are highly radioactive," she explains and scratches at her forehead, lined with worry. "We'll be building something that has never been built in the history of the world. We have worked out the theory, but who knows how it shall work in real-life conditions? It can explode. It can produce a chain reaction that shall never stop—"

"What does that mean?"

Mina shrugs and looks out the window—at the street sweep, at the children, and the dog digging something out from someone's garden plot. "We can accidentally destroy the world."

Taube's gray as ash when Mina finally turns back to him.

"That's why I wanted to know when they shall finish the construction. I wanted to ask of you the biggest favor. I want to see my parents one last time. In case something doesn't go as planned."

He stares at her without blinking, without breathing even. Only his nostrils flare, as though he's incensed by the very fact that one can be so nonchalant about the end of the world. "Does Diebner know of such a possibility?"

Mina smiles at him as one would at a child. "Why, naturally. He's our director."

"Why hasn't he reported it?"

"He has. However, the OKW top brass said the chance is so miniscule that proceeding with the reactor experiment outweighs its risk. Diebner himself is unconcerned as well."

"How miniscule is miniscule?"

"About one percent, according to our calculations. Zero point eight and lots of nines after that, to be precise."

"But there still is a chance that it shall level the earth and we will all die horrific deaths?"

"Zero point eight percent chance, yes."

He's suddenly on his feet. "That's not comforting. That's not comforting at all." He's already groping for his overcoat, which he left hanging over the back of a chair, and pulling it on, missing a sleeve a few times in his rush. "I shall go to Canaris himself. He must be made aware. I shall go to the Führer if needed, but they must cease all experiments until you get a result that shall show zero chance of anything of that sort."

Mina watches him from her seat, the cigarette still smoldering in her hand. "Do go, Herr Hauptmann," she says quietly and with resignation. "I doubt it will do us any good, but do try, if you can. Just take a walk around your headquarters before you go before your higher-ups. Express your concerns as calmly as possible, so that they don't take you off your post for alarmism. You're one of the good ones and I've rather got used to you. I wouldn't want some SS man in charge over me."

He leaves without another word and Mina watches him go, wondering if it's all just a bad dream from which she shall wake up any moment if she pinches herself hard enough.

TWENTY-THREE

In her wildest dreams, Mina couldn't imagine herself heading home to Linz and not just by herself, but with Siggy by her side, and yet here they are, rocking gently on a train gliding languidly south, their legs touching at every curve of the railroad. He came through, Hauptmann Taube, if not with one promise, then with the other.

"You were right," he said in place of a greeting as soon as he stepped through her door, snow-dusted and smelling sharply of pine and frost. "They don't give a toss about possible ramifications. My superiors told me to mind my own business and leave the science to the scientists. And the scientists—I'm talking Dr. Diebner here, of course—laughed me out of their office altogether. Said radium poisoning is a fairy tale some American girls invented during the Great War to conceal their whoring ways and syphilis, and that Madame Curie died of regular cancer and that radiation had nothing to do with it whatsoever. At any rate," he proceeded, digging in the inner pocket of his military overcoat, "here's your official permit for a two-week leave, signed and stamped. And here's your train ticket for Linz. Merry Christmas."

The look he gave Mina as he handed her the paper was one full of sorrow and infinite regret. Her fate was out of his hands now. The brightest minds belonged to the state. This last favor she'd asked from him was all he could do for her.

That, and Siggy waiting for her on the platform with a coy grin and a makeshift bouquet of pine—several fluffy, evergreen branches tied together with a red satin ribbon—with a pinecone at its heart.

It lies on Mina's lap now, heady and unexpectedly soft as she puts her fingers through its needles, stroking it like a cat and almost expecting it to purr in response.

"How did he know?" she asks no one in particular, but Siggy understands her at once.

"He works for the *Abwehr*. It's their business to know everything."

"But the fact that we were friends? That you were coming to visit me?"

"They brought us from the same town, from the same university, from the same faculty even. It would be strange if we didn't know each other."

"But here, in Berlin?"

From Siggy, an unconcerned shrug. "Either an informant living on your floor and reporting all comings and goings or one of their own *Abwehr* people following you around, recording what you've been up to."

Neither is a comforting thought and even the glittering, pristine snowy expanse outside their train car's window doesn't quell Mina's worry.

"Do you really think they follow me?"

"I wouldn't be surprised. You scientists are an infamously unreliable lot. You worship numbers instead of gods and politicians, and therefore, it's notoriously difficult to control you. I wouldn't be surprised if it's your boss who called their attention to you."

Mina freezes momentarily. "Dr. Heisenberg?"

Siggy makes a face. "No, the other one, the one in whose side you put a major thorn when you pulled that trick at the conference."

Siggy's the only person besides Taube from whom Mina has no secrets. It's easy to tell them things, but for different reasons. Taube, he's an authority who can become a voice of reason among warmongering fools, until they do away with him like they always do with those who dare go against them. He's noble and unafraid; he's already lost everything that mattered in his life and doesn't care one way or the other about his own fate in his quest for the truth, and just for that, Mina respects him. Siggy, he simply listens and never judges. As if she can do no wrong by him. He's kinder to her than she is to herself and Mina breathes that kindness like air. Without it, she'll suffocate.

"I didn't pull any tricks," Mina mutters at Siggy's arched brow. "I'm a mathematician. I simply did my job. I calculated."

"Only, those are the calculations he didn't want to hear."

"Rotten luck."

She sees him snort and marvels at the fact that he finds her amusing and witty when she's never thought herself to be any of those things and that, out of the entire university population, it's she who he decided to befriend for whatever mystical reason. He must have seen something in her that she herself didn't see. But then again, he, too, turned out to be nothing like Mina's first impression of him. Under the superficial Nordic handsomeness the Nazi Race Office so admired lies unparalleled talent for finding patterns in the most complicated codes, an intellect sharper than a surgeon's knife and a sense of universal justice that guides his every decision, starting with finding a seat for a slip of a girl in an overcrowded auditorium and ending with a few silent words he created out of thin air just now, in front of Mina's widening eyes.

We need to tell the world.

. . .

Mina watches Siggy from the platform. She stands on her tiptoes to reach her hand to the glass and presses it against his, almost invisible behind the intricate frosty designs. She's back at Linz and he is proceeding all the way to Vienna. Those few hours together for them on the train were all Taube could get for them—it was more than enough and not nearly enough at the same time. There are too many things left unsaid between them and they burn worse than frost on bare skin with their necessity, and still Siggy signs, *Don't say anything at home*, as the last warning and disappears from Mina's sight and into the darkness of the railway tunnel, and suddenly Mina feels much more alone than she did on her first day in Berlin.

Homecomings are always a strange affair. The streets are the same and they're not, distorted somehow as though in a dream and different from the pictures her memory drew. Mina wanders through them with her suitcase in hand and peers into windows and at the faces around her that seem familiar and yet alien at the same time.

A tram trolley rolls to a stop, its yellow eyes now painted blue—the shade of anti-aircraft regulations. Mina grips the pole by its steps and pulls herself inside the familiar car only to find it slightly altered with the same dreamlike quality as well. A rope now separates the front, with a neat plaque "Reserved for military personnel" crowning its seats. And in place of an old plaque, "For Jews only," only a faded rectangle is left at the very back of the tram. Now, women sit there with German Frauen-schaft pins on their coats and argue about something Mina doesn't bother to decipher.

Linz has always prided itself on being the Führer's second hometown. Its new administration must have skipped the Yellow Star decree altogether and decided to set an example for the rest of the Reich by deporting their Jews outright, without any intermediate steps. Where exactly is anyone's guess. They're gone as though they never existed at all, their very memory wiped off from the map of the town.

And not too far north, under Dr. Diebner's keen eye, Dr. Heisenberg is working on the first chain-reaction pile in the new experimental house, Mina thinks as she bites into her chapped lip and splits it, tasting blood, which is befitting somehow. Its sharp metallic tang tastes of a catastrophe of unimaginable proportions that could reduce entire continents to dust. Mina closes her eyes; she doesn't want to believe it—it's much too inconceivable on this bright sunny day with Christmas tinsel flying from every corner and lights strung up in between the streets and people smiling at one another—and yet it's happening and she's a part of it and the thought of it chills Mina's blood.

She stumbles off the tram and makes her way home through familiar streets. They're freshly swept and only the walls of the buildings are pockmarked with snowball artillery. Children practice war on their way to school; they clutch their snow-dusted chests and die theatrically in the snowdrifts. Mina watches their ghosts pass in front of her eyes and wonders how many shall perish in real trenches in just a few short years. Humanity enjoys destroying itself—the only species that does it with pomp and rousing speeches. So, is it truly all that surprising that it craves its ultimate annihilation now? The very last exit from stage, during which the actors shall take the spectators and the entire theater with them to their grave.

Pale and wrought with nerves, Mina knocks on her door and wishes, for one brisk moment, to be able to hear again, just so she'd know if Libby was meowing on the other side, sensing her youngest mistress and rubbing herself against the doorframe in anticipation. But she can hear neither the cat nor the hurried steps along the corridor; only sees the peephole darken momentarily and the door being flung open to reveal her mother in a housedress and woolen socks.

"Mina!" her lips form and she grabs Mina into an embrace that's so full of love it's nearly painful.

Her mother's lips are hot on Mina's frost-kissed cheeks and forehead. She surrenders to their warmth and melts into her mother's hands like she used to do as a child and allows herself to be relieved from her heavy coat and all the layers of scarf and mittens and even boots. There's an inexplicable comfort in returning to one's childhood, where everything was simple and filled with joy, and where the world was at peace instead of dangling on a thread above an abyss of atomic warfare. Where Mina was just one of the girls, instead of one of the atomic reaction designers.

Suddenly, she doesn't want her mother to touch her. She's contaminated somehow with that knowledge, with the complicity; it clings to her in invisible particles of lies and things omitted. They stain the clear air between them as soon as Mina opens her mouth and allows the lies to slip so effortlessly from her tongue, Siggy's stern expression standing before her eyes. *Don't say anything at home.*

Yes, the Berlin Institute is a dream come true. Yes, all of her professors are so very brilliant. Yes, her fellow students are very friendly. The studies are challenging but fascinating. She enjoys it all very much.

She parrots the letters she's been sending, only instead of Taube, it's she, Mina, who censors the truth until it fits into what the government shaped it to be. It's upsetting; eventually, it reduces Mina to tears, but even then, she lies, swiping at her face and calling herself silly and emotional. Yet her mother sees through it all. Mina came out of her flesh and is still very much a part of her. She feels Mina's pain like her own, just like she feels her joy; she always has, and no distance is great enough to extinguish a mother's love.

What's wrong? she signs, as if recognizing the fact that whatever it is that has painted black half-moons under her daughter's eyes and further shaved off flesh of her already bony frame can't be talked about out loud.

Nothing.

Don't lie to me.

Mina tries silence instead, but her mother refuses to have any of that.

Has someone done anything to you? A boy? One of the professors?

Mina tosses her head at once. *No, not at all.*

Her mother nods. She sees it herself that it's not that.

Siggy is there with me, Mina signs, trying to move away from the dangerous ground, but her mother is peering much too closely into her eyes, gray and brimming with water like overcast skies. She reads Mina's very soul through their depths.

That's good. But it's not Siggy trouble, is it?

Slowly, Mina shakes her head. She tries so very hard to stay strong, but it takes one last question from her mother—*Where did they take you really, Mina?*—and she feels her bottom lips trembling and then her chin, and then the entire charade falls apart, because nothing is more powerful than a mother's love.

You need to leave. Mina's fingers signal with a sudden rush of emotion of their own. *You and* Vati, *you need to leave as soon as possible. Go to Switzerland—they're neutral. Lise Meitner went there.*

Who's Lise Meitner?

A nuclear physicist from the Institute. She was Jewish. She left before I was brought there. My team smuggled her out.

Your team?

Yes. We work together on something... terrible.

Is it for the war effort?

Yes.

A weapon?

Mina's hand freezes mid-air before slowly signing the affirmative. *With time, it will be. I don't know for how much longer we can keep it in its current, peaceful state. Leave, but don't make it obvious. Rent a villa for a short vacation. Go with a couple of suitcases only as you ordinarily would. Wear the most valuable jewelry but leave all else. Take as much money as you can but don't empty your bank account.*

Mina's mother's face is paling in front of her eyes. Only her lips press more and more into an unyielding line with every word she reads.

Is it really so serious then? she signs in the end.

Mina could think it over once again, but it would be a waste of time, really. The seriousness of it is all she's been obsessing over every waking hour; all that has robbed her of sleep every restless night. She's a mathematician, calculating is what she does and, after calculating it from every possible angle, Mina nods with a resolution that passes to her mother through the invisible thread they share and always will.

Deadly. Go, before it's too late.

What about you?

When it's safe, I'll follow.

TWENTY-FOUR

BERLIN, GERMANY. JANUARY—FEBRUARY 1941

After the winter holidays, the Institute has an odd feeling about it. It's cold like a tomb and the air is musky and stale, as though it's been abandoned for years instead of days. Along its corridors, the scientists are moving like sleepwalkers. In Dr. Heisenberg's office, the heavy drapes are still drawn, and the blackboard is still black, and the man himself is smoking in the corner, with his gaze directed at the empty space in front of him. On his desk, a fresh photo of him and his wife. They must have taken it in Leipzig where she lives and where he used to live until the Uranium Club claimed him, like it claimed Mina. He misses her already and is suffering from separation much more than from the chain-reacting pile failure. Mina reads the former from his forlorn gaze and the latter from the report casually thrown on the conference table for the rest of the team to peruse.

"You used regular uranium ore for the pile," Mina says, pulling the chair close to him and spreading the report on her lap. "While it does work fine to breed Eka Re—"

"Plutonium," Dr. Heisenberg says with a faraway look about him.

"I beg your pardon?"

"The Americans call it plutonium. Which is a much-better-sounding name, if you ask me."

"They discovered it too?"

"It's always been just a matter of time."

He doesn't want to work today. No one does; they're all in their respective cubicles, feigning activities and secretly wishing to be left alone. At home, they tasted life—sweet, uncomplicated life. Returning from that warmth to the sterile cold of the laboratories is like returning to the front. Only the enemy here is invisible and much more formidable—an ancient pagan demon that has existed from the beginning of time and which they desperately seek to tame.

Mina reads report numbers like words, and through their lens, she watches Dr. Heisenberg's attempts to summon the demon as if through a scrying mirror and hears it laugh at the pitiful human and his pitiful efforts.

Mina shifts her gaze from the report to the nuclear physicist and back, puzzled by his indifference and, what's even more mystifying, such a rookie mistake. Wasn't it he, Heisenberg himself, who used only pure uranium in his equations because only the element's purified form produced results they could actually use in practice?

She wets her lips and probes him, gentle as a feather, "If I may suggest, Herr Professor, purified uranium—"

But he throws her a glance so cold and sharp, it sucks the air itself out of the room. Slowly, the realization dawns on Mina. She bites her tongue and swallows the rest of the sentence like a spy swallows compromising paper and nods deliberately, closing the report and putting it away.

There is no mistake. Dr. Heisenberg is much too brilliant of a scientist to make one. It is a cold-blooded, calculated sabotage right under Director Diebner's nose to rob him of his Eka—

Plutonium, Mina mentally corrects herself.

In this new Germany, people get hanged for less and yet...
And yet.

"How was your trip home?" he asks and shakes the ash from his cigarette into a crystal ashtray perched precariously on the armrest of his chair.

"Good."

"How are your parents?"

"Good." Mina pauses and scans the room, wondering just how much to say. It was Siggy who planted that first seed of paranoia into her—*don't say anything, you never know who's listening*—but now it's grown and sprouted branches deep in the pit of her stomach and there's no ripping them out anytime soon. The Institute stood empty for over a week. Plenty of time to bug its every corner, if it hadn't been bugged already. Undoubtedly, Director Diebner reported Dr. Heisenberg's failure to the War Department and, perhaps, SD as well. Mina recalls Untersturmführer Gürtner's veiled threat about the treatment of saboteurs and looks around, as if searching for traces of his visit here—to "investigate," as he would likely call it.

Dr. Heisenberg is also mistrustful of the familiar walls; else, he wouldn't have interrupted Mina like he did.

She feverishly searches for something else to say, just to throw anyone who could be possibly listening off track. "They're thinking of spending a few weeks in Switzerland in March. *Vati* loves to ski, but they've skied all of Germany and Austria by now. He wants a new challenge."

"A very good choice for any skier," Dr. Heisenberg says but means something entirely different.

Mina nods. "I think so too."

"An old colleague of mine is going there too. First here," he says, reaching for the small globe from one of the bookshelves just beside him. "To here." Mina watches his finger trace an invisible route from Switzerland to the United Kingdom and then the United States. "Very good resorts here, too. Perfect for his health. They specialize in his cases there." He draws a small star over his heart.

A Jewish colleague, and heading precisely where needed.

Mina livens up all at once. "Do you know if he has booked the hotel already?"

"As far as I know, he's packing as we speak," Dr. Heisenberg says and arches a questioning brow.

"Do you think it would be possible for me to go and ask him about the accommodations he booked? I should so love to advise *Vati* on a good place to stay."

"I'm fairly certain he'll be glad to oblige."

He still doesn't understand and Mina grabs a sheet of paper from his desk and quickly scribbles, *"We need to tell him about the Uranium Club and our research,"* before moving it meaningfully toward him. *"If the Americans discovered plutonium, they're working on the same thing as we are. We need to tell them to hurry up. We can't be the first ones to make the bomb. You and I, we both know it."*

Heisenberg reads and quickly tosses his head in horror as he snatches Mina's pencil from her.

"He's a Jew! They'll search him up and down at the border. He can't possibly have any compromising materials on him. They'll off him on sight and all of us right after."

It's Mina's turn to huff in annoyance and seize the pencil back.

"Everything will be coded. What they'll see is an ordinary letter a friend asked to deliver to a friend."

"Do you know coding now?" If sarcasm could be heard from paper, Mina's certain she'd hear it even with her deaf ears.

"A friend does."

Dr. Heisenberg pulls at his hair in a pantomime of sheer disbelief.

"You talk to people about this?" His words scream from the sheet.

"Not people. A friend, I said. Don't you talk to your wife about this?"

"No! So she can sleep better."

"Well, he already can't because he's also roped up in this." The pencil pushes through the paper and leaves a hole instead of a period. *"Do you want to help or shall we wait till Diebner's people figure this out themselves and make the pile work for you? I give them a few months, and that's if you're lucky."*

"You leave it to me to throw them off track. I'll distract them with the 'peaceful' reactor prototype I'm working on in Leipzig. We can always argue that the army can use it too. It'll save them precious fuel they can use on the frontline. It's almost ready, at any rate."

It would be comical, the two of them deciding the fate of the entire world without a single word dropped, if only the situation isn't so damned grave.

Dr. Heisenberg rakes his hands through his hair several times, turning it into an even wilder mop than it usually is, and sits for some time like Rodin's Thinker, head heavy as bronze in his helpless hands. At last, having arrived at the decision, he writes an address on it, which Mina memorizes, then takes the paper from Mina's hands and holds the tip of the cigarette to its corner until it catches fire. Together, they watch it burn and turn to black ash until all that's left of it is gray dust in Dr. Heisenberg's ashtray.

Friday night, long past twelve, Siggy's still flipping the pages of Wells' *The World Set Free* at Mina's dining table. His hunched back is a question mark in the dim amber light of a candle; his brow is a sharp slash of concentration. Fascinated and still as water in a forest lake, Mina watches him work his magic, turning descriptions of the Uranium Club's work into ordinary, innocent words.

Please, tell the interested people the following thing. We are trying hard here, including Heisenberg, to hinder the making of a bomb. But the pressure from above... Heisenberg will not be able to withstand the pressure from the government to go very earnestly and seriously into the making of the bomb for much longer. And say to them, say they should accelerate, if they have already begun the thing... they should accelerate the thing.

By the time Siggy's finished, he can't feel his back. Outside the window with its blackout drapes, not really enforced yet but drawn all the same for their own privacy, the first pink slices of sun-kissed sky are appearing.

Mina pulls the drapes open and blinks the sand out of her eyes. Siggy's eyes are just as red from strain but bright all the same. He's smiling as he turns this way and that in his chair, stretching limbs that have gone to sleep after endless hours of hard work. Mina pulls her arms overhead too and feels her vertebrae creak.

The key to the code is disguised as a phone number—a real one, to one of the inns in Switzerland, if anyone decides to test it. The code itself is in the pages of the book predicting the end of the world. Siggy picked it himself from Mina's abundant collection.

A suitable choice for a physicist, he explained in sign language and, after a moment's hesitation, slashed an English-looking signature on the first page. *For the customs,* he signed in response to Mina's confused look. *They don't understand sentimental value. Now, a copy signed by the author would make sense to them.*

And what if they requisition it?

So what? He'll just find another edition when he arrives in Switzerland.

Mina replays the exchange in her mind as she collects the

fruits of Siggy's labor in her hands. A simple letter, asking the proprietor of the inn to save a room with two beds and preferably a balcony for a colleague's father's friend who shall arrive for a quick vacation in March.

She may have a way with numbers, but he has a much better way with words. Silent, or otherwise.

Mina holds the letter to her heart in a gesture of silent gratitude and then, in a sudden rush of emotion, throws her arms around Siggy and buries her nose in his neck. He hugs her back, gently, aware of the crushing power of his great hands, and pulls away with evident reluctance, tapping the face of his wristwatch.

There will be time for that, still. And now, go, before it's too late and he's gone forever.

Mina goes, runs, breathless and terrified, through the gray Berlin streets that are just waking, and carries Siggy's words next to her heart—from one man who hopes to save the world to another, grateful to be the link in this paramount chain on which the fate of humanity is swaying softly like a pendant.

Dr. Reiche's wife opens the door, fearful and on guard, hands pulling close a robe with a yellow star on its breast. Beside her slipper-clad feet, suitcases are waiting. Her shoulders sag in visible relief when Mina introduces herself and asks to speak to Herr Doktor.

Innocently. About Switzerland.

He listens to her cheerful banter and reads the instructions she writes down for him. The code. How to work it. The phone number—*this you may keep.*

He asks for the names—also in writing; they talk only of mineral waters and Mina's father's bad kidneys—but Mina just regards him with pleading urgency.

He nods his understanding.

Anyone, who will listen. Anyone you can get to. Just speak, scream, if needed, but get them to listen and get them to believe and get them to hurry the devil up if they want to keep the world intact for their children.

With a grave nod, Dr. Reiche takes her hand and squeezes it in silent promise. He'll do whatever it takes. Upon his children's lives, he swears.

TWENTY-FIVE

BERLIN, GERMANY. SPRING 1941

Spring has come to Berlin, wrapping the Kaiser Wilhelm Institute for Physics in a tender embrace of budding leaves and the soft hum of a world reawakening. Yet, within the Institute's stoic walls, the air is heavy with matters far removed from the gentle thaw of the season.

Lost in thought, Mina sits at her cluttered workspace, her fingers absentmindedly tracing the equations that mapped out the invisible forces of the universe. There hasn't been any news of Dr. Reiche's message, no shockwaves through the newspapers. But no news of arrest either. Siggy explained to Mina multiple times that it will take time for the physicist to ever reach the allied shores, let alone pass the message to the people in charge, but Mina is impatient and wrought with nerves and slowly loses her mind over all this uncertainty.

Von Weizsäcker's hand waving in front of her glazed-over gaze pulls her out of her trancelike state. He's smiling, but his eyes are on guard.

"Director Diebner wants us in his office."

It takes a moment for Mina to react. "Theoreticians?"

"No. Just us two."

"Whatever for?"

"I don't know, but I wrote a will on a piece of paper."

Grim humor, but it fits the occasion perfectly.

With a sigh, Mina lifts herself out of her chair and follows von Weizsäcker into the experimenters' wing. They are awaited; Diebner's adjutant escorts them to the director's office at once. There, opposite their superior, a man is seated enjoying Diebner's brandy that the theoreticians have never had the honor to see, let alone taste. The stranger's uniform is immaculate, his face impassive, and his gaze sweeps over the scientists with an unnerving sense of purpose.

Mina's heart tightens in her chest, a premonition of unease settling upon her as she notices a serpent crest on his collar: SS medical corps insignia.

"Ach, Dr. von Weizsäcker, Fräulein Best." Director Diebner's smile is dripping with honey, but all Mina feels is the hornet's sting of his sharp glance. "It's my honor to introduce you to Dr. Blobel. He works directly for the office of Dr. Brandt, our Führer's physician."

"The honor is all ours." Mina watches von Weizsäcker say. "But I'm afraid you have the wrong department. We are physicists, not physicians."

The two men at the table oblige his joke with chuckles.

"We have all the medical expertise we need," Dr. Blobel assures von Weizsäcker. "What we need is someone with good knowledge of X-ray machines." Looking directly at Mina, he articulates his words very slowly as if she's not only hearing- but mentally impaired as well. "Dr. Diebner here says that you attended Dr. Geiger's lectures on radiation?"

"I did," Mina confirms, all self-possession on the outside while inside her veins the blood is slowly beginning to boil. "Half of the Institute did. If you need a truly expert opinion, why not talk to Dr. Geiger himself?"

The SS physician regards her, his eyes completely devoid of

warmth. "Dr. Geiger is in France and the matter is rather urgent. The reason why you're here instead of half of the Institute," he mocks her words, "is because Dr. Diebner called your mathematical skills, I quote, 'unparalleled.'"

There it is, Diebner's revenge, coming to bite her just as Siggy has warned her it would. And Mina feels she already knows what Blobel is here for. Untersturmführer Gürtner was more than explicit in his descriptions of the *Aktion T4* program. Mina's own mother lost her job over it. Euthanasia—the logical daughter of Nazi eugenics everyone in the scientific world has whispered about. The man before her seems the perfect embodiment of those dark whispers.

"Dr. Diebner is too kind," Mina mutters, feeling oddly like a student called in front of the headmaster. They haven't bothered to even offer her or her colleague a seat.

The SS physician smiles briefly before lowering his glass onto the table. Now all of his attention is on Mina, and her alone. "How many roentgens are necessary to achieve sterilization in a human being?"

There is a moment of stunned silence before next to her von Weizsäcker erupts in protest. Mina doesn't see what it is exactly that he's saying, as she's busy staring at the SS physician in front of her. She has been expecting this, and yet there is a sudden chill in the air that has nothing to do with the spring drafts.

"Sterilization?" Mina repeats slowly and deliberately. They've grown much too used to the word, the SS. They throw it around without sensing what it truly entails. She wants him to taste the atrocity of it on his tongue. "May I ask to what end? Our work with radiation is of a theoretical nature, not medical," she says, her tone laced with caution.

The physician smiles, a thin, cold stretch of his lips. "Oh, but it is a theoretical inquiry, of course. Though one that shall demand practical application if we decide it to be the best course of action. We seek to understand the threshold at which radiation can prevent the propagation of defective genes. A matter of public health."

Mina's blood runs hot with quiet fury. She's been living in the shadows of eugenics her entire life, dealing with the discrimination stemming from the twisted ideology that deems some lives more worthy than others. She has seen the laws passed, the propaganda, learned of newborns being murdered after being declared defective. And now, it seems, a part of her work, her science, might become an instrument in that ghastly symphony.

Mina exchanges a loaded look with von Weizsäcker. His face is pale, his usual jovial demeanor replaced by a grave solemnity. Without trading a single word, Mina can tell they both feel the almost physical weight of ethical responsibility pressing down upon them.

"This is not a simple calculation," she offers at length, "and there are significant risks involved in exposing human tissue to high levels of radiation. You may end up killing them. Unless that's your actual intent."

Director Diebner feigns an insulted gasp, but Dr. Blobel only smiles thinly, like the snake on his collar patch. "We have all the euthanasia tools we need. This is for sterilization purposes only, I assure you. Else, why would I need a mathematician's help to figure out the right dose? It's for our own German folk, the ones who are unfortunate to suffer from physical deformities or mental issues, such as alcoholism, schizophrenia, depression... We want the process to be as smooth and painless as possible. We won't even tell them they are being sterilized. They'll think they're undergoing a routine X-ray and go home without any idea that they can no longer pass defective genes on. And when they wish for a child, there are so many they can adopt! You see? It's beneficial for everyone."

Director Diebner pulls forward, calling Mina's attention to

himself. "You can test it on yourself, Fräulein Best, if you're so concerned about accidentally killing someone."

So, it's out in the open between them now.

Mina is about to strike back, but it's von Weizsäcker who comes to her defense instead. "Herr Director, I ought to report you for speaking to one of our scientists in such a manner! Holding a superior position does not give you the right to insult your subordinates, male or female, hearing or not. And we are scientists, not butchers. We're working on improving people's lives, not turning them into human guinea pigs. The idea itself is outrageous, and you know it; else, you wouldn't have been looking for any concealment tactics."

Director Diebner reddens in his rage. He's about to interject something but remembers whose son Dr. von Weizsäcker is, and besides, from his end of the desk Dr. Blobel is already holding out a pacifying hand, calling for a ceasefire.

"I see I've brushed on a sensitive subject I had no business bringing up. No, no; it's quite all right, Dr. Diebner. Your colleagues are correct. It's not their burden to carry, it's ours. We shall figure it out ourselves. Let the young people worry about their science and we'll worry about ours."

As they're dismissed, leaving a trail of icy tension in their wake, Mina feels a surge of alarm. "Should I have agreed to calculate it for him?" she asks, a fistful of von Weizsäcker's sleeve in her hand. "Because you heard him. They'll just start experimenting on the 'disposable' ones until they figure the right dose out."

But von Weizsäcker only shakes his head, solemn like a grave. "No, Mina. We're already carrying a big enough burden around our necks. Don't put another stone on top of it. You'll only drown if you do, and then who'll calculate our way out of that bloodthirsty numbskull's atom bomb ideas?"

Mina's heart aches for the victims, for the faceless masses who might soon suffer under the guise of science. She feels the sting of tears in her eyes, but she blinks them back. He's right, the department's golden boy who has suddenly become so very fearless when she most needed him to; there is no time for sorrow, only for resistance, even if the only resistance available to them is numbers Mina turns in their favor. Well, if that's the case, then she will fight with every breath in her body, with every equation and every discovery. For in a world gone mad, the pursuit of truth, the defense of the defenseless, is the greatest act of rebellion.

And so, Mina throws herself back into her work, her resolve unwavering, her spirit unbroken. For she knows that in the end, it is not the roentgen count that will define this chapter of history, but the courage of those who dare to stand against the darkness.

TWENTY-SIX

BERLIN, GERMANY. SUMMER 1941

In his office wreathed in smoke, Dr. Heisenberg neatly folds the newspaper and drops it into a waste bin under his desk.

"Well, here it is. The war is certainly lost," he announces with some apathetic finality about him.

It's stuffy here and not just because of the muggy end-of-June air, or all of the theoreticians gathered round their senior's desk, or even the cigarette smoke that refuses to filter through the windows thrown open. The atmosphere itself is heavy with some outward pressure that's weighing them down, sitting on their chests like the top of a marble tomb. They disbelieved it long enough; kept writing it off as an ugly rumor—after all, didn't they sign a non-aggression pact with the Soviets only two years ago? Only, here it is, an even uglier reality, staring them square in the eye and cackling at their childish naivete. A collective feeling something akin to the shame of a deceived spouse, too embarrassing to discuss and too evident to be silenced.

Von Weizsäcker is the first to gesture, his signal for attention reminding Mina of a drowning man's hand more than anything. "Perhaps, nothing is lost yet," he says, ever the idealist.

"Tell it to Napoleon." Dr. Heisenberg, the skeptic.

"But then it was winter to blame. It's summer now and if our armies move swiftly enough—"

The discussion grows heated. They all talk at the same time, forgetting to signal to Mina in time and all she catches is snatches of phrases as they fly about the room like scattered electrons.

"—the entire Soviet Union then?"

"—but the Blitzkrieg. It has worked all over Europe—"

"—can't even take that tiny English island—"

"—the war on two fronts! Just what we needed!"

"—haven't learned their lesson twenty years ago, those Feld-marschalls of ours—"

"—but Russia lost then—"

"—didn't. The revolution—"

"—now the OKW shall truly ride us like racehorses until we produce the blasted bomb for them. With the Soviets, they'll need it."

Overwhelmed and in need of some space, Mina leaves the office and walks briskly along the palatial hallways offering anything but respite. She pushes the heavy door open, the one leading to the courtyard, and is nearly blinded by the assault of midsummer sun.

Must have been Himmler's idea, to attack on summer solstice with his love of everything pagan, a thought flashes through Mina's mind as she picks her way through the gravel and bushes until she can safely crouch beside one and hide from it all for a few precious minutes. Just a few minutes to collect herself, to keep herself together and not fall apart. Just a few minutes to breathe in and out and not think of anything else but her breath.

Only, it's easier said than done. All sorts of insects crawl around her feet, her dress is sticking to her back like a snake's unshed skin, wet and abominable, and the thoughts are rushing about her head when she least wants them to—a self-sustained chain reaction.

Mina freezes momentarily on her haunches as something clicks in her mind. She can't quite put her finger on it yet—it's far too ephemeral, much too deep in the darkest corner of her subconsciousness, and the smallest gesture might spook it. Ants climbing her toes suddenly forgotten, Mina listens closely to that elusive thought. Like a hummingbird, it darts from one place to another, its outline just visible on the periphery of Mina's inner vision. A puzzle of seemingly unrelated things begins to slide as if moved by an invisible hand. A piece of von Weizsäcker here, a piece of armies moving east there, a piece with a numerical significance of the invasion and a piece with a bomb at its center.

With utmost care—*just don't disappear!*—Mina pats the ground for a stick and rejoices as her fingers close around one, just the size of a pencil. Moving as though under water, scarcely breathing even, she begins to sketch a formula and, for the first time, it's not uranium that takes the central place but its by-product, the mysterious plutonium, von Weizsäcker's discovery. When uranium splits, here it is, its by-products are always pictured on the right—east!—and now the number needed for the self-sustained reaction—

Despite the singing, pale-gold sun, all blood drains suddenly from Mina's face. She made a mistake the first time, that fateful day at Director Diebner's conference room. No; not her, in fact. She simply used the numbers provided by the experimenters, but those numbers were wrong, Mina sees it clear as day now. They don't need tons of plutonium or some unwieldy apparatus to launch the atom bomb. About ten kilograms would be enough to create a crater one kilometer deep and forty in radius. In the direct vicinity of its explosion, no structure will survive. As for anything living...

...That, Mina doesn't even wish to consider.

Blood pulsing wildly in her temples, Mina rushes back to Dr. Heisenberg's office where the theoreticians are still putting forward their theories about the end of the world and seizes him by the sleeve.

"Need to talk," she breathes in his ear. "Urgent."

Without a word of protest—she must look a sight indeed—he follows her out of the office and into the yard, where she puts him, mystified and sweating from such a sprint, in front of her latest discovery. Heisenberg doesn't seem to realize what he's looking at just yet but soon grows still like a statue and drops on the ground before the numbers sliced into the earth's flesh and stares at them long and hard before wiping them slowly with the palm of his hand.

He mutters something; realizes that Mina can't hear him and turns to her, looking suddenly aged twenty years.

"I'm saying, ten kilograms. To get even ten kilograms—"

"You simply need a working reactor, which shall split regular uranium into its by-products—one of which is pluto-nium. You won't even have to purify it first. You made sure that the pile here, in Berlin, didn't work so Diebner wouldn't have anything to report on the bomb, but you've already built your 'peaceful' reactor prototype, haven't you? The one in Leipzig. Is it working yet?"

In Dr. Heisenberg's eyes, thousands of stars are dying agonizing deaths. They've been worrying about the wrong thing, hiding the wrong thing from the eyes of Director Dieb-ner, when something much more dangerous has been brewing right inside Dr. Heisenberg's reactor. How arrogant it was to consider it a mere ploy, something to divert Diebner's attention with, how entirely blind and idiotic!

He slaps his forehead in helpless desperation and leaves a dark smudge on the wet skin. Silently, Mina kneels next to him and wipes his face with her handkerchief in a gesture of unadul-terated absolution.

"Come to Leipzig with me." His eyes are suddenly all fire. He hasn't surrendered to the fate, not just yet. "There is only my assistant, Döpel, who works on it with me, and Frau Döpel, his wife. And a couple of mechanics, but they just weld stuff; they can't tell a reactor core from their elbow, so they won't be any trouble."

Mina regards him, her thoughts of invitation scattering and making little sense. "You wish me to go to Leipzig and to make sure that reactor works? After what I've just shown you?"

"No. I want you to come with me and make sure it doesn't. For as long as we can."

The crisp, sterile air of the laboratory seems even heavier today, as if weighed down by an invisible burden. Mina moves with a purpose that betrays her inner turmoil, gathering paperwork and inspecting the Geiger counter which is about to join the contents of a little suitcase she packed. A portrait of concentration, her eyes stormy under the harsh fluorescent lights, she doesn't notice Hauptmann Taube stepping into the laboratory.

She sent a request for travel approval through von Weizsäcker, her usual channel, and received Taube's permission promptly. Naturally, she didn't expect her *Abwehr* handler to appear here in person. His presence, once she finally sees him, is certainly a surprise. Mina's grown so used to seeing Taube in her apartment or a museum, it's odd seeing him standing here in his uniform, a stark contrast to the delicate instruments and whispered theories that dance around the room.

"Good afternoon, Mina," he greets her with a slight bow. "I received word you wished to go to Leipzig with Dr. Heisenberg."

Mina nods and brushes off an invisible speck of dust from her lab coat. She feels caught off guard, ambushed somehow.

"Yes, Herr Hauptmann. It's about the reactor prototype project. Dr. Heisenberg has requested my assistance in Leipzig."

"So I heard."

"I've already received your permission and stamped travel pass." *Why are you here?* Mina searches him with her eyes.

"Yes, I made sure to approve them promptly. But—" Taube's brow arches slightly, a signal of his surprise. "Leipzig?" he inquires, his expression a controlled blend of curiosity and caution. "Why there, if I may ask? Don't you have a reactor prototype here in Berlin? In Director Diebner's 'virus house'?"

Mina takes a deep breath, steadying herself for the impending conversation. "That's the entire trouble. I need a respite from Berlin. And from Director Diebner in particular." Her voice is steady, but beneath the surface, it carries the weight of unspoken distress.

Taube's eyes narrow, sensing the gravity behind her words. "Is there something amiss with Diebner?" he probes.

Mina hesitates, her façade of composure wavering. "Do you want the truth or a censored version?"

"I've been censoring far too many things lately," Taube responds. "You're under my charge and protection, Mina. You should know by now that you can tell me anything."

Mina thinks about mentioning Untersturmführer Gürtner claiming the same very thing when he left her his card during his last visit, but then doesn't. With all her loathing of their uniforms, Taube is no Gürtner. Why insult the only officer who may actually be on her side for a change, without any ulterior motives?

Truth it is.

"With all due respect, Herr Hauptmann, I don't want to be asked to calculate how many roentgen it would take to sterilize a human being with undesirable genes," she confesses, the horror of the request lingering on her tongue like a bitter aftertaste. "I already have Untersturmführer Gürtner to deal with. I would really rather not be brought face to face with medic corps SS and posed with questions I find, frankly, revolting, and be threatened with that very sterilization by Director Diebner if I refuse to cooperate." She pours the words out and takes a big gulp of air, both emptier but lighter somehow. *Here's your truth, Herr Hauptmann. You do what you like with it.*

Taube's response is swift, his hand inadvertently clenching into a fist. "I knew nothing of this," he states, the ire rising in his cheeks in pale pink blotches. "No one has the right to threaten scientists under the OKW protection. This is an abomination. You have my word that I will investigate the matter promptly and reprimand all guilty parties."

She watches him, understanding the genuine shock etched across his features. "I appreciate that, Herr Hauptmann, but I'll tell you the same thing I told Dr. von Weizsäcker when he wanted to report the incident to you. You'll only make it worse. No one will remove Dr. Diebner because there's no one here to replace him. Dr. Heisenberg is as politically unreliable as they get. He was fortunate just to be included in the research and only because Director Diebner had no other choice. And the rest, they're brilliant scientists but they lack organizational skills and Director Diebner's connections with all the military higher-ups. Top brass in the OKW like him because he's trying to turn the atom into a weapon. They would never choose some deaf girl over him. So, while I appreciate your concern and desire to help, the best you can do for me now is let me go to Leipzig."

Taube regards her for some time, his mind at war with itself. At last, with great reluctance, he nods, the lines of his face hardening with resolve. "Of course. Go. Take a little break. Leipzig is a beautiful city. At least it was," he adds, more to himself than to Mina. "This war has... twisted many things."

Mina meets his gaze, recognizing the conflict raging within him. "Herr Hauptmann, may I speak freely?" she whispers. If the labs are bugged, she doesn't care one way or the other if the

SD and Gürtner hear what their lapdog Diebner is up to. But Taube's life, she refuses to play with it.

"You always can with me." Mina sees his lips move.

"I know you pride yourself on serving your country; my grandfather was an officer too. God knows, I understand. But this isn't the country you swore allegiance to. This is something altogether different. This is the country where science has been turned into a tool of annihilation instead of hope. You choose where your loyalties lie, Herr Hauptmann. Because, in the future, we'll all have to face the choices we made today."

With those final words, she presses Taube's hand and leaves him to wrestle with the implications of her statement. The silence that follows is deafening, broken only by the faint hum of machinery and the distant echoes of a world at war. Mina doesn't hear them, but hopes that Taube does.

Outside, the city of Berlin bustles under the iron fist of the regime, the streets lined with the stark, imposing architecture of the Third Reich. The sun casts long shadows over the cobblestones, the light struggling against the pervasive sense of oppression that hangs in the air. Mina is more than ready to leave it all behind, even if for a short period of time.

"You're leaving? At this crucial moment, you're leaving."

Von Weizsäcker is following her and his superior's movements around the office with disbelieving eyes.

But Dr. Heisenberg refuses to be fazed. His steps are unhurried and measured, his hands are steady as he gathers together research materials and reports. Mina, a small suitcase with the Geiger counter and all sorts of other machinery stuffed into it in a rush, watches him too and almost applauds Heisenberg's self-control. With each other, they can scream and tear at their hair in full confidence. With others, they ought to show only one face and that face must be as set as stone. Not that von

Weizsäcker can't be trusted, but he's still much too young and ambitious and his father works for Foreign Minister Ribbentrop and such connections are always corrupting to a degree.

"I always leave for Leipzig on Fridays. I have a wife and children, if you remember."

Von Weizsäcker gestures at Heisenberg to Mina, as though in search of support, but Mina can only offer him a smile of consolation and a polite shrug.

"He's dragging you there too," he asks her. "Whatever for?"

"To study radioactivity produced by the reactor and its effect on biological organisms," Mina offers a reply she and Dr. Heisenberg agreed upon.

"We need all the workers here to help us with the chain-reaction pile and you're taking yet another pair of hands with you."

"Fräulein Best doesn't work with the pile at any rate. She only helps you count. And I need her to help me with the reactor because it's the reactor that the OKW is most interested in at the moment, so be grateful I'm not dragging you all to Leipzig."

Von Weizsäcker's wrinkled nose is a perfect indicator of his sentiments toward anything more provincial than Berlin, and with that, he shakes Herr Professor's hand before offering his palm to Mina.

"Don't die of boredom while you're there."

"I'll try not to."

"Radioactivity doesn't affect bio-organisms. He's just bored senseless there and wants company."

Mina thinks of saying that a deaf girl can hardly be called good company but opts for a parting smile and a wave instead.

TWENTY-SEVEN

LEIPZIG, GERMANY. SUMMER 1941

The morning is still young, and out of its usual staff, only Dr. Heisenberg, his assistant Döpel and his wife, and Mina are inside the Leipzig Institute. Mina hasn't slept well: a new place and her nerves have seen to that. Despite Frau Heisenberg's— "Call me Li, dear!"—attentiveness and efforts to make their new houseguest as comfortable as possible, Mina barely slept a wink. When she did, she dreamed of hellish fires and ash falling from the sky.

She left the nightmares in her bed, but the feeling of unease remains now that she is face to face with Leipzig One, the first-of-its-kind reactor prototype.

"Don't fret." Dr. Heisenberg nudges her slightly forward. "It doesn't bite."

"Only because you haven't tested it yet," Mina mutters more to herself, but approaches the apparatus nevertheless, Dr. Geiger's counter at the ready. She holds it like an exorcist would hold a cross, but the counter's needle remains unmoved. The demon is still slumbering, undisturbed, inside its aluminum sarcophagus. "It's smaller than I thought," she admits, treading the laboratory's ground with more confidence now that the counter has put her heart at peace.

After expecting something fearsome and tremendous, Mina's surprised that Dr. Heisenberg's invention is scarcely larger than Graz University canteen's soup cauldron, only with a heavy lid and a single rod protruding from its top.

The nuclear physicist pries it open and reveals to Mina the reactor's uncomplicated guts. "Here's what we have. Two layers of uranium fuel, one inward and one outward, and in between, heavy water to create reactivity."

"Try it with regular water first," Mina fires the sentence that produces a conspirator's smile from Dr. Heisenberg but sends his Leipzig assistant, Döpel, into a state of mute, stunned amazement.

Mina feels for the fellow. He has just arrived in the laboratory, folders with notes under his arm, bright-eyed and excited at the prospect of testing their love child for the very first time, only to find some girl with braided hair and a white lab gown assisting Herr Professor as if she belongs here and demanding nonsensical things that anyone with half a brain knows would result in a failure.

"With all due respect, Herr Professor," Mina watches Döpel's lips move, "why replace heavy water with regular water if it was you who calculated that regular water doesn't work as a moderator?"

It's Mina who responds instead of Herr Professor. On their way from Berlin to Leipzig, they rehearsed Mina's role in all this. She's well prepared to act.

"Because we don't have enough heavy water to waste on experiments. The OKW is generous with its research funds, but there's a war going on if it's news to you. To preserve our resources, we ought to try the cheapest solutions first." Döpel is about to interject something, but Mina stops him with her hand raised. Just like him, she's well aware that such experiments won't bring any results whatsoever and only delay the whole process, but that's precisely what Mina and Dr. Heisenberg need: time. "And if those solutions prove ineffective, that's precisely what we shall report. Only after their ineffectiveness has been proven by experiment, we can move onto more expensive solutions."

Döpel casts Dr. Heisenberg a pleading glance, but the latter only spreads his arms in a helpless gesture.

"Fräulein Best is the OKW's representative here in Leipzig. She's here to supervise the experiment and to report on it. We are to listen."

Döpel must have questions, but he keeps them to himself. So does his wife, Frau Döpel, but at least she doesn't regard Mina with barely concealed contempt. On the contrary, she takes great interest in Mina and her handicap or, to be exact, her ability to read lips. The reactor takes second place in her list of priorities despite the men readying it for its very first test.

"How do you communicate with other deaf people?"

"I..." The realization suddenly dawns on Mina. "I've never actually met another deaf person."

"That's fascinating! But you're so perfectly assimilated. It can't possibly be easy, having to live among the hearing and hearing nothing yourself. Our world is so sound-centric. The radio, the phone... public announcement system. The anti-air raid—do you hear that?"

"Never had to, fortunately."

Out of the corner of her eye, Mina sees Dr. Heisenberg mutter something, but she can't decipher the words. For some reason, she's convinced that it's "we'll all hear them soon enough" that slips from his lips or something similar.

Döpel calls his wife then and the torrent of questions subsides, leaving Mina alone and slightly melancholy. That's what she's always been, and always will be, for everyone around —a nuisance or a curiosity, more of an object of study than a person. Besides her parents, only Siggy sees her for what she is; headfirst, he dove into her world and learned her language and spoke to her tenderly with his great nimble hands. But Siggy is in Berlin—Mina didn't even have a chance to say goodbye before her hasty, temporary departure or explain the circumstances of it—and Mina's parents are also gone, and God only knows when she'll see them again. Hauptmann Taube delivered their last couple of letters, in open envelopes, and had suspicion in his eyes but hasn't voiced it yet. Silently, Mina thanked her mother for her smarts and the perfectly innocent tale she wove in the letters with stamps from Switzerland like a Scheherazade's long-lost sister. *"Vati's health took a turn for the worse. Local doctors, who specialize in his condition, advised us strongly to abstain from travel and certainly from work. So, after giving it a lot of thought, we decided to remain here until he recovers fully. The sanatorium is so very splendid and does wonders for patients like him. They treat them with mineral water and baths and salt chambers—you of all people would love it. Medical science at its finest."*

Mina can't help but think about them as she records Dr. Heisenberg and Dr. Döpel's every step. After filling the reactor with carefully measured water, they close the lid and exchange a last glance of reassurance. From her position at the desk, Mina watches them with a heart that is both strained with tension and yet tender. Two people she managed to save. Now, just to save the rest of the humanity.

Minutes tick by and the oscillograph registers virtually nothing. Inside the aluminum reactor case, no reactivity is happening. No heat is generated. No sign of anything—rather to Mina and Dr. Heisenberg's hidden delight and, oddly, disappointment.

The feeling is controversial and difficult to digest, but it's still there, undeniable and slightly sour. The humanitarians in them pray it doesn't work. The scientists in them crave to see something happen. Inside both, a silent war is raging, and yet, outwardly, they remain still as granite and just as unmoved: Dr. Heisenberg with his arms crossed over his chest and Mina with a pen hovering over the log's page next to the wristwatch slowly dragging its hands in hypnotically identical circles.

Nothing will happen. We're wasting our time, Mina's mind flashes, but instead, she rests her head on her fist, her elbow bent on an angle, and suggests they give it till the end of the month.

"Whatever for?" Tired from the wait, Döpel drops into a chair opposite Mina.

"For, maybe, the reactor needs time and you'll mind it just fine on days when Dr. Heisenberg and I are back in Berlin," Mina counters with a smile that drives Dr. Döpel to distraction and makes him grind his teeth in helpless ire, but OKW's authority is authority all the same. The Prussian with centuries of militarist bloodlines in him triumphs at long last and he surrenders and patiently waits till the end of the month.

Just as patiently, he waits for the next experiment that Dr. Heisenberg writes out and schedules for the following month, this time with only one layer of uranium and two layers of water. Just as patiently, he supervises the construction of a new vessel, and this one shall go with the heavy water—praise the Lord!—but the welders were apparently given the wrong blueprint, the draft of the original that has been since then reworked, and the entire project has to be scrapped. Another month to wait until they build a new aluminum case.

Back in Berlin, which she visits together with Dr. Heisenberg every other week, Mina reports on the Project Reactor Sabotage progress to Siggy, who reacts in positive delight at Herr Professor and Mina's ingenuity. As is their habit, in Mina's apartment, they talk with their hands, leaving words for trivial things only.

So, when's the launch of Leipzig Three?

September. Do you think we'll be in Moscow by then? Mina is biting the nails she's eaten down to the stubs over the course of the summer.

Difficult to say. Siggy shrugs. *Reports from the front say the troops can see the Kremlin through their binoculars.*

The day lingers past six and is sultry and still. Through the open windows, honey-golden light pours onto the rug on which they sit instead of a sofa, cross-legged, knees touching, bathed in that amber glow. Between them, copies of Mina's reports. Originals are with Director Diebner, but these, these are for Siggy. In case something happens to her. Mina isn't afraid for her life per se, but people have a nasty habit of disappearing in Hitler's Germany. It's only logical to share state secrets with someone who doesn't lack the courage to use them properly—against that very state, if needed. And Mina knows whose side Siggy's on. He's proved it time and again.

As if reading her mind, he brightens and quickly signs, *I have something to show you,* before digging inside his military jacket. It's a photocopy of a newspaper clipping and it's in English. Mina's knowledge of it ends with school lessons, but it's enough to understand the gist of the article. In the United States, scientific experiments are being made on a new bomb. The material used in the bomb is uranium, and if the energy contained in this element is released, explosions of heretofore-undreamed-of power could be achieved.

Her mind still processing the news, Mina looks up from the clipping, still warm and slightly wet with Siggy's perspiration.

Do you think it's true? Did Dr. Reiche reach the people in charge and pass on the information?

From Siggy, a boyish one-shoulder shrug. *One can only hope.*

Wherever did you get it?

From the analytics department. Made a copy while they were having lunch.

But do you think it's true? her fingers insist.

Could be true. Could be a bluff to intimidate us.

German scientists?

Germans in general.

Suddenly on her feet, Mina paces the room as she considers both options. She's lightheaded and unsteady. In between train trips from Leipzig to Berlin and back and sleepless nights, she's drained of all strength and running only on nervous energy and fear. That fear, not quite as sharp and animalistic as one would experience from enemy fliers dropping bombs overhead (despite Luftwaffe Chief Göring's boastful promises, they have begun creeping into German territory now), has been following Mina like a shadow for quite some time now. She's used to its dull nagging and tries to ignore it whenever she can, but it's still attached to her like a vampire and bleeds her dry from each tiny new wound it inflicts.

What if we're forced to build the bomb?

What if the Allies build it first?

Would they use it against us?

Would we use it against them?

Would we use it simultaneously and reduce entire continents to radioactive rubble, just like Wells predicted?

But no, Mina tosses her head, forcing herself to get a grip. It's just her skittish nature speaking. Afraid of her own shadow, paranoid and laughed at behind her back by Döpel for refusing to part with her Geiger counter, for talking nonsense about radioactivity and assigning nonexistent illnesses to it. So what if Curie died of blood cancer? His mother died of liver cancer and she never saw uranium ore in her life.

Perhaps that's really what she is, just a girl and a coward who has no business in nuclear physics, who's afraid of something she used to love not that long ago just because she doesn't understand it fully.

But then, no one does, not quite yet, and that's what's so frightening about it.

Unwittingly, Mina pauses by the window and gazes into the setting sun through narrowed eyes and tries to erase some horrible premonition caused by it for whatever strange reason and jumps when arms wrap around her from behind and Siggy's chin comes to rest on top of her head. He's saying something in her ear—she feels his warm breath against the skin, so shiver-inducingly intimate, and she allows herself to melt into his embrace, which is warmer than a thousand suns.

She's grateful that he lets her imagine whatever words she needs to hear right then, and yet, she still wants the truth. That's the scientist in her: always obsessed with the truth, no matter how terrible.

Mina turns to Siggy and stares at him, imploring and insistent. And just as he always has, he understands her without a single word dropped.

"I said, whatever it is, we'll live through this together."

How beautiful his lips are as they form the undying oath.

"And if we don't live through it?"

"Then we shall die." He's calm as a sea right after storm and just as strong as its deepest, invisible currents. "But even if we die, I'll still hold you as I am now."

Her heart a clenched fist of overpowering emotion, Mina rises to her tiptoes and throws her arms around his neck. In the explosion of their kiss, somewhere in the parallel galaxy, a new universe is born.

TWENTY-EIGHT

LEIPZIG, GERMANY. SEPTEMBER 1941

"The radiation," Mina repeats. "It's in your hand, Herr Döpel."

"How can it be in my hand? I have washed it multiple times."

Mina tests the Geiger counter against the controls and then swipes the wand once again against Döpel's burned palm. The headphones are hanging uselessly on her neck—she'll never hear them click—but the needle climbs stubbornly to the right. "I can't explain it, but it is. It's gotten under your skin somehow."

"Geiger himself claims that radiation only clings to inanimate objects. Once in contact with skin, as soon as we wash the residue off, it's gone."

"That's what we have all been taught so far, yes." Mina nods. "However, you can see the reading of the counter for yourself. It hasn't gone anywhere. It's quite literally under your skin."

To think back to it, the day started off all wrong. Dr. Heisenberg's twins came down with a cold the day before. After tending to them all night together with his wife, Dr. Heisenberg either forgot to wind his alarm clock or simply didn't hear it and overslept. So did Mina, despite the fact that she never had an alarm clock to begin with and would often joke that it would do her just as much good as sunglasses would a blind person and instead relied on sunlight to awaken her from the night's slumber. Only, that Saturday dawned so dingy gray and full of cold mist, it was more twilight than morning and, for the first time in months, Mina slept right through without so much as stirring to look at the time.

And then, in the laboratory, Döpel was in such a rush to test Leipzig Three that he waved off Dr. Heisenberg's protocol and Dr. Heisenberg himself, said something from the other side of the aluminum reactor shell that Mina translated as *I know what I'm doing, it shall definitely work this time* and began submerging the container into the vat of heavy water.

From his position at the oscillometer, Dr. Heisenberg gestured to Mina to mark the beginning of the reaction. It did work this time, just as it was supposed to from the beginning, but at least they had salvaged three months by experimenting with regular water, dragged their feet for as long as they could. With her logbook perched on the crook of her elbow, Mina stood just over Dr. Heisenberg's shoulder, reading the numbers and marking the time of the reaction progression. Atop the aluminum case, condensation began to appear.

"It's sweating," Mina whispered to Dr. Heisenberg's shoulder.

He nodded, as fascinated as her. Leipzig Three was officially producing heat.

For a little less than a minute, the numbers followed Dr. Heisenberg's theoretical calculations with admirable precision but then something went horribly wrong.

It's been over two hours now. The fire that the reactor caught is long put out and Döpel's burned hand has been tended to by Frau Döpel and Mina, and they still, with the best will in the world, can't understand what exactly transpired.

"Something inside caught fire," Döpel says, holding his right hand extended and close to an open window.

They're in the experimental facility's library—the lab itself still reeks of smoke, heated aluminum and, sharply, of something metallic. It'll take weeks for it to properly ventilate and for the welders to build a new reactor shell—an additional blessing that came with the failure. How long it shall take for Döpel's hand to heal is anyone's guess.

The burn doesn't look all that terrible—a patch of scalded skin on both sides of the palm with the worst bubble in between his thumb and an index finger, where he grabbed the reactor's lid to throw it open before it would blow up altogether. Not a lethal case by any means, but it bothers Mina for another reason: even after washing Döpel's hand thoroughly, even hours after the incident, Dr. Geiger's counter is reacting to it.

Unlike her, Döpel isn't concerned about it in the slightest. What he wants to know is what could cause spontaneous combustion in his reactor prototype.

"Heavy water doesn't catch fire out of the blue," Dr. Heisenberg says, raking his hand through his hair for the umpteenth time. "So, it has to be uranium."

"Ignited by itself?" Döpel looks doubtful. "With no apparent reason?"

"Has to be contact with oxygen."

"But the reactor was sealed."

"So, it wasn't sealed properly then. There must have been a faulty seam somewhere."

Döpel throws his hands in the air and winces in spite of himself when the wound reminds him of its presence. Back to the windowsill it goes. Let the September breeze cool it off.

"Burns like a devil," Döpel complains and that also catches Mina's attention. Raised by a nurse, she was surrounded by medical encyclopedias and hospital talk from the tenderest age. There was a period in her life when she seriously considered becoming a physician herself, but the love of math won over Mina's interest in chemistry and biology. Still, she remembers well enough that burns are supposed to hurt, not actually cause burning sensations under the skin, as if hundreds of tiny red ants are crawling and gnawing through every cell.

Leaving the two physicists to their devices, Mina heads for the medical section of the library. It's small but full of books of the latest editions, commendations to the Leipzig University administration. Without much trouble, Mina finds what she is after: a full illustrated medical encyclopedia, just like the one *Mutti* used to have. She scans the contents section and flips the page with burns of different degrees. And here, in the descriptions accompanied by images that are both fascinating and gruesome, Mina finds confirmation of her doubts. Something's wrong with Döpel's burn. It doesn't fit under the criteria of a regular, thermal one. So, it has to be nuclear, just like the one Dr. Röntgen sustained during his experiments.

Mina stays quiet for the rest of the day, keeping her concerns close to her heart, but in the evening, when Elisabeth Heisenberg is busy putting the children to bed, Mina seeks her husband out in his study and pulls the chair up close to him. Seeing that the conversation is coming, Dr. Heisenberg puts away the notebook in which he was sketching new reactor prototype designs and sets his gaze on Mina.

"Do you remember what happened when Dr. Röntgen took far too many images of his hand with an X-ray machine?" Mina begins without any preamble.

"Vaguely."

Mina nods. "I remember, almost word for word, the description of the burn that he sustained from one of Dr. Geiger's studies he compiled for me. What Röntgen, himself, later called a radiation burn. He never approached any heat source and yet the skin on his hand first began to redden, then bubble up and then turn black when the necrosis began."

Dr. Heisenberg shifts in his chair.

"And then there was the case of that American who was drinking radium tonic recommended to him by his physician supposedly to help with his sprained wrist. Before his death, when he had already lost all of his teeth and his lower jaw had rotted away, pardon the gruesome imagery, he wrote to different medical journals and regular newspapers to warn others of the dangers, but I don't think anyone paid any attention to his claims, just like they dismissed those girls' claims about radium destroying their mouths and esophagi. You know who I'm talking about, right? The radium girls, whose job during the Great War was to paint numbers on wristwatches for the military with radium paint, so they would glow at night and would be easier to see. To make numbers neater, they were taught to lick the brush to make its tip pointier. The tip with radium paint on it." Mina's voice dips to a mere whisper. Horror seeps through it and saturates the room. "Dr. Heisenberg, I know you made my 'research of radiation on biological organisms' a mere pretext for my coming here with you, as a good joke to the others in Berlin, but has anyone really researched it besides Dr. Walsh who published a study on it, and even that one is so short, there's nothing really to go by? Because Döpel's hand is still radioactive and it shouldn't be. What if radiation got under his skin, like it did with Dr. Röntgen?"

For some time, Dr. Heisenberg seems lost in contemplation. He crosses and uncrosses his legs and rakes his memory for the information—Mina sees it clearly in the sharp line of his tightly drawn brows. At long last, he begins to speak.

"I can understand ingestion, like in the American's case. X-rays, that's... I can't explain that just now. Certainly, gamma rays may..." He loses his train of thought in the dark tunnels of doubts and becomes withdrawn and tongue-tied, like most scientists whenever they come face to face with something out of their field of knowledge. "I don't know with certainty if anyone ever researched it, but I can call the Institute. If something has ever been published on the matter, it shall be in their library in Berlin."

"Dr. Geiger has already given me everything that was in the Institute's library. We need something recent, if such studies even exist. Something from across the border."

Dr. Heisenberg smirks wistfully at that last request—with Germany at war with the entire world, fat chance the world will want to share any scientific discoveries with the Nazis—but then he looks in Mina's eyes and lowers his gaze at the silent plea in them.

"I'll see what can be done. If anyone can get anything from foreign sources that would be von Weizsäcker, through his father's channels."

"What about Dr. Bohr? He's still in Holland, right? Could you possibly call him and talk to him? He was your mentor back in the twenties; surely, he'll be glad to help?"

At the mention of Bohr's name, Dr. Heisenberg only blows out his cheeks with a look of quiet desolation about him. "He won't talk to me, let alone anyone from the Institute."

"Why on earth not?"

Dr. Heisenberg smiles at her with gentle reproach for having to spell it out. "I refused to leave Germany when there was still a chance. In his eyes, that makes me if not a Nazi, then a Nazi sympathizer at the very least. And he's Jewish, Mina. Jewish and without a job because of the Reich's rotten policies in the occupied territories."

Mina contemplates for a few moments and nods to herself. "Call von Weizsäcker then."

"I will."

Mina nods her thanks but doesn't leave, still sitting in her chair expectantly.

With a half-amused, half-resigned shake of his head, Dr. Heisenberg reaches for the black phone that stands on his desk.

"I see that you mean to call him now. All right. Let's hope he's home and not at one of his father's parties."

Mina watches him dial the number and feels a tiny worm of envy twitch inside of her. How fortunate those people are, who can just pick up the phone and speak to a person on the other line, in another city, even the other end of the world if it tickled their fancy. Mina can read lips like others read books, but she'll never be able to do that—place a phone call to someone just to hear their voice. She'll never sing along to a new popular song or know what birds sound like as they nest on the sill of her Berlin apartment. She'll never know what Siggy's voice sounds like, or Dr. Heisenberg's, for that matter.

For a short instant, she feels useless and incomplete some-how, but then reminds herself that if Saint Bernard dogs could save people during the Great War with their little nursing kits and whiskey, she can certainly make her own contribution to the fund of humanity. It is almost inconceivable now, the fact that she hoped to make that contribution by cracking the uranium code just a couple of years ago. She wasn't bright enough for that, and maybe that's good, because now she can if not reverse its research, then stall it enough together with Dr. Heisenberg until they know all the benefits and dangers of it.

And something keeps telling her that once the uranium genie is out of the bottle, there will be no putting it back. And it won't be granting wishes only; it shall demand souls as payment.

Dr. Heisenberg packs for the weekly trip to Berlin, but, for the first time, Mina refuses to go along, Siggy or not. For four days straight, she has been pestering Döpel with questions concerning his hand and all but driven him to distraction as she has checked its state by insisting on replacing the gauze on the wound herself. It's grown wet and seeps yellowish pus smelling faintly of metal and refuses to grow a crust despite all Mina's expectations. It's all because she keeps bothering it, Döpel grumbles, but neither Mina, nor the physician who's treating it, share the same opinion. The physician diagnosed it as a chemical burn, Mina can bet her life it's radiation.

"You think I'm wasting my time?" she asks Dr. Heisenberg as she hands him his trench coat in the hallway of his home. Weighed down with the couple's twins, Elisabeth Heisenberg is watching her husband with infinite love and silent longing.

"Not a single scientist who pursues something that hasn't been discovered before is wasting their time," Dr. Heisenberg says as he places his fedora atop his mop of light hair. "Just keep writing it all down. And when I'm in Berlin, I'll call Li and she'll write down that report on radioactive disease von Weizsäcker uncovered, in addition to the last-century one which you are already familiar with, thanks to Dr. Geiger. This other one is only a few pages long and dates back to '27, but it's better than nothing."

The sweet syrup of his reassurance coats Mina's heart and she steps away to allow the husband and wife their last few moments of privacy. And then off to the laboratory she goes and creeps around the vast room still smelling of smoke and singed metal with her Geiger counter and writes down every twitch of the needle on every square meter of the space. The radiation is still here, much less than before, but it's still clinging to the walls of the vat, now empty of heavy water, to the floor and metal handles of the doors. It's on Döpel's white gown that he wore that day, now lying crumpled and forgotten in the corner. Mina finds a ruler in a desk drawer, uses it to pick up the robe and carries it, away from herself, outside and to the back of the building, where a big garbage container stands. Upon her return, she asks the laboratory assistants to wash the entire experimental room with soap and then lye. And to throw away the mops later. And the buckets. And—this she says after giving it some thought, but who cares, they already consider her mad here—for them to take a shower after they return home.

The assistants, most older than Mina, exchange glances but head toward the janitor's closet for supplies all the same.

In Dr. Heisenberg's office, Mina sits with her counter like a third limb in her hands, and waits to take more measurements. She's a mathematician, after all. That's what she was born to do —to count.

TWENTY-NINE

The evening descends upon Leipzig in the form of a rainstorm. Fat drops, round and luminous like pearls, hit the Heisenberg home windows with force and snake down the glass, rendering the streets outside invisible. In the physicist's study, Elisabeth is taking down the dictation from her husband, the phone's receiver squeezed tight between her shoulder and ear. Standing over her like a shadow, Mina greedily consumes every word coming from under Elisabeth's pen. With each new page, Mina's brows knit tighter and tighter. When at last Elisabeth puts down the phone and turns toward her, Mina recognizes her own fears reflected in Elisabeth's face as if in a mirror.

"I'm no scientist by any means," Dr. Heisenberg's wife says, all big doe eyes and with an unnatural stillness to her posture, "but this sounds, frankly, frightening, if all of it is true."

"What is Dr. Heisenberg saying?"

He, too, has only read the studies for the first time, both written by American scientists, with a nearly thirty-year gap between them. Two cautionary reports—one defining radiation sickness and the second warning of genetic mutations and cancers that can possibly result from it—and in between, years and years of willful ignorance and silence and just a few patents by several prominent pharmaceutical companies advertising radium as a miracle cure. Mina can't help but wonder what he thought of it all.

With a degree of awkwardness, Elisabeth gives a one-shoulder shrug. "He says he's a physicist and not a physician, so he can't really comment on the studies. However, I fear he only said that to put my mind at ease. If it's you he was talking to, it is my deepest conviction he would have said something quite different."

"What makes you think so?"

Elisabeth smiles at her and that smile is both endearing and impossibly tragic. "I'm his wife, you see. He shelters me from everything. Always has. And you, you're a fellow scientist. He can discuss these things with you."

Mina doesn't argue; only gathers the papers lined with Elisabeth's beautiful writing and reads them, slower this time, holding the pages just a tad away from herself as though the symptoms described are somehow inexplicably contagious. She's so engrossed in the reports, she can't help but jump when Elisabeth's hand lands on her wrist, calling for Mina's attention.

"Mina, will you be frank with me? Woman to woman?"

"Naturally." Mina lowers the papers, giving Elisabeth all her attention.

"Is it true? What these scientists are writing, is it true? Do people really get sick from those materials Werner works with? Is it true that they cause cancer and all sorts of horrible deformities in future generations?"

Mina is silent for some time, torn between revealing what's truly on her mind and sparing Elisabeth from the nightmares she has to live with. She's a wife and a mother, Elisabeth. Mina, she has no one dependent on her. She can afford the truth. But Elisabeth...

Finally, she settles on something in between. "I don't know,

Li. The first study by Walsh was published in 1897. That's a long time ago, and Röntgen personally disagreed with it. As for Dr. Muller, who specializes in genetics, he used laboratory animals as his test subjects. He hasn't studied the results in people. Radiation may affect us differently and what can kill a mouse may cause only a brief illness in a person." She smiles at Elisabeth as brightly as she can. "Dr. Heisenberg is perfectly healthy and you two have beautiful, healthy children. I don't think you have anything to worry about."

Elisabeth regards her for a very long moment, a question— *"Why are you worried then?"*—burning in her eyes. But she lowers them eventually and frees the chair for Mina. "I'll go check on the twins. You stay here for as long as you need."

Mina doesn't want to stay here. She wants to run to Döpel's house and stare at his hand from every angle until her eyes grow bloodshot and make his physician draw his blood and send it to Dr. Muller, who understands these things better than she does, and ask him for his opinion.

But the war is going on, and even if the United States aren't involved in it, the Atlantic is infested with German submarines and British warships, and the German mail service has better things to do than risk their lives trying to sneak past the two warring armies. And even if it didn't, by the time blood arrives there, it'll be useless. The American himself could have been long dead. Fourteen years have passed since his findings were published. Many things can happen in fourteen long years.

But what Mina really wants to know is why no one paid the slightest attention to it. If they did, if whatever Dr. Muller discovered is true, they would think twice before developing the bomb that will not only obliterate anything in its vicinity but doom future generations to a slow and terrible death, riddled with diseases and deformities of all imaginable sorts.

For a very long time, she stands in the shower that evening, scrubbing herself raw with soap. And still, when she gets into her bed, she feels tainted somehow, almost expecting her skin to glow faint green as she turns off the lamp.

Winter 1941–1942

Many things can happen in fourteen long years; though, as it turns out, just as many things can happen in two short months. Rather to Döpel's glee, his hand has regrown new skin in place of the old that was coming off it in ribbons. By the end of October, only a few pink scars remained, where ugly, swollen flesh was bursting like cauliflower. By the end of December, just as Japanese suicide bombers attacked Pearl Harbor and the Soviets mounted a counteroffensive near Moscow, he returned to the laboratory to work on a new reactor, Leipzig Four—the fate of its predecessor all but forgotten, purged from the laboratory by disinfectants and countless washes and even a new layer of paint of an ugly shade of yellow that Mina detests with an inexplicable passion.

In Leipzig, Döpel celebrated the government's official abandonment of the peacetime economy and the full switch to the wartime one. Not even Dr. Heisenberg's reserved comments about the lab needing tons of uranium fuel for a full-scale working reactor, and that's if Leipzig Four proved itself to be such a reactor, dampened his mood.

In Berlin, the mood was quite different. Berliners met the news of the United States entering the war with a collective groan—a sentiment that Dr. Heisenberg wholeheartedly shared.

It's now those few days between the declaration of war and winter holidays and Berliners can't quite decide whether to shop for presents or non-perishable items to stock their pantries with. Inside the Institute, the staff are just as lost and crabby. Once again, they gather around the blackboard, but this time with Mina in the middle.

"You're the mathematician here," Director Diebner says,

handing her a piece of chalk with a bow of exaggerated gallantry. "We need to prove to the OKW that our research is essential to the war economy and shall produce swift and decisive results. Make the corresponding numbers so I can show it to them at the meeting in February."

But instead of him or the blackboard, Mina looks at Dr. Heisenberg. He reads the unspoken question in her eyes and pulls on his cigarette, hard, but there's nothing he can say. They've grown used to their sabotage being the subtle kind. But there is nothing subtle about Director Diebner, not now, not with Japan and the United States entering the war and Hitler turning the entire economy on its head. Former textile factories shall be producing uniforms only; former toy plants will be outfitted to bang out bullets so that real soldiers instead of wooden ones will kill and die by them.

"Don't look at him." Director Diebner snaps his fingers in front of Mina's face. "I'm your director. I'm in charge of this team, and if you wish to keep your jobs," he says, roving his heavy gaze across the room—this is meant for every single one of them, "if you wish to remain here instead of the frontline, you shall give me the numbers I request."

"I'm a woman, they wouldn't ship me off to the front," Mina grumbles out of some childish impulse.

"No. They'd put you to work on a factory or some such," Diebner counters, his head cocked. "Instead of a nice, clean laboratory, you'll be pulling twelve-hour shifts in an ice-cold war plant with minimal rationing."

Mina doesn't mind the factory in the slightest, but there are the lives of her fellow scientists to be considered. She gazes around sheepishly and is met with equally sheepish looks.

"Well?" Diebner demands once again. The color is rising in his neck. Mina can see he's growing impatient. "Shall I send for the uniforms now or will you see reason after all?"

"We're working on the reactor," Mina can't hear her own

voice but is convinced, for some reason, that it sounds like a very old, rusty cog turning. "I can only give numbers for the reactor. It's not a wartime—"

Diebner waves her off. "Yes, yes, we've been through this. We can't make a bomb as of yet, we'll need either clean uranium fuel for it or von Weizsäcker's plutonium. Plutonium is produced in the reactor when uranium fissions. You're working on the reactor. Therefore, yes, it is a wartime production. Now, give me numbers. When can I expect this working reactor?"

"Full-scale? Not a prototype?" Mina's hand, with the chalk in it, hovers next to the board without touching it. She's trying to buy some time, for Dr. Heisenberg to come up with something, but Director Diebner steps right in front of her, blocking her immediate superior from view.

"I think it should be understood that, yes, I need a full-scale working reactor. How soon and how much?"

Mina swallows around a barb in her throat and, feeling the weight of the entire world on her shoulders, puts a date on the board.

"That's in six months." Diebner doesn't seem too pleased.

"That's the date for the prototype testing. But if everything goes as planned, it can become a full-scale reactor."

In her mind, Mina is already building sandcastles of possible things that could and must go wrong, but for now, she'll smother Diebner's fire with lies—to keep her fellow scientists safe until...

Until the Soviets distract Hitler's warmongers enough to take the heat off the nuclear physicists or until the Americans build their bomb and obliterate them all—whichever comes first. As long as no one's blood ends up on Mina's hands. That's all she worries about.

"Why so long?" Diebner demands, his index fingers beating a drum atop his crossed arms.

"The third prototype caught fire. We need to ensure it

doesn't happen with the fourth one. Everything must be seamless."

"Fine." Diebner exhales his discontent. "What do you need for it to work seamlessly?"

Director Diebner's face falls as someone says something. When Mina scans the small crowd with her eyes, she realizes that it's Dr. Heisenberg, who has finally recovered his voice lost to the initial shock and threats that followed.

"All of the uranium ore in the Reich and occupied territories," he repeats for her benefit, a barely-there smile creasing the corners of his mad eyes. They're the eyes of a gambler who has just put everything on zero and is praying for a miracle. "Put it on the board for Director Diebner, Fräulein Best. We'll need at least five tons of uranium fuel for the first full-scale reactor. For it to work at least for some time while they mine more ore. I needn't explain that we'll require constant shipments to support the reactor working at all times, need I?"

Diebner looks at him as if the man has lost the last of his marbles.

Mina is already calculating things on the board with ruthless efficiency. It's a delicate balance, putting obscene amounts of uranium ore on one side of the scale and the lives of the physicists on the other and dangling the promise of an atom bomb in front of the OKW's nose just so they'll pay up and keep the scientists safe and alive, all the while knowing that she and her colleagues would rather eat that very plutonium with a spoon than allow a bomb to be made out of its hellish substance. But Herr Freudenberg, the kind old baker, has taught Mina balance all too well. He may have died, but in his name, Mina, as Dr. Heisenberg's team's little bookkeeper, shall remain the keeper of peace, the protector of life itself.

When she's finished, she steps away from the board, tilting her head this way and that, going over the calculation with a satisfied look on her face. "Yes. That should just about do it. You may tell the OKW that if they give us everything we need, they may have enough plutonium to consider a bomb by the end of the next year."

Bright-eyed and immensely pleased with himself, Director Diebner copies the numbers and dates into his notebook and even kisses the top of it as soon as he slams it shut, like an Italian chef kisses the tips of his fingers after he completes a particularly fantastic dish. "Thank you, Dr. Heisenberg, Fräulein Best, gentlemen. I expect the OKW to be most satisfied."

He walks out, but now it's her own fellow theoreticians that mob Mina, all distorted faces and hands in hair. They talk over each other, but the sentiment is the same. *What have you done? Just what have you gone and done?*

Dr. Heisenberg steps between Mina and his colleagues. "Bought you another year away from the trenches. And now, scram and pretend to work, but don't discover something else that fissions by mistake. Dr. von Weizsäcker, Fräulein Best and I have matters to discuss."

THIRTY

February comes and goes, and together with it, the second OKW meeting. This one Dr. Heisenberg attends and returns from it with his back wet with sweat but his mind at ease. Later that evening, with the blackout drapes drawn closed and two mugs of hot ersatz coffee steaming between them, Mina recounts its details to Siggy with her animated hands.

Lots of military brass there, all full of rage for the British bombing Germany and asking for the uranium bomb but, fortunately, having very little idea of the logistics of it. Dr. Heisenberg had no trouble talking his way out of it—at least for the time being. Said we need a working reactor first and that will only be ready in the summer, if everything goes smoothly, which it won't, we'll make sure to see to it. Though, they said they don't mind waiting as long as there's light at the end of the tunnel. Very keen on their miracle weapons, those men. One of them actually suggested for a battleship to cross the Atlantic, then for a fighter plane to take off from it, aim it for New York City, bail while still over the ocean, and then for the submarine to pick the crew up against the backdrop of glorious vengeful flames engulfing the city. Quit laughing, he was speaking in all seriousness, according to Herr Professor.

She watches Siggy throw his head back and slap his knee and can't help but break into a fit of chuckles herself.

And these are the people who lead us, he signs to her while still shaking his head. He hasn't been to a barber in quite some time, busy with the Americans entering the war and the load of his work doubling; a long lock of hair falls over his eye. In the pale light of the dimmed kitchen bulb, it shines like raw platinum ore. *My lady, we are doomed.*

Good for us, Mina signs back and means it. Ever since Hitler came to power together with his unhinged supporters, this country has gone to the devil. *I frankly don't care one way or the other if they obliterate us all.* Her hands freeze midair and drop atop the table as soon as Mina realizes her mistake. Her parents are long gone and safe, waiting the whole mess out in neutral Switzerland, but Siggy's parents are still in Vienna, and they won't budge, the old Imperial guard, no matter how many times Siggy tries to compel them to "travel for the sake of their health." In fact, Siggy's father threatened to disown his son altogether if he brought the subject up ever again. He happens to like this new Hitler's Reich. Finally, everyone fears them and submits to them. Those Zionists are gone, just like those blasted freethinkers and perverts who only knew how to corrupt German youth. What's there to complain about? As for Siggy's mother, it is anyone's guess what she thinks. It's her husband's responsibility, to think. Her responsibility is to take care of the house and not meddle in his affairs. Just how such a couple could produce someone as pure and selfless as Siggy still mystifies Mina to this day.

And yet, family is family, and so, she raises her hand to apologize for the harshness, to explain that this was not what she meant at all, but Siggy catches her wrist before she can. Under his fingers, her pulse is beating its wings like a butterfly intoxicated with the first spring pollen.

I don't care either. As a nation, we deserve it.

They do, too. In front of Mina's eyes, like some macabre silent film from the twenties, snapshots of the past flicker in quick succession. Mina's expulsion from school on the grounds of her disability. Her mother quitting her job on the day when a physician asked her to assist him with the first euthanasia case. Herr Freudenberg on his knees, his bakery going up in flames behind him. SS recruits in universities. The army in charge of science. Von Weizsäcker telling a weasel-faced man in a white gown to get lost when asked, hypothetically, just how many roentgen it would take to sterilize a person without them realizing it. Dr. Heisenberg tasked with creating a bomb that would bring the sun itself to its grave.

Mina shuts her eyes and rubs them until they hurt. She doesn't want to talk about it any longer. She wants to live a life that is ordinary and full of small, everyday wonders, where people aren't set on obliterating each other. She wants her cat Libby and Siggy, and to be able to visit her parents whenever she needs a hug from her mother, and to drink coffee that doesn't taste like spices and hay, and to burn lights all night in her apartment without fear of having an incendiary bomb dropped on top of her head. Is it really that much to ask?

I want to leave here.

She half-expects a judgmental look, but it's Siggy who's sitting across from her. He never judges. Only listens and, somehow, always understands.

Tired? Without another word, he rises to his feet and goes behind her chair and puts his hands on her shoulders. Like warm wax, Mina melts under his touch as he kneads and undoes all the knots her body has twisted itself into in the past few years. A life-length of tension and fear is stored under her skin. She feels ancient and ready to crumble into dust, but

Siggy's hands inject new life into her as they travel from her temples to her shoulders, arms, and back, and all at once, she's vibrating with it and leans into that long-craved intimacy and surrenders herself with sweet abandon.

I'm not going anywhere though.

The morning is still young and crisp when Mina promises it to the man lying next to her through the rings of bluish cigarette smoke. Her bed is much too narrow for two, but they make do. The generation born between two wars, they've never had a habit for comfort.

And not because of Taube, either.

In the predawn twilight, her hands are barely visible. Only the tip of the shared cigarette glows bright in the dark. If Siggy didn't take it from her, she would be certain that she was talking to herself.

She is, in a sense. Talking herself through things that are too painful to think has always been an outlet for her, like a medieval doctor letting a patient's bad blood.

I could have, if I wanted to. If I really put my mind to it. Lise Meitner, she left.

That's the Jewish physicist? Siggy signs. In his right hand, the cigarette tip flashes like a comet disintegrating into cosmic dust.

Mina smiles at the fact that he remembers. Always remembers everything she says, always listens to every name and detail.

Yes. Her fellow scientists got her out.

That was before the war.

He isn't wrong, but Mina is an obstinate little thing and particularly when she gets something into her head. She may be lacking many things, but persistence isn't one of them.

War or no war, they can still travel to occupied and neutral territories to give lectures and whatnot.

Yes, but you're not a professor.

Dr. Heisenberg could take me on as his assistant. Like he did with Leipzig. To Switzerland, if needed. They wouldn't be looking for me either. No one will miss a deaf girl whose biggest talent is to count faster than the others.

A girl who's a part of the Reich uranium project, Siggy signs and passes her the cigarette for the last pull before it's finished.

Mina's lips burn with that last inhale before she stubs it out. In the darkness, she can barely see her own hands as they move. *I could get lost if I really wanted to.*

So why don't you go?

Why doesn't she? Because he's here next to her, and because there's still work to be done, and because maybe, just maybe, she isn't as much of a coward as she has always claimed to be? She is in no way paramount to Dr. Heisenberg's attempts to delay the progress of his research as much as he can or his attempts to keep the men under his charge from becoming cannon fodder for the German war machine. She's ordinary and replaceable, but the truth of the matter is, Mina simply won't be able to live with herself if she leaves now.

Mina is about to put it all into words and turns to Siggy for a split second to check if he isn't sleeping yet—she has been thinking the argument over for quite some time—and realizes that the words here aren't needed. A knowing grin grows on his face as he raises his arm for her to use as a pillow. Mina lifts her head and rests it on his shoulder as he holds her close for a few more precious minutes—before it's time for them to go to their respective workplaces and pretend to be people they're not.

That's a good idea, lectures and whatnot, Siggy suddenly signs, breaking the spell, but there's no rest for the wicked; their brains are always on guard, filtering information, probing the enemy for the new openings in its defenses. That's what's brought them together and that's what bonds them tighter than blood. *I'm thinking, they can pass information to other scientists and particularly in Switzerland. Switzerland is a major spy hub as of now—I should know, I get messages to and fro faster than I can decode them. There are plenty of British and Americans there. But it's the Americans that you're most interested in, right? They're the ones working on the atom bomb, no?*

Yes, Mina nods against his shoulder.

Could you perhaps offer to go there—for a lecture or some such—and pass on whatever messages you want to pass on? And I'll tell you the names of the people who need to hear them so they can reach the other side.

The idea is brilliant, but she didn't expect anything less from someone who smashes codes like dry shells. Mina's skin grows hot against his and it's a beautiful feeling—to be this loved, this understood. To have someone fight alongside you—and die alongside you, if needed.

THIRTY-ONE

SPRING 1942

Like the calm before the storm, the spring of 1942 offers the Uranium Club a bit of a respite. Armed with Siggy's offer (naturally, Mina keeps his name and status to herself—one can never know what can go wrong), the theoreticians hop on the trains heading west and return with faces ignited from within with mutual passion as Mina looks on from the shadows of their Berlin lab. That inner glow is the only trace of their highly dangerous and clandestine activities. For the same reason Mina doesn't talk about Siggy, they keep mum about whom they saw and what information exchanged hands. They may not be in physical trenches, but their invisible war is no less dangerous and, perhaps, even more detrimental to the fate of mankind. With fierce determination, they protect their comrades with their silence. The entire department is suddenly both deaf and mute and Mina can't help but smile at the irony of it all.

In Leipzig, Dr. Heisenberg is putting the finishing touches to the L-IV with the help of Döpel and a couple of loyal mechanics. Even in Berlin, no one bothers with them; Director Diebner is busy currying favor with the new Reich Minister of Armaments and War Production, Albert Speer, and spending more time in restaurants and ministerial offices than in the Institute. Left to their own devices, the theoreticians consider it a blessing.

"I almost forgot just how absolutely splendid it is, to work without army brass and their underlings breathing down my neck," von Weizsäcker declares one afternoon when the sun hangs high in the sky, warm and heavy like a ripe fruit, and the air smells of blossoming lilacs.

"Don't jinx it," Mina warns him, even though it's hard to believe that on a day like this, anything can possibly go wrong.

With lax control and the absence of threats to send them all to the frontline, they've grown tender and relaxed. With sunlight on their faces, it is hard to believe that war is raging all over Europe, and in the Pacific and in Africa as well, and that people are being torn to pieces somewhere just a fighter plane flight away. They still work, but their heart is not in it, not on this obscenely beautiful spring day, splashing color all over the city and saturating the air with its intoxicatingly sweet smell. Instead, they go from office to office and gossip about old times as they drink their chicory coffee and plan outings to Grünewald on the weekend. *You bring beer, I'll bring meat. And Paul shall be in charge of the pastries. His wife makes strudel like nobody's business.*

Von Weizsäcker is invariably in charge of champagne.

"Where shall I get the damned stuff?" he protests as he always does. "You, my good lads, mix things up in your enlightened heads. My father *works* for Minister von Ribbentrop, he's *not* Minister von Ribbentrop. And even if he was, von Ribbentrop has long abandoned his champagne business for the ministerial chair. Been almost ten years now."

They ignore the department's golden child's objections with a wonderful nonchalance about them, knowing that he will indeed come through and procure the required champagne. He simply always does and they've grown used to his reliability in the matter just as they've grown used to seeing the sun rise every day without fail.

But two days prior to the scheduled outing, Dr. Heisenberg suddenly makes an appearance, wild-haired even more than usual and in a suit that hasn't been changed from the previous day. *He must have slept in it on the train*, the thought flashes through Mina's mind as the chief theoretician tears open the envelope and spreads photos of some burning ruins all over von Weizsäcker's desk.

"I don't know what I'm looking at yet, but something tells me that I jinxed it," von Weizsäcker says.

It was meant to be a joke, but no one is laughing. Not even the young man himself.

"What *are* we looking at?" Mina asks.

The pictures are full of smoke and leveled buildings and human bodies buried under heaps of ash—an illustration of Dante's inferno that has somehow transformed into real life from the book's pages.

"Can't even tell, can you?" Dr. Heisenberg's heavy gaze roves over the room, challenging every single one of them.

Besides Mina and von Weizsäcker, there is Otto Hahn and Fritz Strassman and none of them can produce a plausible explanation.

The pause grows so long, Mina begins to shift her gaze from one scientist to another, wondering if they began talking without alerting her first. But no, they're mute as they can be, staring at the photos with disbelieving eyes.

"Is it in Britain somewhere?" Hahn ventures at last, just to say something, just to break that dark spell hanging over their collective heads.

In place of a reply, Dr. Heisenberg lowers himself into a chair as if the strength has suddenly abandoned him. Mina sees his chest heave as he sighs with some devastating finality about him. It's Hahn who posed the question, but out of habit, Dr.

Heisenberg turns to Mina so she can read the words as they leave his pale lips.

"No. I fear, it's our very own Cologne. I don't blame you for not recognizing it. It has pretty much ceased to exist in the state that we knew it."

Mina sucks in a breath. There's a sudden change in the air, as though the temperature just dropped ten degrees.

"It's not an atom bomb." She shakes her head, grasping at photos like straws. "It can't be."

"No, it's not," Dr. Heisenberg agrees, patting himself absently for cigarettes but producing only an empty, crumpled pack. Mina can't help but wonder just how much he smoked on his way from Leipzig to Berlin. He drops the empty pack into the waste bin under the desk and nods his thanks to Strassman as he offers him his cigar case. "The British RAF used incendiary bombs, the first time on such a scale. Devastating, that much is true, but as much as the loss of innocent civilian life and historic buildings breaks my heart, that's not the reason why I brought these here."

He pauses to pull on Strassman's slim brown cigar, eyes gazing through space into nothing.

"That's also not the reason why a well-dressed *Abwehr* gentleman brought these highly confidential photos to me before the first papers printed a less dramatic version for the public circulation. The RAF just went and stuck a stick into the proverbial anthill. Personally, I don't blame them in the slightest—didn't we bomb their cities first, sending half of London's population to hide in their Underground? But that's not the point here. The point is..." He sighs heavily once again and rubs his forehead, wrinkled with angst. "The point is, now the OKW will really want their bomb. The Luftwaffe depleted their resources to mount any significant retaliatory attack on London. They've lost far too many planes to the RAF and aren't building as many replacements as they need.

They're working on long-range rockets or some such, but I don't think those shall make any difference to the final outcome."

Von Weizsäcker raises his hand, his youthful face now just as gray as the ashes of Cologne. "Final outcome as in... winning or losing the war?"

Together with the rest of the team, Mina shifts her eyes to Dr. Heisenberg, searching his face for clues, both expecting and fearing his answer. And knowing the response to it, deep in the pit of her stomach.

"The war has been effectively lost ever since we opened the second front," Dr. Heisenberg says without expression. "It will be lost even sooner now, with the United States getting in the mix, but there has always been one variable that can change the entire game."

"Atom bomb," Mina whispers and feels everyone's eyes on her, full of cold, tangible terror.

Dr. Heisenberg nods and stubs the cigar in the ashtray. "Now that not only we but the war ministers themselves see that the war is lost without it, they'll do anything possible—and impossible—to make us build it." He looks them in the eye, one by one, like an ancient demigod mounting a pitiful resistance to the Olympus rulers themselves, not really believing in victory but asking for them to at least die with honor in the name of life on earth. "Under any circumstance, no matter the threats, no matter the pressure, we cannot make it happen. I don't care if they begin putting red-hot needles under your nails or a gun to your head, don't you dare succumb to them."

They aren't warriors by any means; they are the thinkers, the inventors, the innovation drivers, but they nod all the same and swear their whispered allegiance. There's only one question that still burns through everyone's mind. It's Strassman who voices it, looking almost ashamed for doing so.

"What if they come for our families?"

For a long time, Dr. Heisenberg ponders his response, even though there's nothing really to think over at a time like this.

"It's not my place to decide that for you. I'll just say this: I have a family myself and I would gladly lay my life for their sake. However, when it comes to the fate of the entire world—and this is precisely what's at stake here—I'll put bullets through my wife's and my own children's heads before swallowing one myself, but I'm not handing the weapon of mass destruction into the madman's hands."

By the end of that speech, Mina's entire body is shaking, balancing precariously at the verge of an abyss, and feeling the pull of gravity like never before. They are all lined up here, the guardians of the ultimate secret, and in their chalk-smeared hands, the destiny of humanity quivers.

Mina's living room is still, save for the shadows dancing across the walls, playing with the somber expressions of Siggy and Mina. In the candlelight—the electricity is out due to the blackout regulations—they sit opposite each other, a small dining table separating them, a space filled with both intimacy and an unspoken tension. Siggy's hands tremble slightly as he reaches for his cup, the hot tea untouched, steam no longer rising from its surface.

Mina watches him, her sharp eyes softened with concern. She knows this man, his every gesture, every unspoken thought that flits across his face. Yet tonight, there is a stranger sitting opposite her, all withdrawn into himself, refusing to meet her eyes as if fearing to read a death sentence in them.

He hasn't said two words since he arrived on her doorstep, drenched to the marrow by the spring thunderstorm and looking positively miserable as he signed, *Can I just sit here with you?*

Mina has let him stay silent in his chair for as long as she can bear, but the pain radiating from him begins to prickle her skin, sharp as a needle, striking at the very nerves.

"Siggy, what is it?" Her voice is gentle, a caress meant to soothe. "You can't sit here and expect me to watch you suffer in silence. Tell me what's burdening you. Maybe I can help."

He looks up, and their eyes meet. *You can't help,* he signs. The pain in his gaze is palpable, and it tears into Mina's very heart. *This one is my own cross to bear. I suppose, I didn't expect it to be so heavy.*

Tell me.

No. You'll hate me if I do.

I already hate myself on most days. You may as well join the club.

A faint shadow of a grin briefly passes over Siggy's face. He reaches out and presses Mina's hand, grateful for her taking the edge off, before signing once again.

I have done something... something that I fear may haunt me for the rest of my life.

Mina's mouth presses into a resolute line. *Whatever it is, Siggy, we'll face it together. And now, tell me.*

He takes a deep breath, steadying himself with the warmth of her gaze. *You must have learned of Cologne by now.*

Yes, Dr. Heisenberg showed us the photos today. It's a tragedy. Those poor people—

Mina drops her hands atop the table once she notices tears standing in Siggy's eyes. She freezes where she sits, afraid to make another move, to hammer another nail in the coffin of his heart.

It was me. I decoded intelligence concerning the upcoming RAF raid. His hands tremble something terrible. Mina watches him swallow a few times, but the lump is still there, visible, choking him with emotion. *I had the coordinates, they were for Cologne, but I...* His eyes are pools of torment. *I changed them in my report. I gave my superiors Dresden coordinates instead. I don't know what I was thinking. I didn't have much time to think. I acted on an instinct, wanted to give the Nazis a taste of their own medicine, to let them see what they're doing to people in Britain and France and all over Europe and Africa... But when I realized what I'd done, it was too late to change anything. They didn't even question me the following morning, my superiors. Just went about the office, cursing the "damned Brits" for spreading disinformation on purpose. I murdered thousands of innocent people and no one even reprimanded me, Mina.*

Tears gather under his chin. He doesn't bother wiping them, mortified with himself.

Mina feels her own throat tightening. *You didn't murder anyone,* she signs. *The bombs did.* The predecessors of the bombs Director Diebner so desperately wants them, the physicists, to build. How would she feel if the Luftwaffe dropped them on civilian cities? She'd want to slit her own throat, too, that's how.

I could have warned them. They would have been prepared. Siggy's face is etched with an agony of the soul.

But Mina only shakes her head, all cold logic when he needs it most. *You would have been delaying the inevitable. The war is lost to us, Siggy. The raids will only be coming more and more often, from all directions, until we surrender or they raze the entirety of Germany to the ground, whichever comes first.*

He knows it, deep inside, he does; Mina can see it in his tear-veiled eyes full of infinite torment, but one can't order one's heart what to feel. It is an independent compass. Sometimes it points where you least want it to, but one thing it can never do is lie. It hurts like a bastard, certainly, but, then again, truth always does. Only lies are smooth like honey-laced venom and just as easy to swallow.

You're in the radio corps, Siggy. You're only responsible for one city. What I work on, it can level the world itself. And it will be turned into a weapon. It's just a matter of time. And as someone who contributed to its research, no matter how peaceful, I shall forever carry that burden within myself, just like all of us who have anything to do with atom splitting, starting with Einstein and ending with the Leipzig reactor prototype welders. So, if we're in competition for the most loathed person on earth, I win.

He smiles at her tenderly and kisses her hands and then buries his face in her palms. They sit together, their silence a mutual understanding of the burden they bear, a shared hope that one day the world will know peace again. And in this quiet room in the heart of a Germany torn apart by war, the flickering flames cast a soft glow on two faces, etched with sorrow but clinging desperately to love.

THIRTY-TWO

LEIPZIG, GERMANY. SUMMER 1942

With the upcoming ministers' meeting hanging over his head like an executioner's ax, Dr. Heisenberg contemplates his L-IV with an unreadable expression. It's Mina's profound conviction that in other circumstances he would be excited to the extreme to test this newest invention that could bring the cleanest energy imaginable to his native land and beyond. He would pace the laboratory as Frau Döpel took his dictation and then, later at home, write letters to his colleagues all over the world and type out his ongoing study day by day until the experiment proves successful and celebrate with champagne he'd spray all over Döpel's and the mechanics' heads and then travel for lectures and conferences and share his prototype with his colleagues so that the world would become just a tad cleaner, just a tad brighter, just a tad more affordable for the poorest of regions...

But this is not "other circumstances." This is the Reich and his personal war, and he hates the thing as much as he loves it, and it tears him apart every single minute—Mina feels his suffering deep in her own bones. She, too, used to worship uranium. Now, she's grown to fear and loathe the very sight and smell of it.

"What do your calculations say?" he mouths. He always does when they're alone, now even more paranoid for fear of being listened to.

Mina checks her notebook and taps the numbers instead of a reply. For three weeks, they're safe. The chain reaction in the pile shall proceed as planned. But longer than that and it shall reach dangerous criticality and become unstable.

Dr. Heisenberg nods. He reached the same results with his formulas.

"So, we report progress to the ministers as we promised, get our pats on the back, keep our lads away from the front, and then leave the damned thing here and wait for an accident to happen. Diebner will lose his mind, no doubt, but an accident is an accident. We can't control physics we don't quite understand yet," he talks himself through plausible explanations, planting them hard into his own mind so that they come naturally to him when cornered. "And then we'll promise to work on our mistakes, build a new, improved prototype, and so on and so forth, until the war ends."

"Or until they put us all against the wall for wartime sabotage," Mina whispers ironically and wonders when she acquired such cynicism for life and, also, such disregard for it. No, the disregard, that's for herself only. The others, literal strangers she never met and whose languages she doesn't speak, are the ones she's thinking about. It's for them that Dr. Heisenberg is ruining his own creation he'd otherwise cherish like a child.

"You think they'll name a street after us some twenty years later?"

"And frame the bullet pockmarks?" Mina arches her brow.

"A statue would be nice, too." Gallows humor, but what else is left with one's neck in the noose?

"I wouldn't want one. I don't look good with pigeon drop-pings all over my face."

They share a companionable laugh and nod to each other before Mina goes to fetch Döpel and the mechanics to help them lower L-IV into the vat with water. Then, the countdown shall begin. What comes after, only the devil knows, and some-how, with some suicidal bravery, that suits them just fine.

Berlin, three weeks later

Strolling through the suburb unofficially baptized as the German Oxford has always brought up bittersweet emotions in Mina. Designed and built as a testament to German enlighten-ment, it is another world in itself. Here, even the air is different, or perhaps it just seems so to Mina, but each time she inhales a lungful, she almost tastes limestone, old libraries, carved wood polished with citrus and oil paintings of dignified men, most of them bespectacled and stern, all mixed into one intoxicating infusion. How blessed she would have been to be a part of it in some other life, in some parallel universe, in some science-fiction novel yet to be written. To contribute her own drop to the well of the world's knowledge, to walk the same halls as those men in oil paintings walked and be proud to be a carrier of their torch. Only in place of old crests, Nazi banners now hang above the German Oxford's buildings' entrances, and instead of dignified men, Hitler stares the visitors down, reminding them who the science now works for.

Dr. Heisenberg offers to drive her from the Institute to the Harnack Haus—yet another institution coincidentally named after Max Planck—but today, she needs air. Needs to take it all in before diving off the deep end, possibly to never resurface. A lab coat over her navy dress, Mina sets off through the familiar paths with her hands shoved deep in her pockets. No paper-work for her to carry. She's meant to be a spectator at today's ministers' meeting, invisible and mute and without official opinion.

Von Weizsäcker has high hopes for the meeting. According to him (or, to be more precise, according to gossip he picked up from his father), new Minister of Armaments and War Production, Speer, is an architect and has only been appointed to the position because of Hitler's misplaced fatherly feelings. It was all after Speer built a plaster mock-up of the new Berlin and gifted it to the Führer. The old man got lost in the maze of miniature museums, parade grounds, stadiums, and a grandiose new Reich Chancellery. And then he lost the last of his marbles and appointed the architect to a post for which he isn't qualified in the slightest, and good for them, von Weizsäcker winked. Since Speer knows nothing of physics, he'll just have to listen to what Dr. Heisenberg tells him.

Replaying the conversation that took place earlier that morning at the Institute, Mina wants to be just as hopeful, but can't help but have doubts instead. Von Weizsäcker, he's a golden child, born with a silver spoon in his mouth and raised on a sweet concoction of everyone's adoration. Mina, she's like that ugly duckling who's been pecked at too much. Where von Weizsäcker sees light, she notices shades first and foremost. He's an idealist and Mina's thinking is as critical as can be, but maybe that's the whole reason why Dr. Heisenberg entrusted her with his Leipzig experiments. Accidentally, out of the goodness of his heart and the best intentions, von Weizsäcker would just go and make it work and then it would be all over for them and the entire world. Instead, Mina is Dr. Heisenberg's personal Cassandra, terrifying him with her apocalyptic visions of the future and digging into old and half-abandoned research just to pull out more skeletons from uranium's closet to ensure that the physicist remembers what he's dealing with.

Just as she's mulling all this over, a hand touches her shoulder. The gesture is as light as can be, purposely not meant to startle, but it does all the same. Mina jumps as she comes to an abrupt halt and stares into the face of the man she was just thinking about.

Out of breath and with his suit jacket flung over his shoulder, Dr. Heisenberg offers her a brisk apologetic smile and shoves a thick stack of papers in a leather briefcase under his arm. "Frightened you? I'm sorry."

He must have run out of the lab to catch up with her, it occurs to Mina just then. "No, it's all right." Mina searches the road running parallel to the path she was walking. "Where's your car?"

Dr. Heisenberg waves in the direction from which he came uncommittedly. "Decided to take a stroll too."

"Much too hot for a stroll."

"It'll be even hotter inside the conference hall."

Mina doesn't argue. It likely will be, when the military brass begins to fry them over the promised miracle weapon.

They walk for some time in companionable silence until Dr. Heisenberg says something Mina doesn't quite catch.

"I said, the crickets are going positively mad today," he articulates with yet another apologetic, wistful smile.

Mina nods. She still remembers what crickets sound like in summer, the air vibrating with their sometimes-deafening chirping. Deafening and yet able to lull one to sleep at the same time, particularly when one lies on grass soaked with sun, and even more particularly, when an ivy tree whispers softly over one's head, its low-hanging branches caressing one's skin like feathers. Mina isn't sure where such a distinct memory came from, but she remembers the feeling painfully well and in sharp detail despite the fact that she was a mere child when it imprinted itself into her impressionable young mind.

"What else do you hear?" she asks Dr. Heisenberg, suddenly hungry for sounds she's long grown used to living without.

He cocks his head, likely wondering where to begin.

"Birds."

"Which ones?"

"Swallows," he clarifies and motions to one of the two-story buildings which houses some department having to do with botany. The swallows must nest under the orangery's roof, attracted by the closeness of greenery of all shapes and sizes. "Also, those little black ones with yellow beaks. Don't hide that mocking smile, I see it perfectly well. Birds are not my specialty."

"I wasn't smiling. I don't know what those yellow-beaked ones are called either."

"Yes, you do. You're just taking pity on an old man and are too well-bred to humiliate me. That's the Austrian graciousness in you. You lot drink it with your mother's milk."

"You're not even forty. In what world are you old?"

"When I was your age, anyone twenty years my senior seemed old to me."

"Yes, well, I didn't have much experience with children my age, so my mind is also forty. Or even sixty, after everything the past few years have put me through."

He suddenly stops and regards Mina with an odd expression, his hand shielding his face from the sun.

"We failed you." Mina watches his lips utter after a long pause. "We, the old guard, failed you, the young generation. Instead of a normal childhood, we gave you post-war inflation, market crashes, starvation, and bad lungs. Instead of a normal adulthood, we gave you more ration tickets, more shortages, and a war more devastating than the last, from which so many of you won't return."

"You still can do this one thing for us," Mina says, pulling a weed out of the earth and inhaling its rich scent with her eyes closed. When she opens them, they are dark gray and stormy. "Life is so very beautiful. All of it—the crickets, the swallows, blind moles under our feet. Don't destroy it, please. Sometimes, progress is the worst enemy of natural order. Let's stop here, while we still can."

Dr. Heisenberg is solemn as a grave when he offers Mina his free hand. "Of that, my dear Wilhelmina, you may be sure. For as long as I'm alive, I'll fight against the uranium bomb. I give you my word. I can't speak of others working on it, but that blood shall never be on my hands. That much I can promise you."

With a new resolve in his step, he resumes his walk toward Harnack Haus, Mina in tow. With the same steely determination, he enters the conference hall, where most of the dignitaries have already gathered, and takes a place among his colleagues, leaving the seat next to him for his loyal companion. Apart, they're frightened and unsure, but banded together, they feed off each other's strength and, all at once, they're a united organism with one mind and one goal—survival. Not theirs, but that of the entire homo sapiens species. They close ranks and prepare for war. Next to Mina, von Weizsäcker reaches for her hand and squeezes it in a sudden rush of emotion—a bittersweet childish gesture that she returns. And somewhere in the back of her mind, Siggy's voice: *Don't fret, Einstein. It'll all work out in the end.*

The shadow of Cologne hangs heavy over their heads. Almost every minister begins his speech with a request for a minute of silence for the innocent victims' memory. Though their outrage is artificial somehow. Mina watches them shake their fists like amateur actors in a badly directed play. They bemoan the poor children burned alive in the hellish fire inflicted by the RAF, but all Mina can think of is all the children they agreed to euthanize in their own hospitals, back in the peaceful times, just to keep the genetic pool clean and unmarred by anyone born with the slightest handicap. They cry for the historic cathedrals reduced to ash, and at the same time praise the new long-range rockets that have successfully hit their targets in London. They blame the Americans for meddling in a war they have no business to be in, and at the same time calling for weapons to be built that could rain their vengeance down on the blasted States from far across the ocean.

It's not revenge or peace that they're after. It's more blood-shed, on their own soil and on the soil of the others, until the whole world is engulfed in a hellish fire and the only things that survive are tiny one-cell organisms from prehistoric times.

At last, Dr. Heisenberg is invited to the podium. He takes his stand with a calm assurance about him and nods slightly at his tiny brigade. The sheen of sweat is gone from his forehead. Now is the decisive moment and he's no longer afraid. His eyes, like those of a condemned man finally on a scaffold, are bright and clear. No matter the outcome, it shall be over soon.

He begins on the progress of the peaceful atom and its research over the years, but that's not what the ministers are after. History is of no interest to them. Their unspoken leader, Minister Speer, raises his hand with a pen in it and asks something Mina can't hear. Out of the entire warmongering bunch, he's been the quietest one so far, listening closely and taking notes, his expression contemplative and reserved. He doesn't belong here, it occurs to Mina just then. Much too young, much too wrong for the part, he has the dreamy look of a typical artist about him, in contrast with the severe martinets surrounding him. Most of them are in uniforms; he's in mufti and out of place, and yet, it's his question that momentarily darkens Dr. Heisenberg's countenance.

"I'm afraid, you ought to ask the *Abwehr* that, Herr Minis-ter," Dr. Heisenberg says with a polite incline of his head. "We did see the reports of the Americans working on the uranium bomb as well, but if you would ask for my personal opinion, I consider it a simple provocation."

Speer asks something else and Dr. Heisenberg chews on the answer for a few moments. With so many eyes on him and the Gestapo certainly present in the room disguised as some of the aides, he knows to choose his words carefully.

"I'm not dismissing it completely, Herr Minister. I'm only saying that they would need to throw their entire country's production at the project if they wish to create a working bomb in the nearest future, but even in the highly unlikely case that they do, it would still take them years to build it."

He listens to yet another question, pauses once again.

"I'd say, three to five years. And that's if they put every factory, every plant at the project's disposal, which no country at war and in its right mind will ever do."

Mina shifts in her chair, von Weizsäcker's palm growing wetter by the moment in hers. This is precisely what comes from someone naively not giving someone credit. Speer may be an architect, but he's a highly intelligent one. He's asking the questions Mina feared he'd ask. His lead is invisible and gentle; he's nudging Dr. Heisenberg to the dilemma the latter refused to consider. *What if the enemy develops the bomb before us? What if they do to the rest of Germany what they did to Cologne? What if producing a bomb would act as a deterrent and give Germany the protection it needs? Purely as a defense measure, of course. Speer himself would never condone the use of a uranium bomb on a peaceful population. But surely Dr. Heisenberg sees the benefit of having such a bomb in the Reich's arsenal?*

Dr. Heisenberg nods with a concerned look about him and passionately agrees with everything Minister Speer is saying. *Yes, it would certainly be beneficial. Yes, it would serve as a good deterrent. Yes, the bomb itself won't be all that big, just the size of a pineapple for somewhere like London. Purely hypothetically speaking, of course.*

Of course.

Silence hangs over the room, sticky and hot like tar. Mina feels it coating her throat; it's suddenly difficult to breathe. It's a staring game now between Minister Speer and Dr. Heisenberg. Whoever blinks first, loses.

Mina claws into von Weizsäcker's hand but doesn't notice. Neither does he, even when her nails dig deep into his skin.

"Say, you have unlimited resources," von Weizsäcker mouths to Mina, just as he previously did with Speer's other questions, her personal ventriloquist through which the Minister is speaking. "All the money and materials you need for research. How long will it take in this instance to produce a bomb of that size? According to Director Diebner's report, we may have it by winter."

Dr. Heisenberg is all smiles and apologies. "I'm afraid the report misrepresented slightly what I have said. To produce an atom bomb, we'll need either pure uranium fuel or a fuel produced from uranium's byproduct, the element my colleague von Weizsäcker discovered. We called it Eka Re. Americans call it plutonium. Now, plutonium can only be produced in any significant quantities during the uranium fission process. As of now, my assistants Döpel and Best are testing our latest reactor prototype. For three weeks," he says and checks his wristwatch, "and a few hours, it's been fissioning and producing plutonium, which we shall extract and use in further experiments. I promised Director Diebner enough plutonium fuel for testing by winter and that's if everything goes to plan. I wish we could do it faster, but faster is not always safer, particularly when you don't know what you're dealing with. And we're dealing with something truly unprecedented here. I just want you to understand that."

In his seat, Director Diebner is quietly seething, but, as Mina shifts her gaze from him to Minister Speer, he doesn't appear crestfallen, unlike the rest of his colleagues. Siggy's been

hinting at it for some time, but until now it hasn't really regis-
tered with Mina, the fact that the war isn't going all that well.
True, Germany occupies almost the entire continent now, but,
judging by the military brass' tense expressions, its powers are
stretched thin. The Luftwaffe isn't building enough planes to
compete with the RAF, the war has been seeping into German
territory and, without an atom bomb, it shall be lost sooner or
later. And that's why Minister Speer is suddenly turning in his
seat and then rises altogether, offering the theoreticians gathered at the back a smile of extraordinary charm.

"I've been warned that your leader is an extremely modest
fellow, but I didn't believe it," Speer says and follows it up with
a friendly chuckle. "I had a friend like that, back in my university days. He'd go starving for days between paydays—it was the
twenties, you see—but wouldn't take a single Pfennig from me.
Dr. Heisenberg reminds me of that dear friend of mine. Such
morals and principles are a rarity to find."

There's an ominous undertone to those last words he utters.
Mina feels it weighing heavy on her shoulders as soon the words
leave his lips.

"So, I want you to tell me exactly how much money, what
equipment, and materials you need to build this one little
pineapple-sized bomb."

Von Weizsäcker jumps from his seat and blurts something
out, causing a crease of confusion to mar Minister Speer's high
forehead.

"Ten thousand Reichsmarks?" Mina sees him repeat the
number von Weizsäcker must have offered without thinking. In
her seat, Mina closes her eyes briefly as if to spare herself the
embarrassment. Fortunately, she can't hear a few ministers
chuckle at the miniscule sum, but she's convinced that that's
precisely their reaction. In his desire to take the heat off Dr.
Heisenberg, von Weizsäcker said something so idiotic, no one
will ever take their arguments seriously now.

Mina's supposed to be mute and invisible, and yet, her legs force her up in spite of herself. Wiping her palms on the skirt of her dress, she clears her throat and offers Speer her name and title.

"I apologize for my colleague, Herr Minister. He doesn't deal with financing much and still has pre-war prices on his mind." A few smiling faces around her. From his podium, Dr. Heisenberg is staring at her without blinking. "Our department shall need around forty thousand Reichsmarks and that's to fund research until the end of this year."

Speer nods, looking suddenly relieved, and marks the number down in his notebook.

"We'll also need a working reactor, and I think it's safe to say that we may have one as, unlike its predecessors, it's been working without any incidents for almost a month now."

Another nod from Speer. He motions for her to *continue, please*, looking livelier by the moment.

"Dr. Heisenberg and I have every confidence in a positive outcome. However, L-IV—our current prototype—is very small and produces only a miniscule amount of plutonium. For a working reactor that produces the amount of plutonium needed for a single bomb, we would have to build a nuclear plant with a reactor thousands of times bigger than the one we have now, which would require tons of concrete, steel, aluminum, not taking into consideration all the uranium ore in the Reich and occupied territories and all the heavy water that can be produced at the Norway plant. Then you can have your bomb. In '45—46, I'd say. That's the numbers I gave Director Diebner for his report you're holding in your hands now. Unless that information has been redacted for brevity reasons. As I told you, I'm the department's mathematician. Even my colleagues find my constant calculations insufferable, let alone Herr Director."

Half-turned in his chair, the look Diebner gives her is positively homicidal. Mina can see his jaw tense as he grinds his teeth in helpless fury.

"So, no bomb then in the foreseeable future?" Speer concludes and turns to Dr. Heisenberg for confirmation.

The latter spreads his arms in an apologetic gesture and smiles like a condemned man suddenly pardoned.

When he takes his seat next to Mina, she can feel his entire body quivering with nerves and immense, all-encompassing relief.

No bomb, they let out a collective breath.

No bomb, blood pulses deep in Mina's temples.

No bomb.

No bomb...

THIRTY-THREE

The road to Leipzig is uncharacteristically quiet. In their train compartment, Mina and Dr. Heisenberg refuse the tea and melt into the horsehair upholstery, their limbs are both weightless and impossible to move. It's still light out despite the late hour, and instead of staring at the blackout drapes, Mina gazes out into the fields creeping by and drinks it all in—golden blades of wheat, cows herded home by a bearded shepherd, the edge of the woods looming in the distance, fiery red in the rays of the setting sun.

How perfect everything is, when painted by nature's hand. How splendidly in place everything is and in harmony with itself and achingly precious.

Life.

It's even harder to return to the laboratory after passing through its magical domain. Nearly impossible to enter the room that reeks of metal and chemicals to check on the hateful thing and see it very much alive and breathing, sitting in the vat of water as if nothing is the matter.

Next to Mina, Dr. Heisenberg doubtfully checks his watch.

"I don't know how long it'll take it to reach criticality," Mina whispers a response to his unspoken question.

They are alone here, in the entire building, not counting the guard on duty downstairs and a janitor waxing the bannisters on the staircase. The business can still be bugged for all they know. And so, they read lips and whisper.

"Let's hope it's tonight, when no one is here," Dr. Heisenberg says, backing away from the vat and refusing to turn his back on the L-IV as if out of superstition before some ancient, unpredictable deity.

Mina nods and also retreats in the same manner, without quite realizing it.

But when they return the following morning, the building is still very much standing and so is the lab and so is Döpel, and he isn't running about screaming for help but calmly reports that the L-IV is doing wonderfully as always. Dr. Heisenberg regards him with mistrust and goes to check for himself. As does Mina and, undoubtedly, the reactor prototype sits gleefully and defiantly in its little pool, cooler than the icebox in the Heisenbergs' home.

In front of Döpel, Heisenberg says nothing. Just looks at Mina, and Mina looks at him, but there's nothing doing.

"I have a seminar scheduled," Dr. Heisenberg says after a while. "I suppose I'd better get to it."

Döpel, the reactor's loyal guardian, pulls a chair and waves the physicist off. "You go ahead, Herr Professor. I have it all under control."

Seeing Dr. Heisenberg's hesitation, Mina follows him out the door and into the hallway, once again busy with life. "I'll stay in the room with him, watch the thing," Mina tells him reassuringly. "If anything goes wrong, I'll pull him out and run for you at once."

Dr. Heisenberg still looks mighty uncomfortable with the entire setup but walks away eventually. Before he disappears around the corner, he throws a last glance over his shoulder. In his eyes, there is a tale of a thousand worries.

Mina is back in the laboratory, but there isn't much for her to do, other than check on L-IV every now and then, rather to Döpel's annoyance. He tolerates her circling around the vat until lunch, but then, after taking a bite of a sandwich his wife must have lovingly packed for him, he pushes the waxed paper smelling appetizingly of smoked meat and pickles away and pushes a second chair from under the desk with his foot.

"Will you sit down already? You're making me dizzy, stalking about in circles like a broken record." Sensing Mina's reluctance, he assumes an expression of exaggerated benevolence and holds his right hand up for her. "If you promise to sit still, I'll let you study the scars on my hand."

Mina thinks of making a comment about his unorthodox trading techniques, but, as she finds herself closer to the desk, bites it down and keeps it shut between her teeth. After being driven to distraction by Mina's constant examinations almost a year ago, he has all but outright prohibited ever mentioning the damned hand again. It's unlikely she'll ever get another chance to interrogate him about it, so she decides to take advantage of this one.

Reluctantly leaving the vat behind her back, Mina takes the offered chair and takes Döpel's hand in hers. It has healed nicely, and little remains of the first marks of the terrible injury. In place of angry, red, bursting flesh, there are a few pale pink scars, virtually undiscernible from those that burn victims bear.

"Does it still give you trouble?" Mina asks after studying it closely.

Döpel's quiet for a moment, as if deciding whether to tell Mina the truth or just get her off his back. He must have decided on the first as his face loses that devil-may-care grin and assumes a sober expression.

"It hurts sometimes. Random times. I tried writing down

the occasions, weather, what I ate the day before, if I traveled, if I was at work or home that day, but I still can't arrive at any conclusion. Sometimes it just aches." He flexes and unflexes his fist, stretching the pink glistening skin over his knuckles. "It doesn't limit my abilities in the slightest, so I suppose it's a small price to pay in the name of science."

Mina grins together with him. "How's your general health?"

"Perfect. We have just had our yearly physical here at the institute and I'm glad to report I'm healthy as an ox."

"That's very good."

Döpel picks up his sandwich and resumes his munching, all the while eyeing Mina over its mustard-covered top. "I'm still puzzled as to why you were so concerned about it back then," he says after swallowing a mouthful. "Yes, yes, I remember you citing those studies on radiation disease, or whatever the hell it's called, but..." He cocks his head, regarding her like a child. "Come now, you don't really believe it, do you?"

"What? The fact that radiation travels through human tissues? Ever heard of X-rays?" Mina arches her brow.

But Döpel only waves her sarcasm off. "Certainly it travels through tissue, I'm not arguing that, but as far as causing an actual disease?"

"Surgeons at the end of the past century didn't believe that they had bacteria on their hands either, and shunned their colleague who suggested they wash and sterilize their hands. Lots of people died before they finally put two and two together. The trouble is, no one believes something that challenges their previous worldview. Just think of all the fury that descended on Einstein's head as soon as he published his theory of relativity. And now look at us, applying it in experiments a mere twenty years later."

"The same Einstein declared that releasing energy from splitting atoms wouldn't be possible in his lifetime, and now look at us," he says, using Mina's own words, "splitting atoms in this very room while having this pleasant conversation. Even great men make mistakes, Mina."

"I sincerely hope I'm mistaken here too but until uranium's and its by-products' safety is proven by science, I'll stay as far away from it as possible."

"Then stay away from it." He laughs at her good-naturedly. "Go take a walk, soak up some sun. The weather is marvelous today."

Mina steals a glance at the door but decides against it. "No, it's all right. I'll fetch a book from the library, if you don't mind. Read a little, but here."

"I don't mind in the slightest. Better than standing watch over some idiotic water vat."

Mina still checks the water one last time before hurrying to the library and back. She needn't rush—the water is still as glass, as though L-IV hasn't been informed of any possible criticality it's supposed to reach. Wondering if her calculations were wrong (but then Dr. Heisenberg's have to be wrong too as he arrived at the same conclusion), Mina counts and recounts everything twice in her head, but the results are stubbornly the same.

With a lock of hair in her hand which she keeps twisting and untwisting around her index finger, Mina scans the same page for a hundredth time, the meaning of the words escaping her. On the opposite wall, the clock's hands drag toward the evening, slow and heavy like molasses. In the pit of Mina's stomach, fatigue replaces anxiety. The past few days have taken their toll. She yawns into a closed fist and steals more glances at the clock rather than the vat. It'll strike two soon. And in four hours the watch shall be over and they can all go home and leave L-IV to its devices—

Mina looks up with a start. Döpel is suddenly on his feet, staring back at her with rapt attention.

"What is it?" Mina asks, blinking away the drowsiness.

"What's that noise?" Döpel asks, listening closely to something.

"I'd love to help you identify it or even find its source if I wasn't deaf," Mina reminds him with a smile, but that smile drops at once as soon as she sees him rush toward the vat.

The book tumbling down off her lap, she hurries after Döpel but comes to an abrupt halt at the edge of the vat. From its depths, strings of bubbles are rushing toward the surface, small at first, just like in a pot that was placed on a stove not that long ago.

"Thermal reaction," Mina blurts out, catching Döpel's lips mutter the same thing at the exact same time.

Leaving Mina on watch, Döpel crosses the room in a few lunging steps and returns with a test tube.

"Let's see what we're dealing with here," he mutters under Mina's watchful gaze. "Here, take the matches and light the splint for me while I catch a few bubbles of this unidentified fellow."

"Oxygen?" she suggests. "Like last time?"

With utmost care, Döpel takes a burning splint from her hands and holds it to the tube's opening.

"Hear that?" he asks, triumphantly pulling out the splint.

"Döpel." Mina regards him with reproach.

He slaps his forehead with the hand still holding the splint and laughs. "Forgive the idiot, I'm too excited to think straight. There was a pop. It's hydrogen."

"Hydrogen?" Mina repeats, now completely at a loss. "Wherever did that come from?"

"I haven't the faintest idea and don't want to find out. Go get Paschen. He's the mechanic on duty today. Let's get this thing out of the water first and call Dr. Heisenberg second, so he can decide what to do."

After throwing a concerned glance at the tank but seeing that the bubbles haven't changed in size, Mina hurries to fetch a mechanic. Fortunately for her, Paschen is in his cubicle, digging into the receiver of a black phone he has taken apart. He drops it at once as soon as he hears that Döpel needs help with L-IV and runs back so fast, Mina has trouble keeping up with him.

Once in the lab, he immediately rushes to Döpel's aid and the two hoist the aluminum sphere out of the vat.

"It's warm." Mina sees Paschen remark.

At the same time, Döpel waves at her. "Get Heisenberg!" he yells, but Mina only tosses her head.

Neither Döpel nor Paschen have the faintest clue about their conspiracy. They're an innocent party in all this, people who don't deserve to suffer in case something goes terribly wrong. Neither Mina nor Dr. Heisenberg could predict exactly what would happen to L-IV. It's only fair for her to take responsibility for a decision Döpel had no part in.

"No. You two go," Mina tells him. "I'll stay here and watch."

Döpel thinks of protesting, but then sets off out of the lab and into the corridor toward the seminar room.

"Shall I unscrew the top?" Paschen asks, a wrench at the ready.

"No!" Mina holds up a warning hand. "Don't touch it. Not until Herr Professor is here at any rate."

Perhaps Heisenberg can deduce the mystery of hydrogen suddenly bubbling up all over the sphere. Until then, Mina will keep the mechanic well away from it. The event has no precedent in the entire history of humankind. Only God knows what's brewing inside that devil's kettle.

In no time, Döpel returns with Dr. Heisenberg in tow. The latter is pale but collected as he searches Mina's face for clues. Is this the criticality they had only vague notions about? And if it is, how to deal with it now?

"The sphere is warm," Mina reports. "Shall we open it?"

With a deep crease slashing through his forehead, Dr.

Heisenberg contemplates the sphere for a few seconds, probes its surface with his hand.

"Whatever the reaction is that's taking place inside, we should stop it," he says more to himself than the others.

"But then we'll let the oxygen inside." Mina's heart is suddenly beating erratically somewhere at the bottom of her throat. She tries to swallow and discovers that her mouth has gone completely dry.

"Yes, there's that."

"It can ignite," she continues.

"Do you have any other suggestion?" Dr. Heisenberg snaps, which is so out of character for him and particularly in relation to her, Mina, that it frightens her even more.

"Let it be?" Mina probes and throws a longing look at the door.

Let's all just leave. Lock the lab and let L-IV do whatever it wants as long as it's far away from us, her eyes plead.

Reading the message in them, Dr. Heisenberg steps aside with a gentle smile on his face. "You go, Mina. Go home, help Li make dinner. We'll handle the thing."

The offer is sweeter than honey; Mina can almost taste it, but instead of taking him up on it, she walks over to the corner and takes a fire extinguisher from its designated place. It's the same model the Luftwaffe is using for their aircraft fires and Dr. Heisenberg regards it dubiously.

"Are you quite sure you want to test that on burning uranium?"

"It's been put here for this very purpose," Mina argues.

"It's been put here to douse regular fires," Dr. Heisenberg counters.

"Should liquid chlorobromomethane even be used for dousing radioactive fires?" Döpel is just as suspicious of the bulky container in Mina's small hands as his superior.

Mina just shrugs with one shoulder. "There's one way to

find out, since we know for sure that water won't put it out. Go on then," she says softly to Paschen, aiming the muzzle at the L-IV. "Open it up."

The bolts on top of the sphere are screwed tight. It takes time for Paschen to undo them all. With every bolt undone, the physicists' poses grow more and more rigid. They stare at the sphere like ancient people must have stared at the first fire, fascinated and yet undoubtedly terrified. Beads of sweat gather on Mina's forehead. In her hands, the heavy extinguisher's shaking, but she keeps watch all the same. Paschen pauses before removing the last screw and so do the physicists. After an unbearably long moment, Dr. Heisenberg makes a gesture that is jerky and full of nerves and, given the green light, Paschen throws the lid off.

Here lies the difference between hearing people and those who walk through the world in silence. Upon hearing something unnatural and unimaginably dangerous, they collectively jump away from the sphere, their bodies reacting faster than they can process the danger logically. But Mina, she only feels the sudden change in the air, as if a great vacuum opens up in front of her, threatening to suck her straight into the maw of the beast, and then sees the flames shooting up out of the sphere with a ferocity rivaling only ancient volcanoes. Her face momentarily singed with the heatwave, she squeezes her eyes shot but clasps the extinguisher's trigger all the same, despite burning particles of uranium flying all around her, landing in her hair and on her clothes like some grotesque black snowfall from hell.

Before long, Dr. Heisenberg is beating hot ashes off her shoulders and head with his jacket.

Before long, Paschen hurls a bucket of water on top of the sphere to aid Mina's efforts.

Before long, Döpel is pumping the precious heavy water out of its compartment to save at least that.

And then comes silence. It smells of heated metal and, for some reason, ozone, just like before rain. Mina's face feels hot.

"You were right," Dr. Heisenberg says without any expression. The same shock they all experienced has wiped all other emotions from his face. "It ignited."

"I hate it when she's right, too," Döpel says with a smirk that refuses to look teasing and cheerful. Mina catches him steal a glance at his hand.

"Now what?" she asks, dropping the empty extinguisher to the floor.

"Now what?" Dr. Heisenberg repeats. He doesn't know what now. No one in the entire world does. "We ought to lower the temperature inside the chain-reacting pile. Let's screw the top back on, cut the supply of oxygen, and put it back into water to cool off."

Mina opens her mouth to remind him of the moderator, without which the reaction shall only grow more unpredictable, but then remembers why she's here, why both of them are here, why, while Hitler's in power, Germany can't possibly have a working reactor, as a reactor produces plutonium and plutonium is an atomic bomb material, and even if they step away from the project, the SS will just hurl other physicists to finish their job and then it's the end of them all. The end of the earth as they know it.

And so, Mina says nothing at all. Neither does Döpel, either because he trusts in Dr. Heisenberg's abilities too much to question his decisions, or because he's too protective of whatever heavy water he managed to salvage—Mina can't tell. She can only watch Paschen screw the top back on as tightly as possible, muscles on his forearms bulging like ropes until the final bolt refuses to turn a speck further. Like priests of the ages long gone, they gather in solemn silence and lower the sphere back into the water, all eight hands on its top as though on the altar of matter and thought.

At once, Dr. Heisenberg shoos the others away. Only Mina refuses to budge, remaining by the water tank, which is bubbling up once again. With a sense of apathetic curiosity, as though she has already ceased to exist, Mina watches the vat and catches herself thinking that she was right, that the reactor prototype was running away without a moderator to slow the particle division process. The water is heating up quicker than before. In mere moments, steam begins rising from the water's surface, which is outright boiling. Waves of heat begin to quiver over the sphere itself as if, inside, some wild beast is breathing and pushing against its confines, ready to be set free and devour everything in its path.

Dr. Heisenberg's hand clasps over Mina's wrist, pulling her away.

"Back," she sees his lips cry as he backs away from the tank, pulling her after himself. "Everyone out of this rattrap, now!"

They make another few steps and are just out the doors when the wave of heated air slams them in the backs and sends them scrambling on their hands and knees. Blood pulsing wildly in her ears, Mina looks around in a daze. The entire laboratory is engulfed in flames that creep as far as the ceiling and crawl over the walls, against all laws of nature. Black smoke pours out of the open door, but it's also luminous somehow, sparkling blue against the rays of sun seeping from the hallway window, which, Mina just notices, is without glass. Mesmerized and rooted to the floor, Mina would continue to stare at this new discovery had Dr. Heisenberg not pulled her to her feet and dragged her to the staircase, from which the few people left in the building are poking their heads.

Someone must have called the fire department, for the first firemen pass the physicists on their way in.

"Careful, there's burning uranium in there," Mina squeezes out of herself, but no one pays heed to her words.

Together with the rest of the evacuees, she sits on the grass in front of the university until the firemen emerge from the building. Their chief approaches Dr. Heisenberg and, looking him square in the eye, asks what in the blue hell he, the mad scientist, has been working on.

"Atom smashing," Dr. Heisenberg responds around the pipe Paschen shared with him.

"Congratulations, Herr Professor. You smashed it, all right. Together with your laboratory. And that witch's brew that you have in there, water does nothing to douse it. Neither does foam."

"That's uranium," Mina explains, feeling like a newborn colt on her unsteady, quivering legs.

"Uranium, plutonium," the fireman chief mocks. "Whatever you call it, it tore its container in two. I've never seen anything like it in my life. Is it a new weapon or some such, by any chance?"

"No," Dr. Heisenberg responds in unison with Mina, a bit faster than he should have. "Just an accident. A terrible accident, that's all. It was not meant to act in such a manner."

"Back to the drawing board for us it is," Mina adds, trying to look as bright as possible but barely holding herself together.

By the time they reach the Heisenbergs' home, Mina's skin is crawling with something invisible and vaguely frightening. She notices Dr. Heisenberg scratch under his collar and pull at his sleeve just as he extracts a key from his pocket.

"You have a rear entrance, the one we can access from the kitchen."

"Yes?" Dr. Heisenberg regards her in confusion, exaggerated even further by his exhaustion.

Neither of them has any strength to think, but something deep inside Mina's subconscious urges her to act upon it.

"Let's remove our footwear there and leave it outside. And

then go straight to the bathroom and take a thorough shower. And all the clothes that we have on now, let's just get rid of them. Pile them up and throw them away. And then wash our hands again."

She's expecting him to break into a grin and make a joke about her uranium paranoia, but Dr. Heisenberg is feeling something too, on his very skin.

"Yes," he agrees after a pause. "Let's do just that."

Mina sleeps late the following morning. There is no lab for them to go to and Dr. Heisenberg lets her rest. By the time she wakes, the sun is standing high in the sky and the events of the previous day have washed away like a nightmare that is already losing its color.

Mina stretches, feeling both lazy and refreshed, and remains in bed for a few more delicious minutes. But something keeps nagging at her, tainting the azure beauty of this summer morning. Annoyed with herself, she throws off the blanket and begins inspecting herself, every toe and elbow bend, every patch of skin and strand of hair. To her great relief, there are no marks on her whatsoever, despite a couple of hematomas on her knees, on which she landed so harshly. But, besides that, she is fine, just fine, just like Döpel said yesterday.

Something else twitches inside at the memory of the name. With a feeling of growing unease, Mina heads to the desk where all of her study materials and equipment are stacked and reaches for the Geiger counter. Her hand trembles ever so slightly as she tests it against the control and then, as slowly as possible, directs it toward herself.

It's all right on her exposed skin, just a twitch that is barely there; however, as soon as the wand reaches her hair, the needle jumps and leans to the right as if forced by an invisible hand. But there's nothing invisible in science and the hand that forces the needle is called radiation and Mina's hair is full of it. Without another second wasted, she drops the counter and runs into the bathroom. There, she grabs a pair of scissors and begins cutting thick strand after strand, mutilating the braided crown she's been proudly wearing for years without cutting until all that is left of it resembles a *Hitlerjugend* boy's cut, and a sorry one at that.

When she emerges in the Heisenbergs' dining room and utters her good morning to the family, there's a moment of stunned silence.

Elisabeth Heisenberg is the first to recover herself. Her smile is pale and slightly forced, but just for the effort, Mina is grateful.

"I used to cut my hair this way back in the late twenties," she manages to utter. "My mother was so mad at me, I remember, but I loved it! It looks wonderful on you."

Dr. Heisenberg doesn't comment on what he perfectly understands. From the kitchen's window, right after breakfast as she dries the dishes Elisabeth washed, Mina catches him waving the Geiger counter over the clothes he left in a heap in the garden. Whatever the result is, he uses a stick to pick up the items one by one before piling them into a sack he dragged from the shed. Using the same stick, he hoists the sack into the boot of his car and drives off.

When he returns, they don't discuss the matter.

THIRTY-FOUR

BERLIN, GERMANY. JUNE 1942

Mina opens the door to her apartment with her key and drops it with a start. Seated at the table, in the same precise chair as he occupied at their first meeting, Hauptmann Taube greets her with morose silence. For some time, they study each other, waiting for the other to look away, to break the silence first. But far too many things have changed since that very first fateful meeting. The dynamics of their relationship have shifted. Instead of a frightened young girl, someone quite different faces Taube now. The experiences of the past two years have hardened Mina like plaster, turned her nerves to steel and her gaze into granite. She has already looked death in the eye. For her, there is nothing else to fear.

Taube must sense it too. He assesses her a moment longer— "New haircut?"—and rises to his feet with a look of resignation about him. "Let's go for a walk."

Mina would like to drop on her bed, face buried in the pillow, and sleep for forty hours straight, but Taube's already reaching for the handle of her suitcase. She lets him stash it by the coat rack and pick up the key, wondering why there is a need for it at all if the *Abwehr* and, likely, the SS too, can come and go as they please. A gesture of goodwill, an illusion of freedom for a prisoner who is theirs to do with as they please.

Taube's quiet the entire way to the Grünewald. He's just as quiet well into its emerald expanse, only his hands clasped behind his back betray his tension. Mina follows him as he picks his way into the woods away from the villas and paved roads and only stops when he finally pauses and faces her. This time, his impassive mask is replaced by fire and torrents of fury.

"Now you've done it. You've truly gone and done it."

Mina sighs, finding herself oddly detached from this entire scene, from her own body. "What exactly have I gone and done?"

"Don't play coy with me, Fräulein Best!" On Taube's temple, a blue vein is bulging. "You know perfectly well what I'm talking about. Your and Heisenberg's latest act of sabotage and the boldest one yet." His face suddenly drops, anger replaced by agony. "You've already had it your way. You've persuaded the Minister of Armaments himself that a bomb is impossible. Why did you have to go and blow up the entire business? You almost leveled the entire university. By sheer luck, there weren't any victims. And that stuff that was inside the sphere? It's still boiling, days after the explosion. I've seen it with my own two eyes when I was sent to Leipzig on investigation. What devilish brew have you two concocted there?"

"Reactor fuel," Mina answers plainly. "Uranium and its by-products."

Taube stares at her as he tries to get his breathing under control. "Do you understand what I just said?"

"That it's still boiling? Yes, Dr. Heisenberg figured it won't be put out by ordinary means. Because it's not an ordinary fire. Water or foam won't smother it. The reaction will just have to run its course until there's nothing else in there to fission."

Taube makes a gesture with his hands, exasperated. "I'm not talking about the damned fuel! I said, I was sent there on investigation. *Investigation*," he articulates as if trying to get through to a child. "Into you. And Heisenberg. And his little group of geniuses. And that radio fellow of yours who has been decoding things that got us in trouble instead of the Allies."

Mina has been waiting for this conversation for years. She's had nightmares about it, woken up in a cold sweat and replayed it again and again in her mind, both at work and on her days off, preparing herself for the inevitable. And yet, now that it's come, she discovers that she feels nothing at all, not a twinge of fear for her own fate.

"It was an accident," she says with calm conviction. "An experiment gone awry."

Taube's look is brimming with reproach. "Don't insult me with lies, Fräulein Best. We've always been frank with each other."

"Yes, we have. I thought you were on our side."

"*Our.*" He shakes his head and chuckles to some thoughts of his. "Our who? Red Orchestra? The White Rose?"

Mina's brows draw together at the mention of unfamiliar names.

Taube only waves his hand dismissively. "That's the entire trouble. Resistance and espionage groups are sprouting up all around like mushrooms after rain. Last month, they tried to blow up a Soviet Paradise exhibit here in Berlin. This month, we find these plastered all over the city."

Mina takes a small rectangular sticker Taube has extracted from his pocket. In red letters over light brown paper, it reads, "*Permanent Exhibition: the Nazi Paradise. War, Hunger, Lies, Gestapo. How much longer?*"

"We have nothing to do with these," she says, returning the sticker. "I haven't even seen them around for that matter."

"The Gestapo scrubbed most of them off before the general population could make an issue out of it."

"I haven't heard anything about any orchestras either. Or roses, for that matter."

Taube gazes somewhere over her shoulder as he taps his cigarette pack for a smoke to pop out. "I know you haven't. They have nothing to do with you. I know that, but the Gestapo, they lump it all into one. A traitor is a traitor, no matter the group they belong to. You may not print any leaflets and call for resistance, but if they find out that you're sabotaging the very chance of Germany winning the war, they won't treat you like those leaflet printers. There will be no hanging for you. That's reserved for ordinary criminals. No, Mina; they'll skin you alive for what you're doing."

Mina's only answer is a noncommitted one-shoulder shrug.

"Do you just not care?" Taube asks her in frank disbelief.

"Do you just not see?" Mina asks him instead and bursts out laughing as she points at her shorn head. "I haven't chopped my hair off as a fashion statement, you know. It was irradiated and nothing—and I mean *nothing*—could wash it off. I'm glad they sent you there. I'm glad you saw reactor fuel for yourself. I'm glad you realized that nothing can put it out. Now you know that I wasn't lying or making some alarmist statements when I was saying that if a bomb is made out of uranium or its by-products, it shall not only create fire that shall burn for days, the rays from the blast will spread much further than the impact zone. They will get into people's hair, clothes, skin, and gradually destroy their tissues like radium tonic destroyed that poor American's jaw and throat. Affected tissue will rot and decompose while those people are still breathing. And you wish to put such a weapon into the hands of the country who has the Gestapo for a guard dog?"

Taube shakes his head, his smile as bitter as the smoke he exhales. "No, Mina. I don't. That's the only reason why you're still free and breathing. I just wish you were a tad more subtle about it."

"We had to destroy the reactor, Herr Hauptmann. If what you're saying is true and they indeed suspect us of sabotage, they would come for us sooner or later and, if the reactor was in working order, they would have put someone else in charge of the project and finished what we refused to and then it would be all over for everyone. Now, after they saw what a runaway reactor is capable of, most experimenters will refuse to have anything to do with it until Dr. Heisenberg invents something safer. L-IV had to be a failure and a spectacular one. We risked our own lives to see to it."

"So you did. But now the Gestapo are breathing down my neck about you."

"The theoreticians?"

"No, Mina. You in particular. Dr. Heisenberg's family is here in Germany. It's easy to keep tabs on him. Von Weizsäcker's father is Minister von Ribbentrop's good friend and von Ribbentrop can always vouch for him. Hahn, Strassmann, and the others? All small fry."

"So am I."

"So it would seem, if only Heisenberg hadn't assigned you to his Leipzig project instead of anyone else. Or if your parents hadn't mysteriously disappeared in Switzerland. Or if you weren't keeping company with a former fellow student whose own father has reported him for subversive statements."

For the first time since the beginning of their conversation, Mina's blood runs cold. Herself, she doesn't give a hoot about, but Siggy, he's a different matter entirely. *And his father, that Nazi pig!* With chilling, calculated hatred, Mina presses her jaws together. *Should rub him face first in that reactor fuel and watch his skin melt off his bones like he deserves—*

With a toss of her head, Mina chases away the terrifying image and the very fact that her mind could produce something so violent.

"He's not arrested, is he?" She's barely breathing.

Taube shakes his head. "Almost no one is arrested the instant they are reported. People are watched first. Followed in some cases. Their apartments and phones are bugged. A circle of acquaintances established. Mail monitored."

Mina nods knowingly. "Why catch one fish if you can catch a whole school?"

"Something of that sort."

"So, you're just watching him now?"

"Us and the Gestapo. And I believe I needn't mention that it's the Gestapo you ought to worry about. Now, we have always enjoyed each other's honesty and now, I need it more than ever from you. Tell me frankly: has he been involved in anything treasonous? Either with you and Heisenberg or on his own? I know you're involved with each other and he must have been telling you things."

Taube's the same as on the day Mina first met him. The same eyes forever tainted with pain, the same proud bearing of a career officer from the bloodline of warriors, just like Mina's grandfather was. Mina wants to trust him like she always has, wants to see a friend among an army of enemies, but this entire country is warped beyond recognition, and if fathers report their sons, who can be trusted?

As if reading her thoughts, Taube nods and shifts from one foot to another, betraying his impatience.

Impatience to extract a confession or to help while he still can? Once again, Mina's mind is a battlefield.

"In other circumstances, I would commend your silence and desire to protect. But, Mina, I need an answer and I need it now. Has Siegfried Mann been involved in anything that can be traced and used as evidence against him?"

Mina is still obstinately silent and Taube exhales sharply.

"I'm asking because I need to know whether to extract one person or two, Best!"

Mina isn't sure whether she jolts because of the suggestion

that has never crossed her mind, or the use of her last name without the customary Fräulein preceding it. Taube is in a rush —Mina sees that much in the glance he throws over his shoulder as if to ensure that they haven't been followed. Still, what if it's all just a game? What if, together with herself, she'll drag those she cares about into an abyss?

A ray of sun filtering through the greenery glimmers on Taube's wedding band as he brings the cigarette stub to his lips.

As if before a dive, Mina inhales sharply and makes a decision. "Swear on your wife and child's grave that you're indeed on our side then I'll tell you everything."

Taube's visibly taken aback but recovers himself quickly. "I swear on my wife and child's grave and their eternal life in paradise," he says slowly and solemnly. "I'm a friend, not an enemy."

Mina nods and also looks about before relaying the whole extent of Siggy's involvement with their circle's activities. The letter he coded and passed to Dr. Reiche fleeing Nazi Germany, to be delivered into the Allied intelligence's hands; the names of people traveling theoreticians could come in contact with to leak information on the uranium project; all the wrong coordinates putting Reich submarines square into allied traps and purposely incorrect information relayed to Siggy's higher-ups that allowed enemy fliers to enter German airspace undisturbed.

By the end, Taube's hand is on his forehead, wet with sweat. It is apparent from his look that he has reached his limit. "Was Cologne his doing too? He decoded it as Dresden, they put everyone on high alert, and in the meantime, the RAF reduced the whole of Cologne to rubble?"

That one secret Mina decides to keep to herself. "I don't know anything about that. I had my own troubles to attend to after its bombing."

Taube wipes his hands down his face. It takes time for him

to turn back into his collected self. "You, children, are mad. With all the smarts you have, you are still positively mad."

Mina only smiles at him, the responsibility for the entire world heavy on her shoulders. "They say madness and genius are two sides of the same coin."

"Go home and gather a suitcase for a weekend in the mountains by the Swiss border. Radiation poisoning, you said? I'll tell them it's contagious and you need to air it out of your body. Heisenberg and Döpel shall stay home on quarantine—I'll see that they do. Take your passport for the German-Austrian border control, but don't take anything conspicuous."

"What about Siggy?"

"Let me worry about Siggy."

"If you take me out before him, they can arrest him."

"I said, let me worry about that."

"I won't go anywhere without him."

He looks at her as his jowls work silently, chewing away at her obstinacy and outright defiance. But then, seeing that she won't surrender, this impossible child he has found himself in charge of, Taube softens his gaze and sighs with great emotion.

"It's not just me, Mina. There are others, too. They'll help Siggy."

Feeling as though a blindfold has been ripped from her eyes, Mina stares at Taube with her eyes wide open. Others, in the *Abwehr*? At the heart of the German intelligence organ, resisting from the inside as well? Just how many of them are there, people who are still standing with their heads up, proud in the face of unimaginable evil? In her narrow-minded view, Mina thought it was only them, the scientists, who were doing something to stop this bloodshed, to turn the tide of war so light would triumph over darkness at long last. But, no; others are fighting the same fight and just as bravely and selflessly, and as long as they do, there is still hope for Germany, the real Germany, the country of Schiller and Göethe, the country that gave birth to psychoanalysis and split the atom, the country that has so much brilliant past and future potential... Too bad that its present is strangled in the noose of the red banner with a swastika clinging to it like a spider.

Mina smiles at Taube through the mist in her eyes and takes his hand and presses it suddenly, with all the gratitude and comradely warmth she feels at that moment.

THIRTY-FIVE

AUSTRIAN-SWISS BORDER

Taube takes her "to the mountains" himself, in his *Abwehr* staff car, after clearing the matter with his superiors. The ride is uneventful and shorter than Mina expected. Laid and ironed out just a few years ago, autobahns stretch in front of them like ribbons, weaving their way through forests and meadows still untouched by the war or famine. Taube suggests that she sleeps —she'll need her strength when in Switzerland and traveling on her own—but Mina takes it all in, commits to memory every pasture and village, the sky without a cloud against its perfect, splendid blue, the rivers and lakes and fishermen with bare torsos and farmwomen herding goats for the pasture, their kerchiefed heads turning toward Taube's car flying by.

For long stretches of the road, they're the only ones driving. "All the gasoline goes to the front," Taube explains when they stop at a village inn for a bathroom break and a quick meal. "Only the army staff can afford cars now. They and the businessmen, of course. Herr Krupp's driver shall be driving Frau Krupp shopping even when our tanks are bogged down, dry as a bone, in some Russian wilderness."

Mina digs into a hearty stew of potatoes and pork—how fresher and juicier it is here than in the city!—and mentions the women they passed in the fields.

"Whatever happened to the German housewife and mother dream?"

"That dream is deader than a doorknob," Taube answers with a crooked grin half-hidden behind the spoon he's blowing on. "With all the men at the front, who's going to do their work? There's only so many foreign slave workers the SS can herd here to take up their places."

"I remember when I had just entered the University of Graz," Mina says between bites. "The dean made it a point of honor to make sure I and everyone present knew I took up some promising young man's space." She shakes her head with a fond smile. "I don't know why I just thought of that. I suppose, in the end, one always thinks of the beginning."

"This is not the end for you, Mina. It *is* the beginning," Taube counters with great conviction. "Mann shall have no trouble putting you in contact with the Americans or the British, whoever is closer to your heart. With your experience and all the information you possess, they'll be happy to offer you a job. And then, who knows? Maybe one day I'll look up and see a bomb of your making dropping on top of my head from the skies. What a way to go will that be!"

He's laughing, but there's no mirth in his eyes. It's all for show, to lift Mina's spirits. Only Mina doesn't want any of that now.

"No." She resolutely shakes her head. "No bombs. As long as I live, I'll never work on one. That much I can promise you."

"If not you, then someone else will," Taube says with the serene look of a fatalist about him. "The demon is out of the box. It's not a question of *if*, it's a question of *when* and *who*. And my bet is on the Americans. According to our intelligence, the British aren't all that interested in that. As for the Soviets, they're working on something else entirely. Something that has nothing to do with uranium, but with hydrogen, if I'm not mistaken." He points his spoon at Mina with a wink. "You may pass this information on to your new contacts as well, if you like."

They finish their meal and Taube pays the innkeeper—coincidentally a woman as well, who's likely also a cook and a waitress for the small enterprise. Mina hasn't seen anyone else around while the tall Austrian was hustling in the kitchen and disappeared into it again after placing the steaming dishes in front of the couple.

Once in the car, Taube removes his military jacket and sits without starting the car for some time. Mina knows that this is the last stretch, feels the approaching border in the hairs rising on her bare arms, and suddenly swings round in her seat to face Taube.

"Herr Hauptmann, what about you?" So preoccupied she's been with her future and Siggy's, with picturing her parents' faces in her mind, Mina has completely disregarded the fate of the man sitting next to her now. "You can't possibly return after you smuggle me through the border. They'll arrest you for treason right that instant!"

Taube smiles warmly at her concerns and pats her hand, balled into a fist in alarm, with friendly affection. "Thank you kindly for your worries, but there's no need for them. It's not me who'll be smuggling you through the border. A local farmer," he explains to Mina's inquisitive look. "I'll only leave you at the village and how you manage to escape is beyond my comprehension. Naturally, I'll have to hold your passport while you're in the mountains, as ordered by my superiors. So, hand it over before I forget."

Mina does as she's told despite the confusion swarming her head, making it swim with all this new information.

"But how will I cross without a passport? And that farmer, is he a reliable man? What if he refuses to risk it?"

Instead of a reply, Taube puts the car into gear. Apparently, she shall soon see for herself.

The village emerges after yet another bend in the road—first, the old church with a cross gleaming brightly in the sun, then a cemetery with headstones overgrown with moss and so old, they must still remember the Vikings, and beside it, a field with cows tearing contentedly at the grass. And, finally, farmhouses without fences around them, narrow paths trodden from one house to another and to a small pond in the middle of it all, with ducks swimming in it and two women washing their laundry on its bank, leaning over the water from a makeshift dock consisting of several long planks nailed together.

Driving slowly so as not to run over chickens and geese wandering freely around, Hauptmann Taube pulls up to a house he apparently knows and parks next to a stone well. A green-eyed calico cat is the first one to wander out of the house to greet them. After her, an elderly man with his face brown as tanned leather and just as lined appears on the porch. Through the smoke of his pipe, he squints nearsightedly at the newcomers and smacks his lips, behind which Mina sees no teeth.

"Haven't seen you in a long time, Hauptmann," the farmer says, approaching the couple. Around his legs, the cat is weaving circles. "Thought the devil's strung you up by now."

"Not yet," Taube grins and extends his hand to his acquaintance. "I'm here for a favor."

The old man shifts his gaze to Mina, asking the silent question. "A girl? Now, that's a first."

"Hopefully, it'll be the last," Taube says and also gives Mina a critical once-over. "Her hair is already short. Your grandson, he's fourteen now if I'm not mistaken?"

"Not mistaken," the farmer echoes. "A scrawny little thing. Just like his father was at his age. He would have been forty-three now, my youngest one, had those bastards—"

Some old hatred ignites suddenly in the farmer's eyes, a connection that ties him and Taube into an unorthodox union, but the origins of which neither man explains to Mina. It's not Taube's secret to share, and the farmer, he's a contraband smuggler, and to him, Mina's a debt to repay, whichever debt it is, and that's about it. Why pour his soul out to a stranger?

A gentle tap on her shoulder calls her attention back to Taube. "There's only one trouble with her," he says. "She can read lips, but she's deaf."

The farmer raises a brow but just barely. "So she is then. Why is it such trouble?"

"What if guards ask her anything?"

"Why would they?"

Taube shrugs, but leaves it up to the man. He knows the guards better – he's the smuggler here.

Moving without his usual energy and efficiency, Taube removes Mina's suitcase from the boot of the car and hands it to her. For a few moments, his hand lingers on her shoulder. He looks her closely in the eye, as if committing her face to memory. "You're in good hands, Mina. Just follow Heinrich's directions and you'll be on Swiss land before you know it."

"Thank you for everything, Herr Hauptmann." Mina clasps the suitcase's handle, holding back the tears. "Will you truly be all right? You're not just saying it for my sake, are you?"

"No," he reassures her with a smile. "Not just saying it."

"And Dr. Heisenberg? Will he be all right?"

"He'll be fine. I'll just visit him and explain it to him that it's against his best interests to blow anything else up or participate in any experiments for that matter. He'll linger in the background until the end of the war, feign to do some research or some such, and after all is over... well, I can't say what shall happen then, or if any of us shall live to see that day, but for the time being, yes, Mina, he'll be all right."

They're silent for a few more insufferable moments. Next to them, the farmer is blowing out gray rings into the clear midsummer air and gazes at the horizon with the eyes of an ancient wise man.

"I guess this is goodbye then," Mina utters at length and bites into her trembling lip.

Taube nods, his face also twisted with emotion, and suddenly pulls her close and holds Mina close to his heart.

"Don't kiss my hair, it might still be radioactive," Mina tries to protest through tears, but he does so nevertheless; covers the entire top of her head with kisses before holding her suddenly out in outstretched hands and handing her to the farmer and his knotted, dark-brown hands.

"Go with God, Wilhelmina Best." The last words that leave Hauptmann Taube's lips. Then, a curt nod, a click of the heels as if to a fellow officer, a fellow comrade in arms, and off he drives in his car with its open top until it disappears behind the cemetery, behind the church, behind the bend of the road Mina will never again see.

Feeling lonelier than ever, Mina follows the farmer into his home and cries even harder when the cat begins to rub its head into her legs.

The cat reminds her of Libby, her own family cat, and of the home itself she is forever leaving, and the country which she shall never again call her own. It's more painful than she could have imagined, tearing herself out of her homeland by the roots. It hurts something frightful, but sometimes soil turns sour even in the best of lands. Sometimes, uprooting oneself is the only chance for survival.

"We're leaving tomorrow morning," Heinrich says, once

inside. "I cross this border twice a week, whenever I go to town to sell eggs and milk and deliver hay to a couple of small farms. My grandson always rides with me. You'll wear his clothes." He glances over her frame with a critically narrowed eye. "You two should be the same size."

At dawn, the old farmer's grandson rouses Mina. Silently, he leaves a stack of folded clothes at the foot of her bed and runs off before Mina can thank him. The clothes are obviously worn but freshly washed and smell faintly of lake water. Mina guesses she ought to thank the women she saw yesterday, scrubbing away at their washboards at the lakeside. She wishes she could repay them with something, no matter how miniscule, but, on Taube's advice, she came here with virtually nothing, just a small suitcase with a change of summer clothes.

In front of the house, the farmer and his grandson are already stacking aluminum vats with milk and crates with eggs among the brackets of hay. Once again, Mina considers the suitcase she holds in her hand and then, instead of taking it outside and concealing it under the hay as agreed upon, she opens it and extracts only the notes she amassed during work. All else— summer dresses and underthings and sandals—let the women have it. Leaving with only the clothes on her back seems appropriate somehow.

Unburdened and slightly giddy with anticipation, Mina steps outside and marvels at the dewy grass under her bare feet. An emerald, farewell carpet to see her off. With her papers hidden under her shirt and overalls, Mina approaches the cart and runs her hand along the horse's flank, soft like velvet and reassuringly warm.

The farmer's grandson, having finished his loading business, looks Mina over, then suddenly drops to his haunches and scoops a fistful of earth.

"Much too pale." Mina sees his lips explain before he smears the soil all over her face, bare arms, exposed ankles, and feet.

Mina helps him the best she can and even digs first her toes and then her hands into the ground to get as much dirt under her nails as she can. They must have done a decent job of it as the old farmer nods his approval when Mina climbs clumsily into the cart and takes up a seat next to him. The last thing the farmer's grandson parts with is his cap. He waves it at Mina—"Good luck, sister!"—and throws it into her awaiting hands. With a bittersweet smile, Mina pulls it low onto her forehead and takes a deep breath when the farmer picks up the reins.

With her thoughts directed at a past she is forever parting with, Mina nearly freezes with fright as a border guard booth and a small roadblock come suddenly into view after yet another bend in the road. She thought she'd have more time, but they're here already and the guard is already coming out of his booth while the second one remains inside—Mina simply hasn't had time to prepare herself for it.

Sensing her stiffening next to him, the farmer pulls a straw out of a haystack behind his back and sticks it unceremoniously into Mina's mouth.

Prompted in such an unorthodox manner, Mina begins to chew on it, her dirty hands exposed, soil-covered feet dangling in the air as the horse comes to a halt.

"Morning, father." Mina watches the guard greet the farmer with a look of familiarity about him.

He approaches the cart from the old man's side and makes a show of prodding the hay with a bayonet affixed to his rifle.

"No partisans hiding?" he asks with a coy grin.

"All ran away." The farmer dips his hands into a satchel at his feet and produces a thick wrap tied neatly with rope.

Mina catches a whiff of smoked pork before the parcel trades hands and instantly disappears into the guard's pocket.

"Thank you kindly, father. Safe travels!"

And just like that, the gate opens and they cross into the country where the war is a distant echo, where coffee is real and people are carefree. Where summer feels eternal and a new day has just begun.

It's the closest to paradise Mina has ever felt.

THIRTY-SIX

BERN, SWITZERLAND. SUMMER 1942

Mina walks the cobblestone streets of Bern with an air of detached determination, her mind racing as quickly as her steps. Half-starved and dizzy, her feet full of bloodied blisters, it's a miracle she made it this far in the first place.

The village where Heinrich, Hauptmann Taube's inconspicuous smuggler, let her off was on the very border. A long way from the Swiss capital. With whatever little money she had hidden on her, Mina purchased for herself the cheapest shoes but didn't splurge on the socks to go with them. Instead, she saved all she could for some bread and milk she allowed herself twice a day while begging a ride from the farmers traveling west. No fancy train rides for those in hiding. Without papers and any protection against the Gestapo spies the major transportation hubs were brimming with, humble country roads only for Wilhelmina Best. The trip that could have taken her a few hours turned into an ordeal stretching into days and, soon, weeks. By the time she reached Bern, creeping into the Old City part of it from the outskirts, the boy's overalls were hanging off her. *What a scarecrow*, she thought to herself as she caught sight of her reflection in one of the shop's windows.

It's the summer of '42, and the world is in disarray, but the quaint Swiss city offers an eerie sense of peace amidst the global tumult. The cool breeze carries whispers of neutrality that flutter through the Swiss flags dotting the cityscape. It's both strange and exhilarating, the absence of uniformed men and cascading Nazi banners turning entire streets into one big blood fest.

Mina, however, is far from neutral. Her heart beats to the rhythm of uncertainty, each thump echoing the questions that have gone unanswered since her harrowing escape from Austria.

Have Taube's men managed to smuggle Siggy?

Where could they have possibly brought him?

Is there a search going on for them?

And the most burning, *What to do now? Where to go? Who to ask all of these questions to?*

Mina shrinks into herself even more at the sight of this peacetime prosperity that antagonizes her with its blissful ignorance. She feels filthy, dirt-poor, and out of place among all of these beautiful women with lustrous hair in fancy updos and the gentlemen accompanying them, their linen summer suits, walking canes, and sunglasses making her bristle at the very sight of them. It's even worse when she passes outdoor cafés and sees all of the intricate desserts left uneaten and melting in the hot July sun, when in so many parts of the world now, people would kill for a crust of bread and some clean water to go with it.

She smells fresh dough and thinks of Herr Freudenberg, the kind baker, likely toiling for one SS-run concentration camp kitchen or the other, if he wasn't killed for some minor disobedience, such as not removing his inmate hat fast enough when a guard was passing by. She swears to herself to find out what happened to him, one way or another. But first things first.

She pauses by the entrance to a luxury hotel, bows her head

in a display of utter humility, and approaches the liveried doorman with her hand outstretched. In it, a note that helped her cross the country. "I'm a deaf German refugee looking for my relatives. Please, help me get to—"

Names of different cities, old stricken off and new ones added, map out her travels, together with stains and lines creasing the crumbling piece of paper like some ancient relic. Now, the words "American consulate" punctuate her final destination. So many times has she been chased off like a pesky dog with a swipe of a cane in her general direction but even more times, has she been aided by the people whose hearts are still in the right place.

The liveried doorman appears to belong to the second category. After reading the note carefully, he takes pity on Mina. With a raised finger—wait here!—he disappears inside the hotel and emerges not a minute later, holding out a city map meant for tourists. With a pencil he produces out of his inner pocket, he marks the hotel where Mina is and draws a line—the shortest route—from it to the consulate. Mina's eyes well up in spite of herself when he adds, "Good luck!" at the bottom. Feeling incredibly alone in this entire alien world, she'll need it.

Following the map as closely as possible, Mina weaves her way along the picturesque streets and doesn't even notice the sun beating down on her exposed neck, by now tanned to a bronze color. From time to time, she lifts up her head to consult the street names on the corners. It's on one of those corners that she notices the flag first, the one she thought she'd never see with her own two eyes, fluttering in the wind as if it's been here since the beginning of time, all countless stars and white and red stripes against the azure of the cloudless Swiss sky.

The American consulate.

Mina pauses at the entrance, steadying herself before stepping inside. She expected it to be a hive of activity, a hub for those seeking refuge and answers, but instead it's almost

deserted, with a few bored-looking workers lounging in the cool-
ness of the lobby with little to do. Sharply aware of her offen-
sive-smelling, filthy attire, Mina approaches the man at the
reception and states her name and nationality before warning
him that she's deaf and would rather speak through an interpreter to avoid being misunderstood.

The American picks up the phone and speaks into the
receiver while pushing a form toward Mina to fill out. A stan-
dard refugee affair, Mina concludes from scanning it quickly,
but fills it out all the same.

The American's expression swiftly changes from indifferent
to alert as soon as he reaches the "former occupation" line. The
words "nuclear physicist" got his attention. Or, perhaps, Mina's
personal addition, "working under Dr. Werner Heisenberg on
the German uranium project" did.

In no time, two men in mufti with sharp eyes appear from
one of the side doors and hustle her away inside the consulate,
as if fearing that she'll change her mind and run off back to the
Nazi-land. In one of the rooms, an interpreter is already waiting
by a uniformed man's side. Mina marvels at how different
American uniforms are and downs the water set before her in a
few big gulps before finally dropping into a chair across the
table from the US officer. He doesn't waste time with pleas-
antries, just starts firing questions at her in rapid succession.

Through the interpreter, Mina signs away her entire life
story as more and more uniformed men fill the room. At one
point, one of them replaces her previous interrogator. Bigger
stars on his shoulders. After a couple of hours, Mina's status has
prompted an interference by their top brass.

He cross-examines her together with his predecessor, his
eyes narrow. She's not a scientist, but a provocateur sent in by
the Nazis to throw them, the Allies, off track.

No, Mina shakes her head obstinately. There is really no
German atomic bomb. And there won't be, not while Dr.

Heisenberg is in charge. But could they please help her find her parents?

But they only torment her with their questions some more, reminding Mina of her first day in Berlin. There, too, had been countless questions until she could barely keep herself awake. Only, there's no race office in the US consulate to measure her skull and proclaim her to be of good Aryan stock. However, this makes things only slightly better.

The sun is down by the time they release her from the room but not the consulate grounds. She'll be staying here for now, while her story is being verified, the interpreter explains. Fine by her, Mina nods, and falls onto a cot without bothering to remove the covers. She gave them all the names she could think of, including Dr. Reiche, who was to smuggle the message to these very Americans. The message coded by Siggy.

Mina's last thought is of him, her brave, selfless Siggy, before she drops into a black hole of sleep where no light and no sound exist.

They wake her before dawn but at least have the decency to bring her breakfast before marching her off to yet another interrogation. Mina wolfs down eggs with toast and doesn't even mind when the same top brass greets her in his office. His demeanor is different from the day before, though. He's almost friendly with Mina today. He offers her his hand.

We have to be suspicious; you have to understand, the interpreter signs his words to Mina. *"They" means the OSS*, the same interpreter explains. *Office of Strategic Services.*

Like our Abwehr? Mina signs.

He cringes, doesn't like the comparison. *The intelligence agency, yes.*

Have they reached Dr. Reiche?

They did. He vouched for her. Confirmed her credentials.

Expressed desire to work with Miss Best on US soil as soon as possible.

I'm not going anywhere until I find my parents and Siggy.

The OSS officer brightens at this.

Great news, the interpreter's hands relay his answer. *We have received confirmation from our immigration bureau that Mr. and Mrs. Best were granted refugee visas just two months ago. They are already on American soil, in New York city to be exact. You are more than welcome to join them as soon as you like.*

Mina's relief is palpable. She exhales a breath she feels like she's been holding for two long years and thanks the OSS officer profusely. But there's still the question of Siggy.

What about Siegfried Mann?

The OSS officer chews on the answer for some time.

We haven't found him yet. But we will. But, in the meantime, we could really use a mind like yours for a project back home.

He keeps returning to the subject, like an itch he's dying to scratch. Mina regards him closely. It's her turn to be suspicious. Is he dangling the proverbial carrot with her parents' names on it just to get her across the ocean to work on...? A twitch of suspicion is already prickling the hairs on her nape of what it is precisely they need nuclear physicists for. Their own bomb. Unlike Director Diebner, who's only dreaming of his, they must already be working on theirs and need all the nuclear-minded scientific brains they can get to complete the task. And Mina worked for Dr. Heisenberg himself, the brightest mind of the entire European continent. They must think she has a wealth of German research to offer. And she could use it to her advantage, just to cross the ocean, just to get away from this war and the entire continent slowly going to the devil...

Still, Mina hesitates, her hands folded atop her knees in

their threadbare overalls. She can't fathom leaving without Siggy, not when he's out there, somewhere, his fate unknown.

"I'll go," she finally signs. "But only with Siggy."

The men exchange a glance, an unspoken agreement passing between them. "We'll find him," the intelligence officer assures her through the interpreter. "Trust us."

Days bleed one into another as the waiting game stretches into August. Mina finds herself in an OSS-sponsored apartment not too far from the consulate's grounds. She's finally scrubbed raw and dressed more appropriately for a treasured nuclear physicist, with clothes provided by the American Red Cross, but her new lodgings still feel too much like the ones she fled from. The first-floor apartment is clean and comfortable, but the eyes of her watchers are ever-present, their gazes like shackles around her ankles whenever she sets off for a walk to stretch her legs or just not to go mad from all this uncertainty and infinite angst.

Her handlers bring her international scientific magazines and try to pique her interest with the newest studies, stacking her desk with notebooks and freshly sharpened pencils, but Mina has had enough of that rot to last her several lifetimes. She wants nothing to do with uranium or plutonium or any other element humanity decides to use against itself. Her mind is blissfully empty and oddly at peace with itself. For the first time in years, she gazes at the sunset across the river and actually sees it—the beauty of it all, the rising tides and moon phases, the clouds racing through the sky, the starry nights and dewy grass under her feet. The planet, just living and breathing.

As it has always meant to be.

August is nearly over, but Mina still reads by the window until the sun dips below the horizon, painting the sky in hues of fire and gold. It's that window that the OSS man knocks at, startling her with his hulking frame and sending her heart into a frenzy. She motions him to the front door and opens it, to find him standing there, accompanied by the interpreter as always, a knowing smile on their lips.

"We found your beau," the OSS agent announces and steps away, revealing the man Mina was beginning to lose hope of ever seeing again.

It's Siggy all right, a little worse for wear but whole. Mina rushes to him, just as scrawny and mutt-like as she was after her trek across the country, and inhales the sweet smell of him—*alive!*—their love a force that not even war could sever.

She wants to ask him a thousand questions, but the intelligence officer pulls Siggy away by the shoulder, gently enough but with clear intent, and motions for the interpreter.

"All good? Everyone accounted for?"

The interpreter signs his words.

Mina has nothing else to do but nod. She's still beaming, her entire body vibrating with gratitude, and he makes use of it, the uniformed man. He came through with his end of the deal, now it's Mina's turn.

"We've arranged for you both to travel to the States," the OSS man says. "You'll sail across the Atlantic soon. We're still figuring out the best land route to get you to the shore, but that shouldn't take longer than a couple of days."

That's all they're left with, forty-eight hours at best and a few weeks on land and sea before it's time for Mina to surrender her very soul in payment for the Faustian services.

She keeps the deal to herself and puts on a brave face in front of Siggy, but he sees the clouds gathering in her eyes all the same once he's taken his bath and eaten whatever was in Mina's pantry. Taube's people smuggled him across the French border instead of the Austrian one. He had a much tougher road through the war-torn country than Mina through the Swiss backroads. Now, she understands why the delay.

"It turns out, our common Graz friend Gürtner and his Gestapo pals were already watching me," Siggy recounts between forkfuls of roast potatoes with blood sausage. "Taube's friend, whatever his name is—he didn't introduce himself, naturally—had to 'arrest' me so that the Gestapo couldn't get to me first. He took me to France, in handcuffs and all, supposedly to make me identify some people from the same cell I was a part of, and once we were in Lyon, he allowed me to 'escape,' but not before he gave me the name of the local contact who was to smuggle me across the border. It's good to have friends in intelligence circles, I tell you!"

Mina smiles wistfully at that and Siggy lowers his fork, eyes on her, searching.

"What is it, Einstein?"

He reaches across the table and touches her hand and there is no holding back the tears any longer. And together with them, Mina pours it out, her very soul she promised to sell just to have him by her side once again.

"They want me for their own bomb project, Siggy. It seems there's no escaping it for me."

Once uranium got its claws into her, it haunts her now like a demon until it'll bleed her dry and throw away the empty carcass. And then, it'll latch onto someone else, spreading like cancer all over the world, from one country to another, growing progressively bigger and deadlier, until the war comes to end all wars and drags the sun itself to its grave, swaddling the crater-pockmarked earth in the shroud of the deadly fallout.

"Like in the book," Mina finishes in a whisper, feeling those last words trembling in her throat.

"They're Americans, Einstein."

Mina looks at him, so tender and sure of himself, even after all the hardships he had to go through, and shakes her head. She doesn't understand what he means. What does it matter who they are?

"They aren't our German SS. They can't *make you* do anything against your will. It goes against what they stand for. Land of the free, remember? Free to decide for oneself what to do with one's life. Just say no once we get there. Or, better yet, tell them that Heisenberg will never build a bomb for the Nazis and ask them to forget about theirs. For the world's sake."

It's too good to be true and too good to believe, but Mina does all the same because it's Siggy who said it and Siggy hasn't once been wrong yet and she trusts him more than she trusts herself. Forty-eight hours. She chooses to spend them in his arms instead of thinking of anything nuclear.

Once again, her bed is only built for one, but they make do, two halves of the whole, once again reunited.

Their voyage is marked by a mingling of hope and trepidation, the uncertainty of their future as vast as the ocean itself. German submarines circling round like sharks, heavy bombers flying overhead. The world is still at war and cares little that two young people are holding hands and hoping to make it across just to see peace for themselves at least for one day. Then, they can die happy.

There are a few close calls, but they make it across after all. Mina's eyes mist over at the sight of the Statue of Liberty greeting them at New York Harbor. Somewhere here, in this half of the world, her parents are. So far, the OSS have been vague about permitting Mina any contact with them for whatever reasons they have, but still, the thought of *Mutti* and *Vati* living in safety from the Nazis is pacifying.

The air is salty and humid and haze swaddles the city despite September counting off its last days. Awestruck and lightheaded, Mina watches the concrete forest of buildings rising in front of them while they dock and presses Siggy's hands tighter.

"And they wanted to bomb it all," she mutters and sees him nod out of the corner of her eye. He knows exactly who she's talking about. Top Nazi brass, who wouldn't think twice about leveling this extraordinary beauty to the ground just for the thrill of it.

But what shall the Americans do when they have their bomb?

Mina is presented with a chance to find out for herself as soon as her feet touch American soil. Together with Siggy, they're whisked away to a place right there in the city, only Siggy is left to wait in the car while Mina is escorted into a meeting where the veil of secrecy is finally lifted.

There are four men facing an empty chair, two in uniforms and two in civilian clothing, and the memories of the Graz ambush in the dean's office resurface in Mina's mind once again as she takes the chair. Only, this time she knows who she is and what she wants—for herself and the entire planet. She's seen what uranium is capable of when mishandled. Mere humans don't intimidate her any longer.

"I suppose, you know, or at least suspect why you're here," one of the uniforms says. The one next to him interprets it from English to silent. "Welcome to Manhattan. Can I go as far as say, welcome to the Manhattan Project?"

They don't beat around the bush, the Americans. Mina is almost impressed with such boldness.

"Is that what you decided to call it?" she asks. "I sincerely hope you aren't building it here. One false move and you'll poison the entire city with radiation."

They all smile at her indulgently after exchanging glances. *Come, now, Miss, we aren't stupid.*

"We're building it everywhere," follows the evasive reply. Evasive but revealing at the same time. What Germany was severely lacking—the resources and infrastructure—the US has in spades. It appears, they indeed threw their all at it. All the factories, all the facilities at their disposal, just to produce a weapon of mass destruction before the Nazis do. *If only they saw Dr. Heisenberg's pitiful reactor,* Mina thinks to herself.

She doesn't begin with an outright refusal. Treading as mildly as she can, she tries to explain it to them, that there is no need to be in such a rush; that such a weapon won't bring anything but evil in its wake; that they have nothing to fear from the Germans. The Germans have other troubles than bombs on their mind now.

But they don't believe her, refuse to listen to reason.

"This atom bomb will end the war and save the world."

Mina's heart plummets at their argument. The very idea of such a weapon being used as anything but a vague threat chills her to the bone. "No," she says vehemently. "It'll only destroy. Such weapons should never be made."

The room falls silent, the weight of her conviction palpable. There's talk of duty and necessity, but Mina remains resolute. "I'm more than happy to help you, but not in the role you've mapped out for me."

It's the men in civilian clothing who tilt their heads in silent question. The uniforms have long lost all interest in her.

"While in Germany, I've been studying the effects of radiation on people. One of the studies was written by an American hematologist. You must have studies going on and particularly now. Allow me to join them. With you developing such a weapon, and on the scale that you're developing it, accidents are bound to happen. Allow me to help people who may suffer from them. My chemistry is good enough, and I'll study as hard as I can, of that you can be sure, but please, allow me to work on something that heals instead of destroys."

There is a moment of silence in the room. In Mina's ears, her own pulse is beating wildly.

At last, one of the uniforms rises to his feet, stacking the papers he brought. "Women. Figures. All right. Send her to the suitable department, I guess."

The words weren't meant for Mina's ears, but the interpreter still relays them to Mina, prompting a smile out of her that lights up the entire room. Her relief is profound, her determination unwavering. She will not be a pawn in a game of destruction. Instead, she will dedicate herself to healing, to understanding, to preserving life in a world that seems hell-bent on annihilating it.

And so, with Siggy by her side and her future ahead, Mina embarks on a new journey, one that promises not the thunder of bombs, but the quiet hope of discovery and the steadfast glow of humanity.

MOTHER

HIROSHIMA. JAPAN, 1946

Somewhere in the world, it's business as usual: people rise with the alarm and groan at yet another workday outside. They shuffle to their bathrooms and brush their teeth and make their coffee before making their breakfast. They scan a morning newspaper while still in their pajamas and complain about politicians and the world going in completely the wrong direction and the weather promising a rainy weekend—what else is new?—and worry about all the mundane things they take for granted. And meanwhile, here, in the ghost town of Hiroshima, any survivor would have given anything to worry about taxes and weather on weekends instead of wondering if they will make it to 1947.

We're losing them one by one, the ones who haven't died right after the explosion but are succumbing to the effects of radiation only now, months later. It's devastating to see healthy-looking women suddenly losing their gorgeous, lustrous hair in clumps and wondering why their necks are so swollen whenever they visit us, the doctors they think know what they're doing. Some arrive with their husbands in tow and show the photos taken a year or two ago and the man in front of us is completely unrecognizable from the one forever frozen in time on the black-and-white film. Their eyes are bulging, pulled forcefully toward the temples by a tumor growing inside their skulls. Their noses are all misshapen and rotting. Their mouths are open wounds with ulcers that refuse to heal and only seep more pus and blood into their stomachs with each swallow, poisoning them slowly, and I don't have enough words to explain to them that there is no cure for what they're suffering from. It's always like this with us, humans: we let the plague out of Pandora's box just to realize that we haven't the faintest idea of how to put it back inside or at least shield ourselves from it.

I'm still typing a report for my latest patient when Dr. Sato appears in the door with a smile that is such a rarity to see on his face. I forget the typewriter in a moment.

"Is something the matter?" I ask him.

"Great news, Dr. Best. The hematologists from Berkeley are finally here."

That *is* great news. We've almost lost all hope of seeing them here, the fabled miracle scientists they've been promising us for months now. Supposedly, they've been studying radiation effects on human organisms for as long as their counterparts were working on the atomic bomb. Supposedly, they can even cure it, depending on the dose of roentgen a patient received.

I rise from my chair, ready to follow Dr. Sato to these Berkeley demigods, but he, smiling even wider, only steps aside, and there she stands, my daughter Mina, a white medical gown and a suitcase in hand.

I'm as stunned as though by a physical blow. I've lost all faculty of speech. I'm paralyzed and don't remember how to breathe properly and I'm so very afraid to blink because she can disappear, my dear lost child, the sweetest mirage my heart can scarcely bear.

But then she speaks, "Hello, Mommy," in her sweet brand-new English, and the spell is finally broken.

I'm upon her in an instant, hugging, touching, inspecting every strand of hair, every dimple in her cheeks. No, not a child anymore. A young woman, with eyes full of fearless wisdom and hands smelling faintly of disinfectant. Just like mine.

"Mina... you?" I ask, stroking her hair, still in blissful disbelief. "One of them? The hematologists?"

She nods with a coy look about her and sets the suitcase on the floor. Behind her back, Dr. Sato is delicately receding into the depths of the building, leaving us to share the precious moment away from any prying eyes.

"I am, yes." She's all smiles, all California suntan and freckles over the bridge of her nose—not just returned from the dead but risen from the ashes like a phoenix, brighter, healthier, brimming with life. "A certain war broke out and I decided to switch majors halfway through."

She's joking so easily now, my daughter who's always been so serious. There's a lightness to her, as if she finally shed the old skin and spread her wings and became what she was always meant to be.

"I've been looking for you," I say. "Ever since I arrived in America."

"They wouldn't let you find me," she replies softly. "During the war, my department was classified as one adjacent to the Manhattan Project."

"They didn't make you—"

"No, no," she rushes to assure me. "I told them from the start that I'll have nothing to do with the bomb."

"Did the Americans smuggle you out from Germany?"

"No. Our own German, one of the few with a conscience, smuggled me from Germany to Switzerland. And from Switzerland, that was the OSS. They were updating me on your progress, even though they wouldn't let me talk to you or visit. I wasn't directly involved with the Manhattan Project but knew of it. I suppose I was more fortunate than the scientists confined to their little atomic village for the duration of two years, but I was still restricted to Berkeley facilities only and under strict no-travel orders. You know what they were thinking then, loose lips sink ships and all that. And I'm an Austrian on top of things. They were watching me very closely." She waves the past off with an almost believable nonchalance. "But enough about me. Let's talk about you. A full-fledged physician now, *Mutti*? Congratulations."

"Been long overdue."

"Yes, it has. I expected to find you here. Wasn't even surprised when I saw your name on the list of the first volunteers they shared with us in Berkeley."

I try to wave her off, but she only doubles down in response.

"No, no, quit it with the modesty. You've always been the one to rush to anyone's aid. I told everyone in Berkeley how my mom had a fully stacked pharmacy in our kitchen and how our neighbors chose to go to you over an actual hospital."

"You thought they were taking advantage of my good nature."

"I was wrong. They simply sensed a person who cared."

"You also thought the medical field was not for you."

"I was wrong about that too."

At home, in my temporary lodgings, we stay up well into the night while Mina tells me all about the turns her life has taken—from Graz to Berlin to Leipzig, from Austria to Switzerland, and from Europe to North America. From a nuclear physicist, to a hematologist. She swallowed the course that should have taken years in half its time and graduated with honors before practicing first in the States and finally heading here.

"Dr. Best?" I arch a brow at her.

In her cheeks, those coy dimples again. "Dr. Mann," she

corrects me and lifts her left hand for me to inspect, with a narrow gold band circling her ring finger.

He came with her to the States and remained by her side throughout her studies, Siegfried Mann, her first true friend and, now, her new husband.

"The OSS people gave him the opportunity to join their radio division, but he would have to stay in the Pentagon for that while I was in Berkeley. So, he told them he was honored by the offer, but he had just discovered that he can make some mean lasagna and would stay with me in California instead. To practice culinary art."

I laugh together with her, liking this boy I've never met more and more by the second.

"He'll be here shortly, my Siggy," Mina adds, as if reading my mind. "They allow us to bring families here. And guess who else I found through the Red Cross and who's teaching Siggy how to bake desserts? Herr Freudenberg!"

"The baker? *Your* baker? Your former employer?" My voice drops in spite of myself. I buried him in my mind almost right after the *Kristallnacht*, after Mina confessed to me all about her tragic business with him. How could he have possibly survived all these years?

"The very same." Her smile is radiating light like a little sunbeam. "Siggy was right about him. The SS put him on kitchen duty in Dachau. That's how he survived. He's in California now, gaining back the weight and working in the cupcake shop he opened together with his brother, who's back from China. Siggy helps them there on weekends. Herr Freudenberg adores him like a son. He'll miss him when he's gone."

"Hopefully, we'll all be back before long."

"Yes. Hopefully."

"I miss your father. Don't tell him though, it'll go to his head," I add in jest.

"I bet he doesn't miss us, having the house all to himself and all the free time in the world on his hands," Mina responds in the same key.

"He took up gardening."

"*Vati?* No!"

"Oh, yes."

"Now that, I'll need to see in person."

"You will. Soon."

We don't know what the future shall bring and hope is all we have, but at least that we have it in spades. Hope brought me my daughter back. It's quite a miracle worker.

"So, there will be a hematology department at long last?" I ask her.

Mina nods, spreads the research she produced from her valise on the table before me, and once again it stuns me to see a young woman where I remember only a child. How I tried to shelter her, to keep her from harm, my handicapped child everyone pitied me for. I shouldn't have worried. She's so much stronger than me, so much braver! It turns my stomach to think how many irreplaceable talents like hers have been forever lost to the Nazi euthanasia program just because someone in the government deemed them genetically inferior.

"I think we finally found where radiation goes once it penetrates the body. So far, we recognize three different affected zones: bone marrow and blood count resulting from it, the digestive tract, and the nervous system. Radiation affects them unevenly; it all depends on the length of exposure, the dose received." She waves her hand—*let's not go into details now*. "The point is, once we pin it down, see exactly what it does to the body of each particular patient and how, we'll be able to treat it."

In her eyes, a thousand suns of hope are burning. I look into them as though into a mirror and am once again reminded that there will always be people who create means of annihilation but, thankfully, there will always be those looking for a cure instead. And as long as there are more of the latter, we, human-ity, still have a chance of survival.

We just have to choose life over death.

Nature over machinery.

Love over power.

After all, we are all brothers and sisters. We may speak different languages, but we have so much to say to each other if we only listen. How much better it is than the silence of a world laid to waste. I can only hope it will never go quiet.

A LETTER FROM ELLIE

Dear reader,

I want to say a huge thank you for choosing to read *When the World Went Silent*. If you did enjoy it, and want to keep up to date with all my latest releases, just sign up at the following link. Your email address will never be shared and you can unsubscribe at any time.

www.bookouture.com/ellie-midwood

I hope you loved *When the World Went Silent* and if you did I would be very grateful if you could write a review. I'd love to hear what you think, and it makes such a difference helping new readers to discover one of my books for the first time.

I love hearing from my readers – you can get in touch through social media, or my website.

Thanks,

Ellie

www.elliemidwood.com

facebook.com/EllieMidwood

instagram.com/elliemidwood

A NOTE ON HISTORY

Dear reader,

Thank you so much for making this journey with me—I can't even tell you how much I appreciate you choosing Mina's story to learn about the German atomic bomb program. Even if the story is fiction, the events surrounding Mina's involvement with the uranium program are based on true events. After splitting the atom in the late thirties, German scientists indeed formed a so-called Uranium Club, whose aim was to harness the fission process and hopefully produce a new type of engine that would produce "clean" energy without the use of fossil fuels. However, with the beginning of the war and the Uranium Club coming under the direct control of the German army, its aim took a more sinister turn. Believing that the bomb could be developed using the same fission process, Director Diebner hoped to produce one for the government. It's only then that Dr. Werner Heisenberg was invited to join the Club. Even Diebner understood that without the most brilliant German physicist, the Club had little chance of succeeding.

The reason behind Dr. Heisenberg's initial exclusion from

the project was his political unreliability. Not only did he refuse to join the Party, but he also spoke adamantly against the expulsion of Jewish scientists from their positions when Hitler came to power, and even went as far as circulating a petition to protest such discriminatory actions. He also fiercely believed in Einstein's theory of relativity and stood by his position even when other scientists all but declared a war on him for supporting "Jewish physics." The anecdote that von Weizsäcker shared with Mina about Reichsführer Himmler's mother interfering on Heisenberg's behalf is based on true fact.

Just before the outbreak of the war, Heisenberg had a chance to immigrate to England or the United States; however, he refused his colleagues' offers, explaining that he believed that he could do more for German science from the inside rather than from across the border. Perhaps, it was this decision that essentially saved the world from a real catastrophe: if it wasn't Heisenberg who was appointed a chief theoretician of the uranium project but some zealous Nazi supporter, we can only speculate how it all would have turned out for the planet.

From his first days at the Kaiser Wilhelm Institute, Werner Heisenberg worked solely on a reactor prototype, developing the blueprint of the so-called "peaceful atom" instead of following Diebner's lead and trying to create a weapon. More than that, he was convinced that a weapon of such lethal capabilities in the Nazis' hands would spell disaster for the entire world, and so, he did all he could to warn the Allies: the episode with Dr. Reiche and the message he was to pass to the Allies once he crossed the border is based on fact, and the message itself is quoted word to original word. It was also Heisenberg who told Minister Speer that a bomb couldn't be made in any foreseeable future, despite Speer offering him pretty much unlimited resources in order to create one.

Most of the supporting characters are also based on real people and organizations active during that time frame. Von

Weizsäcker's father really worked for Minister von Ribbentrop's office and later became a part of the German Resistance cell that were responsible for Operation Valkyrie. Hauptmann Taube's character is also based on the internal German resistance cell operating inside the German intelligence service, the *Abwehr*. As for the scientists themselves, while not officially belonging to any resistance circles, they resisted the Nazi regime in their own way, traveling to occupied countries and passing information to Allies via their colleagues, just as described in the novel.

As for the nuclear physics development and anecdotes surrounding it, I also tried to stick to the real historical timeline to the best of my abilities. It was astounding to learn that the physicists worked with uranium and its highly radioactive by-products without any protection and didn't consider radiation to be any danger to their health. It's no wonder, as only a couple of studies on radiation sickness existed and its real research began only after thousands of people perished from it after the Hiroshima and Nagasaki attacks. Mina's character is based on all the pacifist scientists who spoke out against an atomic bomb and all the physicians who dedicated themselves to the study of the radiation's often lethal consequences.

Again, thank you so much for choosing Mina's story! If you want a deeper look into the German atomic program, I highly recommend reading *Heisenberg's War* by Thomas Powers. Hopefully, such stories will keep reminding us just how fragile and precious peace is. Let's protect it for the sake of life on the entire planet.

A NOTE FROM THE AUTHOR

To my fellow ADHD folk, both diagnosed early and later in life. I finally wrote a protagonist who shares our "neuro-spicy" brain.

I see you. You matter. You are quirky and unorthodox and creative and make the world a much more vibrant place. Don't let anyone ever tell you otherwise.

ACKNOWLEDGMENTS

First and foremost, I want to thank my incredible editor, Claire Simmonds, for helping me bring Mina's story to light. She truly made Mina's character come to life and, through her invaluable insights, helped me turn the very first rough draft into the novel that you're holding in your hands today. I wouldn't have been able to do this without her unwavering support and encouragement.

To everyone in my lovely publishing family at Bookouture for working relentlessly to help my book babies reach the world. Jen Shannon, Mandy Kullar, Jade Craddock, Jane Donovan—thank you for shaping my ramblings into a coherent novel! Richard and Peta, you made it possible to have my babies translated into twenty(!) languages. I know I'm an author, but I honestly have no words to fully express my gratitude to you.

Huge thanks to Jess Readett and Sarah Hardy for organizing the best blog tours ever and securing the most interesting interviews for each new release. Even for an introvert like me, you make publicity a breeze. Working with you is a sheer delight!

Ronnie—thank you for all your support and for being the best husband ever! And for keeping all three dogs quiet when I work. I know, it's not easy given how crazy they are. I love being on this journey with you.

Vlada and Ana—my sisters from other misters—thank you for all the adventures and the best memories we've already created and keep creating. I don't know how I got so lucky to have you in my life.

Pupper, Joannie and Camille—thank you for all the doggie kisses and for not spilling coffee on Mommy's laptop even during your countless zoomies. You'll always be my best four-legged muses.

And, of course, the hugest thanks, from the bottom of my heart, to all of you, my wonderful readers. I can never explain how much it means to me, that not only have you taken time out of your busy schedules, but you chose one of my books to read out of millions of others. I write for you. Thank you so much for reading my stories. I love you all.

Finally, I owe my biggest thanks to all the brave people who continue to inspire my novels. Some of you survived the Holocaust and the Second World War, some of you perished, but it's your incredible courage, resilience, and self-sacrifice that will live on in our hearts. Your example will always inspire us to be better people, to stand up for what is right, to give a voice to the ones who have been silenced, to protect the ones who cannot protect themselves. You all are true heroes. Thank you.

PUBLISHING TEAM

Turning a manuscript into a book requires the efforts of many people. The publishing team at Bookouture would like to acknowledge everyone who contributed to this publication.

Audio
Alba Proko
Sinead O'Connor
Melissa Tran

Commercial
Lauren Morrissette
Hannah Richmond
Imogen Allport

Cover design
Eileen Carey

Data and analysis
Mark Alder
Mohamed Bussuri

Editorial
Ruth Jones
Sinead O'Connor